WINNER'S CUT

WINNER'S CUT

Preston Pairo

Richardson & Steirman
New York
1986

Copyright © 1986 by Preston Pairo

ISBN 0-931933-32-3

Library of Congress Catalog Number: 86-082398

Winner's Cut by Preston Pairo is Published by Richardson & Steirman, 246 Fifth Avenue, New York, NY 10001

Second Printing

Distributed to the trade by:
Kampmann & Company, Inc.
New York, New York

WINNER'S CUT

One

Eddie Gant propped his iguana-skin cowboy boots on top his desk beside a cup of yesterday's coffee. He sat back in his chair, sighed, and began counting typos in his arrest report. He got to fifteen, then thought, *Screw it.* No scumbag PCP peddler deserved better typing. It was some punk kid from Ohio without any priors, so he'd walk with probation whether Gant's report was penned in Old English script or crayon.

Gant was the only one in the detective's squadroom. Everyone else had either gone home to start the weekend with a case of Coors and hot dogs on the grill, or was already out on the street looking to get an early start on Friday night's action.

His report finished—or as finished as it was going to get— Gant kicked in his bottom desk drawer with the pointed toe of his exotic boot, and walked across the empty squadroom into Captain Marler's office. He deposited his ill-typed report in the center of the desk that Marler had cleared of the week's accumulated papers less than three hours ago by running his huge arm over it like a big windshield wiper, putting everything not secured in place into the trash can.

The captain's window was open, bringing in a humid breeze and the sound of revving car engines on the parking lot two stories below.

Gant leaned outside and saw a fire red Porsche 944 being parked in a spot close to the door. "Hey, Wingate," Gant shouted. He waved. "Up here, you asshole."

The tall black detective looked up across the face of the stucco building and saw Gant hanging out from the waist up. "Whachew know, Slick?"

Gant shrugged. The heat had the back of his baggy Hawaiian-print shirt stuck to his shoulders. "Looks like you're gonna do some serious ass cruising tonight, *homme*. The young mommas, they love those Por-sheys. You'll be in their pants by third gear."

"Ain't she pretty? Just got her off an impound order. Belonged to that guy we took three pounds off last week down near Homestead—that stakeout at the airport."

Gant shook his head. "Makes you think we're on the wrong side of the law, don't it?"

"Doesn't make me think about it at all, Eddie. I *know* we on the wrong side of the law."

Gant looked over the rest of the impound section of the lot: half a dozen Mercedeses, a handful of Caddies, two other Porsches, a Trans Am, and an Alfa. All cars used by drug dealers—mostly middlemen: runners, mules, and contacts. The vehicles were now property of Dade County, Florida, thanks to forfeiture statutes enacted into law by the state legislature up in Tallahassee, and enforced with a vengeance by a gung-ho district attorney's office hell-bent on doing all they could to make life as pure a hell as possible for those in the drug trade.

Gant ducked back inside the window. He went to his desk and retrieved his Persuader riot gun, an efficient short-barreled pistol-grip shotgun with an eight-shot capacity. He slung the Persuader's leather strap over his shoulder, then picked up the ankle holster containing his Colt Combat Commander .45.

If anyone saw him outside the squadroom carrying those weapons, they'd phone the cops in a minute, never suspecting he was one. With dark-tanned skin and wavy sun-bleached hair that hung down over the back of his shirt collar, Eddie fit the drug-runner role perfectly. He had the build of an athlete: muscular arms from constant physical activity—not weights—a trim waist, and runner's legs defined from countless miles around the track at Palmetto High. At thirty-two, he still looked young enough for women to think him cute, especially when he turned on the smiles. Gant was a smooth dealer—Slick, as Wingate called him—and had a knack for being able to talk his way into almost anything.

Once out on the parking lot, Eddie walked over to the Porsche 944 Wingate had brought in. Shading his eyes, he peered inside at the smooth all-leather interior, the classic design of the instrument panel, the wooden gearshift knob. "Damned nice car." He shook his head, walking away. "Jesus . . . thirty grand."

Gant didn't make that much in a year. After taxes, he didn't make it in two. After taxes *and* expenses, he couldn't cover it in five. Working undercover for Dade-Metro, setting up drug buys, catching the unknowing minnows in small traps in order to bait them out for the sharks that swam in off the coast from the Bahamas, Jamaica, Bolivia, and a hundred other locales of origin just wasn't lucrative work.

But undercover had its thrills. Trying to look, act, and live like a drug dealer gave Gant the use of a car—something he did not otherwise own. And, best of all, it wasn't just any car. It was a great goddamned set of blow-your-buckets-off wheels: a Lotus Esprit Turbo that Gant always kept in the rear section of the lot, where nobody would park near it and scrape the hell out of the doors. Price-tagged at $60,000, she ran from zero to sixty in a short hair over six seconds. And every time Gant got behind the wheel, he felt the desire in him swell.

The desire was for many things: speed, adventure, conflict, sex, and to have enough money—cash money—to walk into wherever they sold fantasy machines like this and buy one.

Working undercover filled his wish list, except for the last item. One day, though . . . His eyes were always open.

As Gant turned over the Lotus's engine, his desires surged in tune to the power of the motor. He backed aggressively out of the parking space, cutting the wheel, making the front end come around a little. Shoving it into gear, he accelerated across a hundred feet of parking lot, turbochargers roaring. He sped out onto South Dixie Highway in front of a handful of uniform cops who stood by weather-beaten patrol cars. Gant went by them feeling as though the Lotus was his—really his. And the uniforms looked on with envy.

Lots of times, the ego trip worked, especially at times when one rotten day ran smack into the next, but, mostly, he knew it was bullshit—fun bullshit, though.

Out on South Dixie, the main artery from Miami down through the Keys, the jam of rush hour had passed. Instead of five people turning left on every red light, there were only three.

Eddie sat with the windows down at the light near the University of Miami, wondering how he was going to spend this Friday night. The college girls were thinning out up in Lauderdale now, but cruising A1A in the Lotus always attracted the right kind of attention. Still, he didn't really feel like doing that.

Weird how the body changes, he thought. If someone had told him two years ago that, at some future date, he might be sitting in a $60,000 foreign sports car, on a warm Florida weekend night, not out looking for at least one—if not two—of the country's fastest, horniest women, he'd have said, "No way, *homme,*" and ordered another beer. Now he just smiled. "Gettin' old, Eddie," he said softly to himself.

The light changed. Half a mile up South Dixie, Gant saw the red and blue flashers of a Dade-Metro patrol car stopped alongside the curb. Gant saw one of the uniform boys with his ticket book already out, walking up the driver's side of the white Corvette. A smartass-looking Cuban was slouched behind the Vette's wheel.

"Go get 'em, hotshot," Gant said, driving past, trying to catch the uniform's face in his right side-view mirror. *Probably one of the new overzealous types,* he thought.

Seconds later, he heard the pop. To the untrained ear, it could have been mistaken for a car backfiring. But it wasn't. Eddie felt his muscles tensing, adrenal glands jolting in response, accelerating his heartbeat so quickly that he could feel it in his throat.

He glanced into the rear-view mirror. Behind him, cars swerved sideways. One steered into the concrete median, smashing its front end into the concrete lane divider. Brakes screeched as other cars tried to keep from becoming a part of the pile. Metal crunched into metal, glass broke, horns blew loudly—and it all happened so fast.

Through the twisted snarl of cars, the Vette came speeding through, smacking the tail end of a compact car that was stopped across two lanes of traffic near the front of the pack. The white Corvette came up on Eddie fast, knifing into the slow lane to pass him.

Gant downshifted and cut the Lotus right, trying to cut him off. But the Cuban responded quickly, never slowing, wheeling back to the fast lane. He came onto Eddie's rear bumper—then shot by.

Eddie got only a glance at him, but it was enough. The driver was definitely Cuban, with short, wavy hair, squinting eyes, looking about twenty-five—maybe thirty—wearing a white short-sleeved shirt.

Gant accelerated the Lotus up behind the Corvette smoothly, until they nearly touched bumpers. The Cuban saw him, swerved right, then left again. Gant was about to ram him when the Cuban went out wide into the slow lane. Gant kept on his tail, but then the Cuban braked hard, turned left, and shot through the small gap in the cement median divider. The Vette's ass end went out momentarily at the peak of its 180°-turn, but the Cuban straightened it out and stamped on the gas going south.

Eddie had too much forward momentum and not enough time to make the same move. Instead, he raced up South

Dixie, flashing his lights, leaning on the horn, palms sweating as he steered tightly through traffic. At the next intersection, the light was red. Traffic was crossing. Eddie jumped the Lotus up onto the curb, caught the edge of a metal newspaper box, and sent it sprawling in pieces across the intersection. A Camaro cut in front of him, braking, skidding; the driver lost control and slid sideways into a street lamp, crushing the passenger-side door.

But Gant's move had him through traffic now. He went wide around the Camaro, finished off a U-turn, then worked the Lotus into fourth in a hurry, hitting 85. He strained to see through the half-dozen cars ahead of him, looking for the white Vette.

On the other side of the road, he saw the parked Dade-Metro car, its lights still flashing in tired-looked rotations. There was a small crowd gathering in an uneven circle. In a split second, looking between the bystanders' legs, he saw the uniformed body sprawled lifelessly across the macadem.

Eddie felt the fear, but blocked it out. Fear was dangerous, distracting. He fought it, driving faster. He wanted that Corvette.

Three blocks down, he saw it turn west onto Galloway Road. Eddie ran up onto the grass plot, skirting it, fighting to keep the Lotus straight, then crossed railroad tracks with three jarring shakes, bottoming out the Lotus. He got back onto paved road in time to see the Vette make another turn, going into a residential section.

Eddie made an adroit shift between brake and clutch to hit the turn at maximum speed. He was closing in the distance now on the Cuban, racing across flat single-lane roads with palm trees and fenced yards whizzing past him on both sides.

Up ahead, the road ended at an intersection controlled by a traffic light. It was red. Cars were crossing in front of the Vette from both directions, but the Cuban gambled. He hit the crossroad full speed—no horn, no warning whatsoever. The Vette cleared traffic, but spun out making the turn. Too much car for too tight an angle. The right rear corner panel smashed into a cement wall, and Eddie saw the impact jerk the Cuban's head.

Eddie slammed the Lotus to a stop. Quickly, he got out of the sports car, running toward the intersection, Persuader riot gun leveled on the Corvette, its first shell already in the chamber. His finger was tensed, rubbing quickly up and down the smooth trigger.

The Cuban saw him coming—saw the gun—and he dropped down in his seat, out of sight for a moment, but then jerked back into view.

Instinctively, Eddie dove to the ground just before hearing the loud blast from the Cuban's handgun. Eddie allowed his momentum to carry him into a roll across loose gravel. Then he fired through the intersection. The hard scatter of buckshot pierced the side of a minivan going through the light. There was a scream as the van continued forward, skidding off the road. Gant saw clear to the Cuban and fired again, then again, one shot on top of the other.

Two

"What were you looking at—*exactly,* detective, when you fired shot number one?" It was the third time the lieutenant from the Internal Affairs Shooting Team had asked the question, only this time he added the 'exactly' part.

Gant no longer looked at the IA man. What was the use? Eddie didn't see a face there—it was only a blue suit and white shirt, with a gold tie bar pinched tight around the hard little knot of a blood red silk tie.

"I was looking at the intersection," Gant replied wearily.

"The whole intersection?" The lieutenant did not sound like a believer.

"Yes."

"Your field of vision was of the entire intersection? The whole intersection? To the right and to the left of it?"

Slouched in the hard wooden chair, Eddie wanted to tell the lieutenant to put a quarter in a different machine and ride somebody else's ass for a while; but, knowing better, he just rubbed his eyes.

"Well? Were you able to see the whole intersection or not?"

Gant scratched inside the opened front of his shirt with the Hawaiian flowers printed in the fabric. "Lieutenant, I can't tell you how much of the intersection I saw, I saw so much. Every goddamned square inch of it. I saw every goddamned stone, pebble, and speck of dust. I know which way the ants were crawling. I know what mosquito was fucking what." Gant ran his hands through the length of his sun-streaked hair. "I'm the goddamnedest expert on that intersection you'd ever want to see."

"Then tell me," the lieutenant said, even more smugly now, "how is it that for all this detail you saw, you didn't realize you were going to fire a round into the side of a civilian vehicle? If you saw you were about to put half a load of shot into the left hip of a thirty-eight-year-old woman on her way to pick up her daughter from ballet school, how come you pulled the trigger? Didn't you like the looks of her?"

Eddie exhaled deeply. "I thought I was clear. I thought I had the shot."

"So—you *did* see the passenger vehicle moving into your line of fire?"

"Yeah."

"But you fired anyway."

"I thought I had a shot," Gant said. "I thought it was clear."

"So you . . . what? Miscalculated?"

Gant's jaw clenched. "I don't know, lieutenant. Why don't you tell me, huh? You tell me what I did, because no matter what I say—how I describe it—it'll wind up in your god-damned report looking like I fucked up."

"Did you?"

"I'll tell you what I did. I chased after a wired motherfucking Cuban, who'd just downed a cop, for about two miles. He crashed his car and came up with a gun. He fired at me. I fired back. From the time I got out of the car till the time the Cuban got killed took about seven seconds. And during that time someone drove into the cross fire." Gant paused. "Now, lieutenant, you tell me what that is. You pick the words for your report. I'm not picking them for you."

The lieutenant waited, as though wanting to make sure Eddie had nothing else to say; then, he wrote in longhand on a yellow pad of paper that was perched at a slight tilt across the desk. His handwriting was neat, small letters printed slowly, carefully, like a scribe precisely transposing each symbol.

The two men were in Captain Marler's office. The IA lieutenant had met Gant at the shooting and instructed him to meet back here for the interrogation that was now one hour old.

Before returning to the squadroom, Eddie had stayed at the scene with the technical members of the shooting team until they had all their facts, diagraming from where each shot was fired, where it struck, and the result.

It had been difficult to assess whether Gant's second or third shot had killed the Cuban. Both had impacted together tightly. The majority of shot had gone through the Corvette's open driver-side window and hit the Cuban's left side between three inches below his shoulder and the top of his head. Either shot alone would have probably been fatal—at least that's what the little guy on the shooting team had said. The second shot just made things a little messier.

The little guy also said it was lucky for Gant that his first shot had been aimed lower than two and three; otherwise the woman in the van would have been killed. Gant had thought it peculiar the guy said it was lucky for him—what about lucky for the woman?

As it was, she had about a dozen pieces of shot in the side of her leg, from knee to hip. She'd panicked at the scene, clutching onto the first member of the ambulance crew to reach her, then screaming when Gant approached, shotgun in hand. She cried about how she'd told her husband they should leave south Florida. How it was full of killers and dope dealers and people who would slit your throat for the gold in your teeth.

Gant felt sorry for her. He knew from experience that he'd see her face for a long time. He'd wonder, once the stress of all this was passed, if the woman was getting along all right. If the scars on her leg had healed. And he'd think about calling her, to have a conversation that might ease his conscience a little. But he'd never call. He'd just keep thinking about her until there were so many others in her place—the innocent and unlucky—that she would blend with the rest.

Now Gant felt the heat in Captain Marler's office. The lieutenant had closed the window behind Marler's desk, scowling at the fact that it had been left open while the air conditioning strained loudly to overcome the night's humidity.

Gant peeled his shirt away from his underarms, turning sideways in the seat across the desk from the lieutenant.

The blue-suited IA man had only a fine line of sweat across the almost-unseen line of his upper lip. "You've had a lot of experience with shooting scenes, haven't you, Gant?"

Eddie didn't answer. The lieutenant was obviously well-informed on the subject. Maybe he'd spent weeks looking over the department's files, compiling names of officers involved in more than the average number of "shots fired." And maybe he'd seen some of the three dozen times Gant had been in shooting situations, and decided that if he ever had the chance, he'd put it to him. Because the lieutenant looked like the kind of guy who would walk into the statehouse and tell the governor that he thought passing laws to take guns away from cops and give them nightsticks instead—like in England—was a grand, smashing idea.

The IA lieutenant hadn't opened the folder he'd brought into Marler's office with him. It had remained closed at his elbow for the hour they'd been sitting here. Gant had wondered before what was in there; now he had an idea.

"You lost a partner six months ago, didn't you, Gant? Kyler Phipps. He was shot during a drug buy in Coconut Grove."

Eddie felt the lieutenant's stare.

"Phipps went in alone to meet the seller."

"It's all in your report, lieutenant. Why don't you stop playing games with me and open up your little folder there? I know IA's never closed its investigation on it because the guy who smoked Phipps never got caught."

"That's not Internal Affairs' concern." The rim of sweat

along his upper lip glistened. "What bothers me is why you weren't close enough to back up Detective Phipps."

"That's in the reports, too."

"I've read the reports, detective. I want to hear it from you." The lieutenant stared back at him contemptuously, but then his glare shifted upwards.

Behind him, Gant heard the door to Marler's office open without anyone having knocked.

The lieutenant stood abruptly. "Can I help you?"

"Yeah." The voice was gruff. "You can tell me what the fuck you're doing sittin' in my chair."

Gant looked over his shoulder and saw the massive frame of Captain Floyd Marler overtaking the office.

Marler walked behind where Gant sat and opened the small corner cabinet. There was the familiar sound of a bottle scraping over the shelf, and Gant could picture the captain's huge hand engulfing a squat bottle of Crown Royal whiskey, unscrewing it using only his thumb and forefinger. As a long flow of liquid gurgled from bottle to glass, Eddie watched the IA lieutenant try not to react to Marler's presence.

"I'm sorry, captain," the man from IA said, sounding very military. "I didn't recognize you. I'm Lieutenant Simpson. We've never met."

"Good." Marler finished pouring, screwed the top back on the Crown Royal, and replaced it inside the cabinet. "How you doin' tonight, Eddie?" the captain asked, his phrasing deep and slow. "Hear we had a shooting."

Eddie nodded.

Marler crossed behind Gant and came around the side of his desk, moving just close enough for the lieutenant to realize how much shorter he was than Floyd Marler's 6'8"; how much less he weighed than Marler's 280; how much smaller around his wrists were than Marler's 13 inches.

Sipping warm Crown Royal from a water glass, Marler opened the slim folder that Simpson had kept closed and read the cover page.

Simpson said, "That's classified information, captain. Regulations." The lieutenant started reaching for the file, expecting Marler to close it, then wasn't sure what to do when Marler kept reading.

"Oh, don't worry, lieutenant. I won't tell anyone. Besides, I'm an old man. I'll probably forget whatever I read here within a few hours. The short-term memory goes first." Marler smiled almost benevolently, his gray pencil-thin moustache turning up slightly. His eyes even held a momentary sparkle, making Marler seem quite the huge, bald fifty-seven-year-old teddy bear. "Internal Affairs, huh?"

"Yes. I'm part of the shooting-team assignment."

"Yeah? How 'bout that. Big fucking deal." Marler left Simpson to waddle in a bit of shock as he continued going through the classified file, turning each page patiently, reading a few words, then going on. "You write this bullshit in here, Simpson?" Marler looked up from the file, leaving his big finger resting in the middle of a page.

"Sir, I'm going to have to insist that you close that file."

Gant was impressed; Simpson sounded more assertive than most coming up against Marler.

The captain sipped his Crown Royal. Wearing his usual white short-sleeved shirt, no tie, Marler's thick arms looked like well-wrapped bands of steel primed by years of lifting and workouts with a heavy bag. His skin was tanned dark, despite warnings from his doctor that continued exposure to South Florida's sun would only cause more operations like the ones that already had left scars of removed skin cancers along his arms and shoulders too numerous to count. Marler walked around Simpson and opened the window behind his desk. Then he pulled his chair back from where Simpson stood. "I don't like people sitting in my chair."

Picking his file and pad of lined yellow paper off the desk, Simpson moved off to the side, near the two straight-back chairs that lined the empty wall to Marler's left.

The captain rested his drink on the seat of the oversized office chair his wife had bought him at Burdine's Clearance Center. "You know anything about architecture, lieutenant?"

"What do you mean, sir?"

Gant was enjoying the conversation as he sat across the desk from where Captain Marler stood.

"I mean," Marler repeated, "do you know about architecture? You know, the design of buildings? That sort of thing?"

"To some extent." Simpson seemed at a loss to make sense of this.

"That's good," Marler nodded. "Knowledge like that's very helpful to a policeman. Because—now, I'm no expert on architecture—but I'd say there are two ways out of this room. There's the door. And the window." Marler took another swallow of Crown Royal. "But you see something, Lieutenant Simpson. You have to know more than just architecture, because if all you knew was architecture, you wouldn't know that walking out that door was pretty safe, but going out the window—hell, you'd probably break your neck. See? You have to know something about gravity, too."

"Sir," Simpson spoke during the pause. "If you would rather I continue my conference with Detective Gant somewhere else, I can certainly accommodate you."

"I don't want you to accommodate anything. I want your ass to disappear. And you can forget talking any more to my detective—about this or any other case. Especially this crap I saw in that file about Phipps. You see, lieutenant," Marler said, a certain malice entering his words now, the muscles in his thick neck tightening like twisted cord, "you come around here looking to bark up my tree, you're gonna find a big snarling dog sitting on the first branch ready to piss in your face. Because I think Internal Affairs is a fucking joke. A bunch of tight-assed college boys running around in queer-ass Key West suits who wouldn't know what to do with a hard pecker if they had a road map. Now, most of your boys in IA, they know how I feel. But you're obviously new at this and eager to impress somebody. So we can give you a quick lesson. My men get good shooting reports, or the asshole who writes them up bad learns the difference between architecture" —Marler gestured to the door—"and gravity." He pointed a long, muscular arm toward the window, then leaned forward against the desk, still standing taller than Simpson. "Somebody around here fucks up while they're under me, their ass is mine. By the time IA shows, I'll have already eaten them up and shit them out like last night's pork and beans." Marler finished his Crown Royal.

Simpson, standing motionless, but obviously burning, said, "Is it all right if I leave now, sir? I have my reports to file." And, from the snip in his voice, it was clear that these reports would include Marler's threats.

"Sure thing," Marler smiled, turning into a teddy bear again very quickly. "Try the door . . . this time."

Simpson turned on his heels and left. He walked briskly between the empty scattered desks that made up the detectives' squadroom, yanking open the stairwell door, then disappearing as the metal door closed behind him.

Gant said, "Thanks, captain." He closed his eyes. "I'd had about all I could take just about the shooting. Then he brought up Kyler." He shook his head, sighing. "You know, sometimes, when I'm in a room that's quiet, I can still hear Kyler's voice like it came over the wire we had on him that night. He's begging for that bastard not to shoot him. He's actually sobbing, begging for his life. God . . . And I was in the van listening through the headphones, not even knowing where the hell he was inside that abandoned building. Then the shots came. Goddamn! They were loud even through the wire. Three shots, and I shook with each one."

"You want a drink?" Marler walked back to the cabinet and took out the Crown Royal for another pour.

Gant shook his head.

Captain Marler—Uncle Floyd, as the detectives he commanded referred to him fondly when he wasn't in earshot—sat in his oversized desk chair with a fresh glass of smooth whiskey. Seeing him sitting there, Gant now realized that the big seat had actually dwarfed Simpson when the IA lieutenant had been in it.

Marler swiveled so that he faced the open window, away from Eddie. He leaned back so that all Gant could see of him was the smooth crown of his dark-tanned bald head.

Uncle Floyd seemed perfectly content to look out at the scattered gold and white lights shining in the haze across the night outside. Now and then, the chair would move slightly when Uncle Floyd raised his massive arm and took another swallow or two.

Gant had worked under Floyd Marler for five years now. The first time he'd ever seen Marler explode at a superior, or act with total disregard for regulations he considered asinine, Gant was sure the big man would get reamed inside and out. But it didn't happen. Not then. And never since.

Once Gant had been with Wingate, the black detective who'd driven the new Porsche 944 into the lot earlier this evening, and the two men had talked in amusement about the way Marler got away with acting the way he did.

Gant said he had it figured that Uncle Floyd must have pictures of every higher-up in the department doing it doggie-style with seventy-five-year-old hookers.

Wingate had laughed, then said, "Uncle Floyd reminds me of the gorilla in the story about the world's strongest gorilla in the world's strongest cage. See, this gorilla's in a zoo, and the zoo's got two zookeepers—a new zookeeper on the job for his first day, and an old zookeeper who's been there long as the gorilla.

"After the zoo's closed, and all the people've gone, the two zookeepers are sittin' up in their office lookin' out over the whole zoo. The new zookeeper jumps up and points at the world's strongest gorilla who's pullin' open the bars to the world's strongest cage. The old zookeeper watches, too, but he doesn't seem too surprised.

"Now, the gorilla bends open the bars and steps out of his cage. Then he walks kind of slow across the zoo, looking at all the other animals in their cages. He stops at the water fountain and has himself a drink. Then he climbs up a tree that looks outside the zoo, shakes around up there, scratches his balls. Then he swings down out of the tree, walks back to his cage, gets in, and straightens out the bars again so that no one will realize what he's done.

"Well, the new zookeeper, he's about wettin' his pants. He's jumping up and down, nervous and frantic—obviously a white zookeeper. And he says to the old zookeeper, 'Did you see what that gorilla did? That's not right. He can't go 'round lettin' himself out of his cage and going out all over the zoo.' And the old zookeeper says, 'He does it every day. Has for ten years. That's why, at half-past seven, once we close and everyone's gone, I come up here and sit in the office.'

" 'But he just can't do that!' the new zookeeper says. 'It isn't right. It goes against everything they ever taught me in zoo school. Animals can't be allowed to walk around outside their cages. That gorilla can't do that.' And then the old zookeeper looks at the new zookeeper and says, 'Fine. You tell him.' "

When Wingate had told him that story back then, Gant hadn't made much sense of it. Now he understood perfectly.

"All the new kids are pretty upset downstairs," Uncle Floyd said. He was still looking out his opened window, rocking easily in his huge desk chair. He and Gant had been sitting in silence since shortly after Lieutenant Simpson had gone. "Did you know Rogers?"

"Who?" Gant asked quietly, having fallen into a calming stare at the array of Uncle Floyd's football trophies—mementos of the captains' days at FSU as an all-American defensive lineman.

"Kent Rogers. He was out of the academy about two years, I guess. Been working patrol. Good record. Good cop. He's the one got hit out on One tonight by that Cuban."

"He okay?"

"Hospital had him as critical an hour ago. Maybe I should call. No, shit, those bastard doctors won't know anything new yet. They'll just want to know who to send the bill to." Marler took another healthy sip of whiskey. "He took one just about dead center in the chest. Didn't hit his heart directly, but seemed to open up a pretty good artery somewhere. Shit. Fucking Cuban madman. You know why he shot Rogers? For a lousy half-key of smack buried ass-deep in the trunk. I'm tellin' you, Eddie. This fucking world . . . And then, then you got dicks like that Simpson . . . Jesus. He's a cop? Like he's out of the Oral Roberts Police Academy or something. Christ . . . I'll tell you."

"You think Simpson might give you some trouble? I'm pretty sure he's gonna tell somebody how you treated him."

"He's lucky he's not being scraped off the cement out front." Marler finished the final inch of Crown Royal, then said, "So? Good shooting tonight, Eddie?"

"I think so."

Marler let Gant's answer hang in the air a few moments. "You didn't see the van coming through the intersection, did you?"

Gant saw the scene again in his mind: getting out of the Lotus, running to the intersection, Persuader cocked and ready; then the shot from the Cuban, Eddie diving to the ground, rolling over once completely, firing as soon as he came out of the roll. And there was the van between him and the Cuban. It had been the first thing he saw when he looked up, when he looked up *after* pulling the trigger.

"I'd already fired when I saw it," he admitted.

"You fired too quick," Uncle Floyd said, matter-of-factly. "You felt the pressure, and a little bit of panic made you shoot too fast."

With Marler's back still to him, Gant felt as though the criticism was being spoken to the wall, ricocheting back at him as opposed to a direct hit.

"Not bad judgment on your part, Eddie. Not given the circumstances. But not perfect, either. Which is why I'm telling you. You deserve a clean shooting report—and you'll get one. I don't want you to misunderstand—it's always got to be your life first. Your ass is the one on the line. That first shot you fired was a defensive shot, though. You weren't shooting at a target, you were shooting for a reason—trying to keep that Cuban from shooting at you again. The problem was going to the ground the way you did. You lost sight of your target. You made yourself have to fire blind. You should have gone straight down, sniper-prone, and fired from that angle.

The way you rolled, you just about put your back against the cinderblock dividing wall."

Gant realized now that Uncle Floyd's being here in the middle of a Friday night was no coincidence. Somehow Marler had found out that one of his men had been hit and that another was involved in a subsequent chase and shootout. From all that Marler knew of the fire between Gant and the Cuban, Eddie knew that Marler had already been to the scene and checked things out. "You want me on desk duty until my hearing?"

"No. Fuck, that's a stupid goddamn regulation. I'm short manpower as it is, anyway." Uncle Floyd considered his empty glass, then said, "Tell me something, Eddie. How long since you've seen Janice?"

That one caught Gant from behind. "Almost three weeks."

"Uh-huh. Been that long." Uncle Floyd waited.

"She's been taking some extra flights until Pan Am can switch her to more overseas routes. She said she was getting tired of the Florida-Caribbean circuit."

"You two have a disagreement—or just want to make new living arrangements?"

"I guess a little of both," Eddie said, a half-truth.

"Well, that's too bad. The night the two of you came over for dinner, Alice Ann thought you made a nice couple. Now, me, I wouldn't know much about stuff like what's a nice couple and what isn't, but I figured if there was such a thing as somebody who could be with you so that you were a part of a nice couple, she was probably it." Uncle Floyd pulled himself up from his big chair; his body seemed to grow out of it, overpowering the room and everything in it. "Eddie, it's been a long night, son. I'm gonna head home. Why don't you do the same? Get some sleep. Then maybe Monday morning we'll talk about switching you out of narcotics for a while. Maybe you might even want to take a week or two off and get out of the humidity around here—maybe catch a Pan Am flight down to the islands. Hell, it's off season, and they got nice breezes down there."

"Captain, I like narcotics. I don't think you should move me just because of this."

"Got nothing to do with it. I told you, it was a good shoot. Damned good shoot. I just think maybe it's time you give yourself a break. You haven't had a vacation in what—two years?" Marler walked through his open office door into the detectives' squadroom, leaving Gant in his office. "But we'll talk about it Monday, Eddie. Whatever you want to do . . ."

Three

Eddie Gant put down the Lotus's windows to let the night air flow through the car on the drive home. He took U.S. 1—South Dixie Highway—toward Kendall, past Miller Road, where he'd turned after the Cuban several hours earlier. Goddamn strange how his paths for work so often crossed those for home. Maybe it was because all he did any more was work. Even if he wasn't officially on duty, he was always sniffing around, cruising, looking to make a buy, finding out if a deal was going down. Where? When? How much? How soon? Who's moving it? Jesus, maybe Uncle Floyd was right. Maybe he should transfer out of narcotics for a while—or at least take a vacation.

Turning right onto SW 88th Street, he rolled through the red light without stopping, glancing left quick to make sure no one was coming. Then he gunned the Turbo, hitting 65 fast. Cheap thrill, but he needed it.

Eddie's home was a terrace-level apartment in a sprawling complex called Spanish Isles. There wasn't an island in sight, and the only water was a man-made lake that looked smaller than some Palm Beach bathtubs Eddie had seen. But the architecture—like every other square inch of Florida from Orlando south—was Spanish, or Mediterranean, or whatever the builders had been told by their ad people to call it now to make the things rent or sell faster.

The exterior walls were finished in fancy stucco patterns and the roofs were honest-to-God red-clay tile in the older section where Gant lived. The newer sections were roofed with sheets of aluminum molded and painted to look like tile—probably a high-tech Japanese innovation threatening to outmode an entire culture of Mayan clay workers.

The closest parking space was three buildings away. The housing code called for a minimum number of parking spaces per apartment, but apparently there was no limit to the number of cars—or people—assignable to a single unit. Or if there was, management seemed happier with fifteen Marielite refugees who could scrape up the $300 rent than two Haitians whom they had to take to court every month.

Eddie was too tired to feel conspicuous carrying his Persuader riot gun over his arm. Most everyone was either asleep or prone to mind their own business this hour of the night anyway.

Walking down the chipped concrete walk, Eddie glanced casually into apartment windows where lights were on. It was surprising what you could see if you paid attention and knew what to look for. A few weeks back, he'd caught half a dozen guys uncarting bricks of marijuana on their dining-room table. They'd been so casual about it; breaking open the containers, weighing it, rewrapping it in ounce bags. Eddie had just stood outside the window and waited for backup to arrive to make the bust. Then there was that cute little *señorita* he'd spied undressing in her bedroom while he was on stakeout down in Perrine a few months back. The little mama was playing mule, smuggling some mid-level-seller's coke through customs at Miami International in body belts. She'd been getting past the dogs at the airport because of a very strong, yet surprisingly inoffensive body odor that had saved her from being sniffed out.

Eddie unlocked his mailbox and took out the single envelope that he recognized immediately as a reminder that his rent was past due. He got one every month, because Dade-Metro paid on the fifteenth and thirtieth and rent was due the twenty-first. His check on the fifteenth always took care of his other bills, so the rent had to wait nine days until his second pay period of the month.

His apartment was a one-bedroom that was down five steps from the landing. There was always a little puddle between his door and his neighbor's; it sat just to the neighbor's side of a small drain, where the concrete was a noticeable inch lower than the drain itself. And three mornings out of five, Gant would hear the guy next door—a moronic-looking man who told Gant he sold mutual funds, when Eddie knew for a fact he was an assistant manager at Jefferson's discount store—swear loudly when he stepped in the puddle.

Inside, Eddie turned on the standing lamp in the living room. He hung his riot gun and the holstered .45 on the brass coatrack Janice had given him for his birthday, then dropped the rent notice on the coffee table next to the Swanson's frozen spaghetti and meatballs he'd had the other day for lunch. When his hand jostled the aluminum tray, a palmetto bug scooted out from beneath it. Eddie swatted at it with his hand, missed, then grabbed a week-old section of the *Miami Herald* sports page and took a wild backhand swing at the roach as it darted to safety in a crack in the floor molding.

"Little shit," Gant swore, throwing the newspaper after it. He picked up the remains of the TV dinner, walked it to the kitchen, and dumped it in the trash.

Another palmetto bug scurried out from beneath the trash can, ran up the wall a few inches, then got smeared over the plaster when Eddie squashed him with the toe of his iguana-skin boot.

"One for two," Eddie said, wiping off his boot and the wall with a paper towel, not quite removing all of the bug remains from either. "Rickey Henderson ain't that good."

Back in the living room, he pushed aside the sun-faded

curtains that hung an inch too long, dragging over the carpet. He made sure the terrace door was locked, then went into the bedroom.

Sitting on the unmade side of the double bed, he pulled off his boots with some effort. He looked at the 8″ × 10″ photograph of Janice in the imitation tortoise-shell frame on the nightstand. He'd been telling himself to put that in a drawer someplace, but he really liked the way her eyes looked at him.

He took that shot the weekend they drove over to Naples on the Gulf Coast. That had only been three months ago—damn, just a month after he'd met her. Yet it seemed as if he'd known her for so long. Sometimes it was like that; you'd meet someone, and in a week it was like you'd spent the past ten years together. Other people you could know a lifetime and never know them at all.

God. Janice. One pretty lady. He stared at that picture. He missed her laugh.

The telephone sat right beside the standing frame, and next to that was the glowing red face of his clock radio that displayed a digital 2:17. Not that late. He picked up the phone, punching in the numbers without having to check where he'd written them down, as he had the first week after she'd gone.

A very sleepy and slightly irritated woman answered at the other end.

"Janice?"

"No." The reply was dulled by sleep, yet still angry. "Who is this? Eddie?"

Gant recognized Beth's voice now. Janice had moved in with her a couple of days after Beth had kicked out her boyfriend. The timing looked conspiratorial as hell to Eddie, as though the two of them had decided to dump their old men at the same time, then rely on one another for emotional support to get through the breakup.

"Jesus Christ, Eddie. It's two-fifteen in the goddamned morning. The rest of the world doesn't work cop hours, you know."

"Is Janice there?"

"No." Then, as if just remembering, Beth added, "She's laid over in Antigua."

"She get her transfer yet?"

"No, unh-unh."

"Does she still want it, or hasn't it come through?"

Beth breathed steadily, sleepily into the phone. "She'll be back in Miami early tomorrow, but she's got another flight. She might stop home, she might not. Maybe you could try the airport, Eddie."

Gant started to ask again about the transfer, but Beth hung up.

Eddie awakened Saturday around noon, feeling as if he could use another two hours sleep; but after tossing and turning for fifteen minutes, he decided it was useless. He sat on the edge of the bed and scratched his scalp, waiting for the blood to flow before standing. There was a small scab on his left wrist he hadn't noticed before. He picked at it a few times, trying unsuccessfully to figure out where it could have come from.

He showered, letting cool water spray in his face, waking him up. Not bothering to towel completely dry, he put on a pair of blue gym shorts and lay on the living-room carpet, forcing his way through some sit-ups, getting to fifteen before becoming completely bored.

Opening the curtains to another beautiful Florida day, he was not impressed. The sunlight shining into his living room only served to turn up half a dozen palmetto bugs making a dash for the kitchen. By the time Gant picked out one of them to target with his foot, they were all gone. Some things just were not better by the light of day.

There were no eggs and the milk was sour, so he had corn flakes with orange juice poured over them, adding slices of a soft banana to try and overcome the strange combination. He ate slowly and tried to think of something to do today, figuring he'd probably just ride around a little while, then go into the station.

By the time he finished eating, no better choice had come to mind, so he put on a pair of denim OP shorts, a sleeveless

T-shirt, and Nike three-quarter-top basketball shoes with athletic socks pushed down around his ankles. He carried his riot gun and .45 to the car in an athletic bag. On the sidewalk out front, he made a one-handed interception of a football thrown wobbly through the air by a pair of ten-year-old boys with white-blond hair. "Snake Stabler," he said, throwing the ball back to one of them.

And the other one said, "Who?"

Eddie drove half a mile from his apartment, then decided to stop kidding himself. This wasn't any casual drive around Dade County; he was going to Janice's.

It was too hot to keep riding with the windows down, so Eddie turned the air conditioning on full, willing to let some of the Lotus's turbocharged power get sucked off for his luxury. He put the radio on a mellow rock station, turned up a Kenny Loggins song loud, and worked to keep from getting run off the road by the crazed driving of Latino housewives in their Jaguars and BMWs. He even managed to smile the whole way down U.S. 1, thinking, if he was still on patrol, he could write up an entire ticket book in half an hour.

Janice's black Mustang convertible was parked in front of the plain-looking three-story apartment house. It didn't mean she was home because she usually got a ride to the airport or took a cab instead of paying ten bucks a day to park. Still, Eddie saw it as a good sign.

He took up two spaces with the Lotus parked sideways. He climbed the stairs to the third floor two at a time, wondering if he should've brought flowers. Stuff like this always went better if you brought flowers.

Eddie knocked on the door, putting his hand over the peephole. Listening, he heard footsteps coming toward the door. Then it was quiet as he pictured whoever was inside trying to look out, maybe rubbing the lens with their fingers and wondering why they still couldn't see anything. "I have a warrant for your arrest," he said.

The deadbolt was clicked, and the door opened about a foot.

Janice stood in the doorway wearing a white terrycloth robe that made her tan look even darker. Her hair was wet, looking freshly washed. "Hello, Eddie," she said without emotion, keeping a hand on the doorknob.

"It's been a while."

She nodded.

"Can I come in?" he asked, hesitant now, the carefree feeling he'd felt coming up the stairs lost to the chill of her response.

"I don't think so. I have to be at MIA in an hour."

"Oh." He stuck his hands in the pockets of his OPs. "How's the Caribbean? Off season now, right?"

"Yes."

He looked at her. God, she was gorgeous. Janice had mysterious wide brown eyes that were almost almond-shaped, and thick, silky brown hair, high cheekbones that accentuated her face so dramatically. Her breasts were full, her hips curving nicely from a waist that was lean without being skinny. Eddie had asked her a couple of times how old she was, and her answer had always been the same: she'd laugh, look off into the distance, as though calculating how old she *felt,* then pick a number as she'd pull him close in a loving hug. Once he thought about stealing her driver's license to check it out for sure, but stopped himself. He liked not knowing her age; that way, the times he wanted her to be young, she could be young, when he wanted her older, she was. Age was such a funny thing anyway.

Janice started to close the door. "I have to go, Eddie."

"I thought . . . ," he hurried into the sentence, not really knowing what to say, just not wanting her to shut the damned door.

She waited for him to finish.

"Goddammit," he sighed, frustrated. "Can't you talk a couple minutes? I really want to see you again . . . I miss you."

"Eddie," she said plainly, looking down, hiding her eyes, "I don't think we should do this to each other anymore. Okay? It's just not fair. I don't want to keep going over and over it when nothing's going to change."

"What? Tell me. I *can* change. I just don't know . . . I don't know what you want."

She shook her head. "What I want is not to have some other woman pick up the phone whenever I call you from out of town."

Shit, he'd told them never to answer his phone. They could stay, but just don't answer the fucking phone; he'd always told them that. "I'm sorry. I really——"

"It's too late to apologize, Eddie, it won't change things. I know we said we were just going to try out living together. No commitments. No strings. No nothing. But it didn't work for me—okay? I just couldn't handle it like that. I never felt like I belonged. I was just the person who slept beside you *most* of the time. Maybe it wasn't even that much—I don't know. Who knows what you were doing when I was away."

"Why didn't you tell me then?"

"Oh, Eddie. My God! I did. *Constantly.*" Janice combed her fingers through her hair, sweeping it back.

"What? When?"

She looked at him dumbfounded. How could he have missed it?

Eddie said, "What? Tell me. When did you ever tell me what was wrong—what was bothering you?"

"I don't want this to get ugly. I have to get to the airport. I'm sorry if I never spelled it out in big bold letters for you to read. I guess I should have taken out an ad in the sports section—okay? I'm sorry. It must have been all my fault that you're screwing every teenager who walks down the block."

"Goddammit, Janice, that's not fair."

"Do you know what it feels like to be five hundred miles away and call the person you've been thinking about for the past four hours, the person you can't wait to talk to, and then some goddamned *bimbo* answers the phone—answers it in the bedroom where I slept the night before? Do you know what that feels like? Huh, Eddie? Do you?" The graceful curves of her almond eyes filled with tears.

Looking at her, Eddie hurt.

"I loved you, Eddie. And I thought you loved me. Forget

about the *arrangement,* I thought you *loved* me." She wiped the tear that ran down her cheek with the soft sleeve of her robe. "I have to go now, Eddie. I'm sorry."

She closed the door quietly, but the sound of the deadbolt locking made him jump as if it were the jailhouse doors slamming shut.

Four

He was born Javier Mendez in 1951, in the Dominican Republic, but he had not answered to that name for fifteen years. In fact, he had trained himself not to respond to that name in any way, because it could have caused problems.

He now used many names, but never the same one twice. The police—the feds—they tended to let a person's aliases get knee-deep in their computers, and if you slipped and went back to a favorite one, the data banks might kick you out if you got pulled over for a speeding ticket or tried to clear customs.

He considered his ability to change identities with pride. He could go for months using one name, and, in the process, fabricate a biography so detailed that he would begin to believe it himself. Sometimes, looking back on his life, he wouldn't be exactly sure what had been real or made up.

He also knew he was very lucky, but thought of himself as twice again as daring as he was fortunate. He had, as Americans would call it, balls. He had keen perception and icy nerves that fought off the natural inclination to panic under intense—even life-threatening—pressure.

He'd needed the talent to survive those first runs of coke through U.S. Customs back in the early 1970s. Barely twenty years old, he'd brought in as much as ten pounds at a time, literally strolling through customs. Back then, the law-enforcement manpower hadn't been there to worry with drugs; skyjackings had been the crime of public outrage.

By the time the airports became sensitive to drug smugglers, he had already moved onto other deceits, staying a step ahead. He used boats to island-hop southern waters, moving huge loads at a time right up Florida's Intracoastal, making door-to-door deliveries from Bolivian docks to the private piers of million-dollar estates in Boca Raton.

Always innovative, he claimed to be the first to use what he termed a "blind mule": a smuggler who didn't know he was smuggling. Blind mules had been used before Mendez was born—although for other things—but the fact that he thought of it without any historical references made him feel that title to the idea was his.

His typical blind-mule setup would begin in Caribbean tourist islands. He would stuff cocaine in an unsuspecting tourist's luggage, then board the same flight to the States. He'd make sure the blind mule cleared customs, then rip off the luggage. He'd gotten in as much as twenty pounds at a time that way. And the risk had been minimal, while the profit—between '77 and '79, before the prices started drifting down—bordered on the incredible.

But he didn't smuggle drugs anymore. He'd started using on a little more than a casual basis, getting into the American coke scene, cruising into clubs wearing tight leather pants. He'd be pocketing envelopes full of toot and leaving with a girl on each arm. That had been stupid, risky as shit. He'd been busted twice and jumped bail each time, leaving behind FTA warrants in New York and L.A. Not only that, but he'd found it harder to keep his head clear: facts began to muddle, his lies became confused, and his cons started coming apart as a result. So he got clean of all that two years ago.

He'd begun to realize that for as good at what he did as he considered himself, he wasn't getting anywhere. He was bringing in 70 to 80 Gs a year, but it was always an agent's share of profits for taking most of the risk. He was nickel-diming working freelance for the big guys who were raking it in big because of his efforts, his genius.

He told himself he was too smart to be somebody else's boy. He wanted the big money. *Really* big money. The lion's share of the deal. The winner's cut.

So he'd started looking for a big deal he could work for himself. And he'd found one. It was big and it was dirty.

That's why he was in Key Biscayne now.

On Saturday afternoon, Javier Mendez sat poolside at Sonesta Beach wearing a tight nylon bathing suit, red with orange stripes, that left no secret that the flaccid six-inch bulge was lying to the left of his balls. Javier was proud of his talents, and proud of his equipment, all of which he considered God-given.

Reading the Spanish edition of the *Miami Herald*, ordering rum and cokes from the pool boy in a rich South American accent, his dark-tanned fit-looking body slathered with coconut oil, it seemed almost obvious that he truly *was* Aurelio Santiago, the Costa Rican businessman his passport said he was. He was just another Latin enjoying a vacation between international ventures here in Key Biscayne.

The hotel, Mendez, a/k/a Santiago, figured, was only about half-full. It was the beginning of the off season, the first week in June, when all the snowbirds had gone back north, leaving south Florida to its natives and those who couldn't afford to get away in high season.

Key Biscayne, though, was expensive all year round. Santiago's spacious oceanfront room with the two double beds, rattan furniture, and designer bedspread was $175 a day. But that was all right. He was giving himself a lavish bankroll for this job. It was his first solo venture and it would also be his last—a big enough deal to retire on.

He smiled, thinking that, turning a page of the People section of the *Herald*.

An hour ago, walking through the hotel lobby, he'd seen half a dozen pieces of Louis Vuitton luggage lined up near the glass doors, waiting for the courtesy bus to the airport. In his earlier days he would have marked bags like that to use for blind mules, knowing that customs agents often had hell to pay if they did more than a cursory search of some rich lady's suitcase. The rich, he had learned, liked to see customs doing their job—it gave them a feeling of security in an insecure world—but if law enforcement touched them so closely as to make them feel suspect, the rich turned shitty fast.

He was glad he didn't do that anymore. It had been fun and exciting back in days when he didn't know that $1,000 American was barely enough money to hire someone to scratch your ass.

This job now, this one was worth a guaranteed quarter-million—maybe lots more, depending on how hard he wanted to play it. He'd have to be ready to deal with the real big boys, one on one. This was a hell of a jump, from dealing with guys running the drug markets, way beyond them.

His first step was less than twenty-four hours away: She was sitting right there on the beach.

Her name was Amy Lansing, a cute twenty-year-old with soft brunette hair that caressed her shoulders. She wore a bold-colored bikini that barely contained her small breasts, and the bottoms rode up high over her narrow hipbones, exposing half her ass.

She had arrived alone, as he'd been told she would, yesterday—Friday—afternoon, driving a yellow Triumph Spitfire. She'd checked in with a canvas bag slung over her shoulder, paying the single rate for two nights in advance with a gold American Express card.

By 7:00 last night, however, she was no longer alone. Santiago had been sitting by the pool watching her. The young man walking down the beach had alerted Santiago's eye moments earlier, but then he'd ignored the athletic-looking man until seeing him approach Amy Lansing.

She'd embraced him with a welcoming hug, pulling him down onto her beach towel, laughing loudly enough for her voice to carry the sixty yards that separated her from Santiago. Her hands had gone inside the young man's blue oxford shirt, caressing his chest as she kissed him passionately.

Her lover had then removed his black plastic-frame sunglasses and rolled on top of her. To the obvious disgust of an older couple seated in beach loungers nearby, he and Amy groped away for about half an hour, then had the good taste to go to her room.

Santiago had followed them, riding up in the same elevator, smiling at her when she'd looked with embarrassment at where her boyfriend's hands held her. Santiago stayed on once the pair exited on the fifth floor, then he got off on ten and walked down the stairs.

On the fifth floor, he'd walked by Amy Lansing's room and heard passionate giggles without having to press his ear to the door. The girl made the most enticing cries of pleasure, as though surprised how her body reacted to sexual touches.

Santiago figured the "Do Not Disturb" sign on the knob was stupid, considering all the noise they were making.

Taking the elevator back to the lobby, Santiago had wondered whether Amy Lansing was an experienced lover. Would she scratch her fingernails down her lover's back when she came? Would she stretch out vulnerably in a spread eagle and let him do her? Or maybe wrap her legs up around his waist, giving him a full downward angle to thrust inside her? Was she experienced enough to press a fingertip gently around her lover's ass just as he was about to come? Or would she seem awkward with it all—enjoying it, but not practiced enough to know just what to do?

Santiago had thought about this again later Friday night— when he was down on the beach, secluded from view by a small clump of palm trees, looking through binoculars up to Amy Lansing's room. His intentions had not been those of a voyeur; his purpose was far less honorable.

Now it was 5:00 P.M., Saturday, and Santiago's mind was

concerned more with Amy Lansing as applied to the business at hand. Her young man—lover—was still here, having spent last night and the entire day today on the beach with her. If he was going to stay over again, Santiago's plan would have to be changed.

Santiago left his Spanish edition of the *Miami Herald* quarter-folded on the deck beside his chaise. He slipped on the striped Albert Nipon shirt he'd paid $50 for at Saks in La Galleria Mall and strapped his gold Rolex Presidential watch around his wrist. He also wore a thick 18K S-chain, that had been worth $3,000 back in the sky-high-gold-price days, when he'd ripped it off some faggot interior designer in L.A.

Santiago walked to the Sonesta lobby. At the desk, a very attractive young woman worked alone; she had her hands full with a middle-aged woman wearing a tent-sized flower-print dress who couldn't believe that a hotel charging "these ridiculous rates" would make her pay for a thirty-minute toll call to her sister Myrtle in Duluth.

Waiting for the flowered cow to get the hell out of the lobby or drop dead—he didn't care which—Santiago browsed the gift shop, looking over shelves of overpriced silk shirts.

When the woman finally left, Santiago walked straight to the front desk, starting to smile at the neatly dressed young lady behind the counter when he was halfway across the tiled lobby.

She seemed relieved to see an unfrowning face. "Can I help you?" she asked. Her thick brunette hair hung nearly to her waist, a slight hint of henna running through it. She wore a starched white blouse with a small red bow tie that was knotted efficiently.

"I hope that you can, my dear." Santiago shifted into his prime, suave wealthy-South-American format, speaking the way his bosses had talked when they were trying to con someone. "I was wondering if it would be possible to change my room."

"Is something wrong?"

Santiago liked the way her eyes showed interest. He was very much attracted to eyes, and hers were the softest shade of light brown. He saw a quality there that was tamed, yet still animalistic.

"No. The room is"—he paused dramatically, as though searching for the right word—"simply lovely." He said it with such flair and charm, painting a picture with his tongue. "But, you see, it is not very high from the ground. Only the third floor. And the small children ... well, very early in the morning they are in the pool splashing and ... carrying on. It makes it most difficult to sleep." His hands went through the air as though swimming, and he smiled, describing it. "You see?" he laughed. "They swim like this. Although others, they don't swim so good. More like this." He held his nose and made a face as though he were drowning.

The young lady behind the desk laughed.

"Ah, you have a laugh as pretty as your face." He reached over the counter and touched her hand. Her expression showed the slightest interest, so he raised her hand to his lips, kissing it softly, then seemed embarrassed to have done so. "I am sorry. You are here working, and I am acting like a foolish man."

"That's okay," she smiled, leaning forward on the counter. "To tell you the truth, this has been a rotten day."

Looking over the counter, Santiago could see her entire body now. She had a lean figure, a body not at all unlike that of the Lansing girl he had been watching: the same slim waist, although larger breasts that pressed into the front of her blouse, and she was perhaps seven or eight years older.

She seemed flattered by the attention of this obviously wealthy man who looked much nearer her age than the old farts who came clutching after her when their wives were taking a nap. "You asked about changing your room." She paused, letting him look at her some more before turning to the rows of cubbyholes that lined the wall behind her; some containing keys, some mail, some empty altogether. "I could move you up to the seventh floor," she said, stopping at one of the slots.

"Seventh floor. That may be a bit too high. I don't mean to be any trouble to you, Miss ... ?"

"Meyers. I'm Allie Meyers." She came back to the counter smiling fondly, holding out her slim hand to shake his.

He started to kiss the back of her fingers again, but stopped.

Allie held an oval-shaped key ring of sea blue plastic; the number 609 was embossed on it in white. "Is the sixth floor okay?"

"Six is lovely," he replied, pleased. 609. Amy Lansing was in 511—one floor below, two to the north—even closer than he had hoped.

Allie picked up a registration form. "I need your name and current room number."

He chatted idly as she did the paper work. He remarked how different the weather was here in Florida from that in Costa Rica. There was always a mild afternoon rain in the mountains around his estate that cooled things off. "I never close the windows. They stay open all the time. And the birds"—he fluttered his hands through the air—"they fly through all day long. They are the most beautiful color, those birds. Ahhh, such things of beauty. They spoil me. They make my standards very high. I am not so easily attracted as I was as a young boy. Although still as eager."

When she finished, Allie offered him a duplicate key. "Will you need this?"

He leaned forward, whispering. "I am here alone. You keep it. Use it when you come by later to show me the pretty new dress you buy." Santiago laid his hand flat on the counter. "Make sure it is a pretty dress." He winked and lifted his hand, leaving a crisp $100 bill on the counter.

Allie gasped. She hadn't even noticed his hand reach into his pocket.

Five

On Saturday evening, Santiago dined on the patio of a neighboring hotel. The sun was setting behind the uneven row of high-rise hotels and condominiums to his left while a mild inland breeze made it comfortable outside. Now it was almost as nice as the afternoon rains at his estate in Costa Rica, he thought, amusing himself, proud of such spur-of-the-moment imagery.

As an appetizer, Santiago had cracked stone-crab claws with mustard sauce; the crab was good, but the sauce was lousy, so he scraped it off the crabmeat with his fork. His main course was poached grouper in champagne sauce, and, with this, too, the fish was wonderful—firm and white—but the sauce was awful. What was it, he wondered, that made them want to ruin a perfectly good bit of food with some fancy-assed sauce that tasted like cheap cologne?

After his meal, he sat back, as he figured any wealthy Costa Rican business magnate would, and smoked a Cuban cigar. It was an honest-to-God Cuban cigar, too, sent as a present by a Central American friend. He blew the sweet-smelling smoke into the air and watched it fan out in the breeze.

He paid cash for his bill and left a twenty-percent tip. Feeling as if he belonged on the Key, with his linen pants, a dark pink cotton shirt, tan Polo socks, and burgundy tassled loafers, Santiago strolled Biscayne Boulevard. At the shopping center across the street from the driveway to his hotel, he went into the hardware store and browsed the aisles.

The shop's few customers were all men fifty or older who had the look of year-round residents: retired mid-level executives fed up with the unreliable and outrageously expensive repairmen who fed on condo owners like vultures circling dying rabbits. Handymen drafted into service by necessity and an ample but closely guarded "fixed income," these fellows in their pale blue sun hats poked through shelves looking for just the right thing to tackle the latest in a never-ending series of odd jobs around home.

Conversations tended to spring up between strangers going through the same cardboard slots of assorted screws and nails. A relaxed rapport would often develop that would carry through a stroll down to the marina bar, a few drinks, and before they knew it, another day had gone by without fixing that damned leaky showerhead.

To Santiago, it seemed not relaxing, but depressing. What was life without excitement, danger? It wasn't living, it was taking up space—a playing piece on a board that didn't participate, only observed.

Near the rear of the store, Santiago found the nylon rope he was looking for. There was a good assortment. He tried tying a square knot in the ends of the stronger-looking rope, then settled on one and measured off thirty feet. About to slice the rope with cutters that hung from a display pole, Santiago recalculated, deciding to give himself another five feet just to be sure. He paid cash for the rope, taking the receipt out of the bag and throwing it in the trash can just outside the store.

Back at Sonesta Beach, he went up to the fifth floor and walked by Amy Lansing's room. The "Do Not Disturb" sign was gone, and Santiago became concerned. Had he been too casual? Maybe he shouldn't have left the hotel for dinner, but should have stayed where he could watch her.

Not showing the urgency he felt, he took the elevator down to the lobby and walked through the hotel restaurant, then the coffee shop. Amy and her lover weren't there.

He went out by the swimming pool, scanning the dark beach. About seventy yards to his right, he saw them leaning against the bent trunk of a palm tree.

Santiago sat on the railing, feeling foolish holding the over-sized bag of rope; but he didn't want to break contact with Amy Lansing again. Besides, there was no one around to notice.

Almost twenty minutes passed before Amy Lansing and her lover came walking arm-in-arm back to the hotel. Santiago moved into the shadows of the pool bar, waiting until they had gone inside the hotel before following them. He didn't board the same elevator, but remained in the lobby, watching the indicator of their car, making sure it stopped on the fifth floor.

Satisfied, Santiago went to his new room on six. Once there, he put the rope in the closet. He crumpled the brown paper bag into the diameter of a basketball, then walked down the hall to the service closet and dropped it into the trash chute.

It was now a few minutes before 9:00.

He dialed room service and told them to bring up a bottle of champagne on ice and two glasses around 10:30. He ordered a second bottle of champagne, telling them to deliver it now. Yes, also on ice, also with two glasses, but to be delivered to room 511. "Don't tell them who it's from. Just say, 'With our compliments.' Have you got that? 'With our compliments.' Don't say anything else, and don't wait for a tip. I'll take care of that later."

The person taking the order claimed to understand.

Santiago made another call. He pushed the "9" button on his phone, waiting briefly for an outside line before dialing.

On the second ring, a woman answered. "Six-five-oh-nine."

"Tonight."

"Pardon me, sir?"

"That's the message: Tonight."

"Who should I say is calling, sir?" the woman asked, sounding as if she thought he had some kind of problem.

"The whole message is just one word. *Tonight*. Got that?"

The woman tried to hide her sigh. "Yes, sir. Tonight."

Santiago put down the phone and went into the closet. He took the small hard-sided suitcase from the top shelf. Removing a few pairs of underwear, he lifted up the false bottom; it was not a rig designed to get through airport security or customs, it was just an inconspicuous-looking piece of baggage that carried whatever Santiago required of it successfully, without drawing undue attention. A shopping bag or Louis Vuitton suitcase could have worked equally well.

Under the false bottom, Santiago pulled out the SIG-Sauer P-230 pistol, a compact little West German .380 measuring only 6.5 inches from stock to barrel tip. He popped out the slide, making sure all eight cartridges were in place, then set it back inside the stock.

He carried the pistol into the bathroom, setting it on the counter. He removed the can of hair spray from his travel kit and banged it against the doorknob. The bottom popped out, and Santiago reached up inside the hollowed-out can, removing a wrapping of coarse toilet paper from the silencer that fit the P-230.

Silencers and pistols, he'd found, were always best carried separately. Effort should be made to conceal both, but far more time should be spent hiding the silencer, because the pistol, while illegal, could always be explained as belonging to an insecure tourist, while the silencer had "assassination" written all over it.

"I absolutely fell in love with it as soon as I saw it. Do you like it?" Allie Meyers pirouetted at the foot of the bed for Santiago. She wore a bright pink minidress that had black leopard spots angling from her right shoulder down to her left thigh. It had a deep scooped back that revealed lots of warm-looking skin, and the way her nipples poked into the front made it obvious that she wore the dress without a bra.

"Yes," Santiago smiled, looking at her long, lean legs. "I

like it . . . very much." He had known she would come, that she would use the key he had left with her at the desk.

"Is it exotic or erotic?" Allie asked, much more playful now, posing coyly for him, hands holding her thighs, almost caressing them.

"I find it both." Santiago positioned himself on the bed so that the crotch of his linen pants would grab tightly around his genitals, making an obvious outline. He waited until he was sure that Allie had seen the lengthy bulge before changing positions. "Some champagne?" he asked, rising off the bed.

The ice bucket was sweating a wide ring on the veneer tabletop. Grasping the cold neck of the bottle, Santiago twisted it crisply back and forth through the ice, then drew it out dramatically, as though hoisting a sword. Expertly, he tugged out the cork with a loud pop. Foamy suds gushed over the stem, and Allie hurried over to drink the overflow.

She swallowed quickly, then started laughing, trying to take too much of the frothy liquid that ran over her lips. "Look at me!" she cried, shaking off her hands and arms. "Swimming in champagne." The front of her dress was splashed wet, the material sticking to her.

Santiago held the bottle high. "The most expensive swimming pool in the world." He poured two glasses, making sure to hold his drink in the hand that showed off his Rolex watch as he toasted her. "To the most beautiful bird ever to enter my estate." He touched the glass to his lips, but did no more than taste the champagne.

Allie, a hint of blushing warm over her face, met his eyes. Looking very much taken with him, she drank half her glass, which Santiago then refilled quickly.

They stood close and she leaned against him. "This is going right to my head." She tossed back her long hair. "I haven't eaten. It was too much fun trying on the clothes." She hesitated, tracing a fingernail lightly over his chest. "I bought something else . . . although I don't know if I should show you . . . not now, anyway."

"Why won't you show me?" He pretended his feelings were hurt, reaching behind her, stroking her silky hair.

"Because"—she toyed with the thick gold chain he wore, sipping more champagne—"you can see right through it."

Santiago grinned. "Ahh, then I in*sist* you show me. You don't have to put it on. Just show me."

"I'll put it on . . . later." She let him hug her, feeling his chest against her breasts. She returned the soft kiss he pressed to her lips, touching his tongue with hers, then easing her mouth away. "But I want to know about you. You sound like you have such a fascinating life." Looking up at him, she could smell the subtle allure of his cologne, feel the pressure of his phallus against her loins.

"My life is actually very frustrating. My business puts very hard demands on me." His hand slid down her back, resting on her ass.

"But you have your home—your estate—in the mountains where it rains every afternoon and the birds fly through."

"Unfortunately, I am only able to spend a few months a year there. There is not much business to be done in Costa Rica alone. Most of my dealings require my being in the United States or Europe."

"Mmmm," she sighed, sipping. "I've never been to Europe. What's it like?"

Santiago poured more champagne for her, never leaving her embrace. "Oh, my dear. Europe! It is as fascinating and varied as each country, each city, each street. You cannot possibly describe Europe. You can only experience it."

"I would *love* to do that. I feel so dull. I was born in Florida. Married and divorced in Florida. I've been as far as Georgia . . . *once*." She looked almost hypnotized, staring at the rich gold color of his necklace. "I just can't seem to get out of this state. And you've been so many places."

"Maybe someday you would come with me."

"I would *love* to. I really would." She kissed him, excited by the thought. "Where would you take me?"

"Anyplace. Every place! Wherever you wanted to go." He nearly sang the words.

"Ow! I love it. *Anyplace!"* She broke his embrace, twirling a small circle, holding her glass high over her head. Champagne splashed down her arm and she licked it off her skin. Finishing that glass, Santiago offered to pour another, and she accepted.

He looked suddenly melancholy. "I do not mean to ruin our evening, but I feel that I must tell you something. It is part of what I meant earlier about the demands of my business." He touched her cheek softly. "I received a telegram not long ago . . ."

The sparkle in her eyes faded slightly and she looked away. "You have to leave," she realized.

Santiago nodded sorrowfully.

"When?"

"Tomorrow . . . for Switzerland." He released her and turned away. "I'm sorry. I see I am disappointing you. I shouldn't have said anything . . . because now I have ruined your evening."

Allie put down her glass and turned him back toward her, rejoining their embrace. She kissed him. "Actually, I'm glad you *did* tell me. It shows me that I'm not wrong about you."

"Wrong about me? I don't understand."

She kissed him, easing out of their hug, then picked up the small pink shopping bag she'd left by the door. "Most men wouldn't have said they were leaving. They would have gone off in the morning without a word, and I would have never heard from them again."

"I would not do that." He feigned offense, then spoke quickly with excitement. "Sometime soon after tomorrow, I will come back and we will spend more time together. Or maybe, if I cannot come to Florida quickly enough"—he snapped his fingers—"you will come to Costa Rica. I will send you a plane ticket."

Allie pushed her tongue fully through his lips, tasting like champagne. "I would meet you anywhere you wanted. Right now, I'm going into the bathroom to change." She pulled a sheer beige chemise from her pink bag, holding it briefly for him to see. It had a deep V-cut in the front and looked barely long enough to cover her ass. "If you want," Allie said, "my

driver's license has my address on it. It's in my pocketbook.
You'll have to call information for the phone number, though,
'cause it's disconnected right now and by the time I can afford
to have them hook it back up, I'll probably be assigned a new
number."

In a few moments, Allie emerged from the bathroom in her
sheer chemise. She remained close to the wall, touching herself, letting Santiago realize he could clearly see her pale
rose-colored nipples and her auburn triangle.

She waited there as he undressed with the lights on, her
eyes fascinated by the length of his erection. When his pants
were off, she knelt in front of him, wrapping both hands
around its smooth head, taking it between her lips. She sucked
on him until she could taste a hint of semen on her tongue,
then she eased away, lying on the bed.

Santiago undressed her, finding Allie moist and eager; she
was even more so as he kissed between her legs, gently separating her folds with his fingertips, putting his tongue into
her seam, until she writhed passionately, coming, clawing at
his shoulders.

She was still breathing deeply when Santiago entered her,
patiently letting her grow accustomed to his size. They moved
in a perfect rhythm, climaxing together, then stayed in each
other's arms until Allie fell asleep, her breath still sweet of
champagne.

Santiago slid open the balcony door. Before stepping outside, he looked back to the bed.

Allie was there naked, asleep atop rumpled sheets, her
breasts pressed closed together.

Quietly, he went onto the balcony, dressed in a black tennis
shirt, Levi's, and dark shoes. His legs felt the effects of the
sex, and he wondered if having her to his room had been such
a good idea. But he decided it was meant to be. Not only had
she proven an excellent lover, but she would soon be a reli-
able alibi.

Santiago looked down the smooth white face of the building

to Amy Lansing's balcony one level down and two rooms north. He did not see any lights on, nor were there any lights shining from other balconies nearby. Over the grounds in front of Sonesta Beach, the pool and beach areas were illuminated by bright floodlights mounted along the roof line of the hotel. No people were in sight—so far, so good.

His P-230 held in a makeshift holster in the small of his back, Santiago put a knot in a fifteen-foot section of the rope he'd bought at the hardware store. Dropping enough of it over the railing to reach down to the fifth floor, Santiago tied off the other end to one of the main support frames of his balcony railing. He tugged hard on the rope a few times to make sure it would hold. Then, moving quickly, he went over the edge, expertly scaling down the line, swinging himself into the balcony beneath his own.

Pulling the rope off to the side, he tied it off near the dividing wall between balconies. That way, if security guards strolling the grounds would happen to look up, they'd be less likely to notice it.

He leaned around the concrete wall to the balcony to his right. No lights on—curtains drawn closed. Hooking one leg over the railing, holding on tightly, feeling some strength sapped from his legs, he pulled himself over, never looking down as he made the move from one balcony to the other, concentrating only on the coordination of arms and legs.

He paused momentarily, catching his breath, steadying it. He looked out over the hotel grounds once more, still not seeing anyone there.

He leaned over the railing to view Amy Lansing's balcony. The glass sliding door was open; the curtains blew against the screen door. The young couple was making things much easier for him. Much, much easier. He pulled himself around onto the Lansing girl's balcony, taking a final look down at the hotel grounds to make sure it was safe. Then, he listened at the screen, hearing nothing more than the curtain rustling gently against it.

He touched the handle to the screen door, trying to slide it easily, opening it smoothly for about six inches before it caught. Santiago couldn't tell if it was a rusty spot in the track or if the curtain was caught. He tried forcing it a little. Suddenly the door moved an entire foot all at once, making a scraping sound.

Santiago jumped back, reaching behind his back for his gun, drawing it. He waited, listened. The noise didn't seem to have alerted anyone inside.

Carefully, he reached inside the door and pulled back the curtain. Amy and her lover were on the bed less than ten feet in front of him, a slice of light from outside now shining dimly across their bodies. The young man wore only a pair of light blue briefs as he slept face down, head turned away from the girl. She was drawn into the fetal position, wearing an over-sized T-shirt pulled down around her buttocks. Both of them breathed steadily.

There was an empty bottle of champagne on the nightstand, the table still wet where bubbly fluid had apparently overrun when opened. Santiago had hoped the drink would have the effect of inducing sleep. Apparently it had.

There was already a shell in the chamber of the P-230 as Santiago stepped quietly into the room. He pulled back the hammer with his thumb as he approached the bed. He placed the end of the silencer less than an inch from the young man's temple, then pulled the trigger twice in succession. The boy's head and shoulders jerked from the impact, then laid lifelessly—breathlessly—in an increasing pool of blood.

The girl had not awakened, so Santiago replaced his pistol in its holster and went to work.

Six

On Sunday morning, the telephone rang. For a few seconds, Eddie Gant wasn't sure where he was. Once it came back to him, he wasn't especially thrilled with the reality.

In the second it took him to pick up the receiver and put it to his ear, he had the hopeful thought it would be Janice—that she had reconsidered what she'd said yesterday.

"Son"—it was Captain Marler—"I hate to bother you on the weekend, but—"

In the background, Gant heard the sounds of a hectic squadroom.

"——we have a bit of a situation here." Uncle Floyd spoke in his usual slow half-drawl. "The moon must've been full last night. We've had five shootings since dusk—three fatals—and I'm pretty thin homicide-wise. To show you just how bad it is, I'm sending Donald to cover one out on Key Biscayne. He's about wetting his pants, saying this is his big break—you know Donald—and I'm sure he's gonna screw something up." Marler paused, taking a drink of something, most likely Crown Royal. "I'd really appreciate it if you'd go over there and look over Donald's shoulder—make sure he doesn't mess it up too bad. You don't have to get involved if you don't want to. You're still narcotics, not homicide. Just make sure Donald zips the corpse in the body bag face up. You know how the boys at the coroner's office hate to have to roll them over. And so as not to hurt the boy's feelings . . . tell Donald you're just there to see if it's drug related. That way he won't feel like I don't have any faith in him. I'm gonna make him a decent detective if it goddamned kills me."

Gant read the digital face of his clock: 9:42. Well, he'd gotten seven hours sleep, anyway. "Where'm I going?" he asked, managing to pull himself up into a slouched-over position, rubbing his face.

"Sonesta Beach Hotel out on Key Biscayne. One of their guests got two bullets in the temple at point-blank."

"Pro hit?"

"Don't know details. I leave them up to you . . . *and* Donald." There was a sense of self-amusement in Marler's voice.

Gant drove the Lotus into the valet parking lane of the Sonesta Beach Hotel and told the attendant he was with the police. He asked if it would be okay to keep the car parked where it was for about half an hour, having full intentions of keeping it there anyway, regardless of the attendant's response.

The well-groomed youngster looked like a freshman accounting major with this car-parking job to help mom and dad with tuition. He seemed doubtful about Gant's being a cop—with Eddie wearing Nike Air Jordan warm-up pants, three-quarter-top basketball shoes, and a sleeveless T-shirt with the UM Hurricanes' logo—so Eddie went into his hip pocket and pulled out his red surfer's wallet. He yanked open the velcro fastener and displayed his shield.

"Gimme a break, will you, kid? It's supposed to be my day off."

The attendant shrugged. "I guess it'll be okay. We're not busy."

"Great." Gant gave him a dollar since his wallet was already open. "And don't let anybody fuck with it, okay. There's a shotgun in the trunk." Eddie went up the front steps to the lobby two at a time.

"If you're here about the shooting, it's up on five," the parking attendant called after him.

Gant waved thanks over his shoulder. He took the elevator up along with a beautiful woman in a one-piece bathing suit that practically had no back to it at all. She had a rock of a diamond in a yellow-gold setting for a wedding band. Gant sighed to himself, Ahhh, *money!*

The woman got off on three and Gant watched her ass. "Hope you and your husband have a nice day," he said to her back.

It was easy to spot the right room on the fifth floor. There was a line of hotel employees outside the door: cooks, maids, office-type personnel, bellhops, security guards—about a dozen in all, everyone of them looking pissed off.

Gant smiled as they glared back. The big black man in cook's whites looked especially dangerous. "This the viewing line?" Gant asked, his idea of a joke, yanking open the door to 511, going inside.

"What the hell——!" Detective Donald Stripes jumped up at the interruption of someone's coming in unannounced. He stood angrily behind a small table. Opposite him was an old man in a gray uniform with a hotel security patch sewn to the shoulder. "Gant, it's you. What're you doing here?"

Stripes wore a shit-brown three-piece polyester mix-and-match suit that had a long pull down the right sleeve. The knot in his mustard-colored tie was as thick as a child's fist, making a silver tie pin strain to hook the ends of his shirt collar together. On the table he'd positioned himself behind sat a legal-sized pad of lined paper with at least half a dozen pages turned over the spine already; there were also three Bic finepoint pens laid out neatly, a fourth in Donald's fleshy fingers.

Eddie didn't see fingerprint powder dusted over the room, no department photographers snapping away shots of every square inch of the scene, no medical examiner; just a body lying on the bed covered by a white sheet. With all the shooting action overnight, he guessed that Donald might be waiting a while for technical support.

As Eddie pulled the sheet down to the victim's shoulders, Stripes excused himself from the elderly guard and came by Eddie's side. "Captain send you over here on this?" he asked, whispering. "I told him I could handle it my——"

"Just here to see if it's drug related. That's all." Gant brushed back his hair as the ends of it fell around his eyes.

Stripes seemed relieved. "This is my big break, Eddie. A chance to take a case by the balls and swing with it."

Oh, Christ! Gant thought. Stripes not only dressed like a mannequin from the K-Mart men's department, but he talked like one, too—at least, he talked as Eddie imagined a K-Mart mannequin would, if given vocal cords.

"You go get 'em, Donald."

Reassured, Stripes returned to his self-established position of authority behind the veneer table. He drilled the old man in the security uniform, having to repeat each question at least twice before the guard could hear him.

Eddie wondered just how long Stripes expected to keep those people waiting in the hall. Most likely they were night-shift and had been off hotel time for about three hours now. Even if any one of them had any helpful information, they'd probably say they didn't know shit, just so they could be done with it and go home. The time to question people was when they were working. People love being questioned on somebody else's time because it's a legitimate excuse not to do anything that their boss can bitch about.

But that was Donald's problem. He wanted his big break. Here it was. Gant only hoped that Donald didn't come close to accusing that black cook out there of anything, because Eddie figured the cook would go searching for Stripes' gonads by way of his throat and pull him inside out in the process.

Eddie tried to ignore the fact that Donald would most likely fuck up this investigation, and contained his interest to the body. The victim was male, white, young—maybe not even twenty—a good-looking kid with an expensive haircut that was now caked with dark-red blood. The shots had definitely been very close-range—probably inside six inches, from the powder burns left on the body's ash-white temples. Gant pulled the sheet all the way down in order to see the rest of the body. There was no other signs of wounds—just a few light purple scratch marks across his upper back.

Gant recovered the body, then considered the rest of the room. On the night table there was a bucket half-full of cold water, an empty champagne bottle, and two empty glasses lying on their side. Okay, somebody had a little party. Maybe the young fellow here had up a hooker—that would explain the scratches on his back and the champagne. Maybe she rolled him, or else was working with a partner who came in and nailed the poor kid once he'd had his jollies. It had been done before—lots of times.

The closet was empty: no signs of any luggage or clothes. The drawers were all empty as well, and there wasn't a shaving kit in the bathroom. It looked more and more like a sexual rendezvous all the time; but then he found the woman's panties hanging on the back of the bathroom door, and all that changed.

First of all, the panties were plain white cotton—the kind a little girl might wear. They had a freshly washed scent to them, like when your mother does your laundry. It was definitely not hooker underwear—no lace or cutaway holes, not even a racy color, unless you were into the Catholic schoolgirl bit. Besides, if a hooker had worn the panties in, why didn't she put them on for the trip home? Underwear was not the kind of thing one forgot, even in a rush. Although the panic felt after a shooting could explain lots of things, it didn't seem to apply here. This killing was pro, calculated: close range and two shots. That took some stomach and keen nerves. Panic by the shooter was an unlikely element, so the white panties didn't fit in.

In the bathtub, Gant picked out dry hairs that had congealed over the drain screen. He separated them. A few hairs were short and blond—probably the victim's—but others were very long and brown. He laid the hairs back in the tub, hoping to remember to tell the lab boys that he'd messed with them.

Nothing much else of interest struck him, and Donald was still hashing it out with the guard—Donald speaking very loudly, repeating himself, and the old guy answering with a lot of *ehs?* and *huhs?*, so Gant left without saying good-bye.

Out in the hall, the eyes of those waiting to be questioned by Donald Stripes glared at him again, only now with a more noticeable intensity. The 6'6"-plus black cook reached down and grabbed Eddie's arm. "How much longuh we 'spected to stan' out heah?"

"Shouldn't be too long. I think the guard's in there confessing."

"You think tha's funny, huh, man?" the cook said, not letting go.

"No, but unless you get your fuckin' hands off me I'm gonna put seven rounds of .45s in your big fat gut."

The cook stared meanly, then released Gant's arm. "Fuckin' cop. Ah hope whoevuh iced that muthufucka, he be gone."

Everyone else seemed to share that sentiment. Donald's methods were great PR for Dade-Metro.

As Gant walked to the elevator, he didn't think it prudent— for fear they might turn riotous—to tell the line of hotel employees that chances were the killer never would be caught. Murders not solved within twelve hours were tough. Unsolveds older than twenty-four hours were damned hard. And once you got past two days, the chances really took on longshot odds. Gant wasn't sure Donald would even get through questioning the old guard in twelve hours.

Jesus, maybe he was on the wrong side of the law.

The two fag desk clerks working Sunday morning at Sonesta Beach found it perfectly scandalous that there had been a murder in the hotel. "It's right out of *Dynasty*," the tall skinny one—Stanley—clamored. His shorter counterpart agreed.

Both fellows were dressed neat as pins, wearing black pants, white shirts, and red ties that Gant guessed as the basic color pattern for hotel office personnel. They had near-identical close-trimmed hair and neatly combed moustaches, and each was eager to do whatever they could for Gant. "It's so exciting to be involved," Stanley said, getting another agreeing nod from shorty.

Gant scanned the computer printout of the guest registry, finding it difficult to check whether the rooms surrounding 511 were occupied because guests were listed alphabetically. But there weren't that many names—only about fifty—so Gant took his time, using a pen and some hotel stationery, which Stanley had been happy to supply, to make notes. Most rooms were registered to Mr. and Mrs.; only five were being billed at the single rate, and just that many again as triples and quads.

"Is this right?" Gant asked, tapping the pen against the name registered in 511.

The boys leaned so close across the counter Eddie could smell spearmint mouthwash on one of them.

"This room is registered to a Ms. Amy Lansing?" Gant asked.

"Yes. That's correct," Stanley said. "She checked in Friday around two, and paid for two days in advance with a charge card. American Express," he said efficiently, reading coded numbers on the green-and-white-striped perforated paper.

"Did you happen to get a look at her?"

Stanley said, "I didn't. Were you here, Bobby?"

"No, Stan, I wasn't," Bobby replied, the more effeminate of the pair. "I think Allie was working then. Let's see, Friday, two-ish, I would have been back in the office."

"Is Allie here now?" Gant asked.

"Comes on at noon," Stanley said.

"Know her last name?"

"Meyers." Stanley spelled it like he was turning in someone for cheating on a final exam.

"You said she charged the room?"

"Yes. American Express."

"Could I see the charge slip?"

"Certainly," Stanley said, and sent Bobby off to get it.

Eddie said, "Who found the body?"

"Oh, that would be poor Lillian. Little Cuban girl who's flightly as they come." Stanley talked fast when he got on a roll. "She's always running a day and a dollar late. Apparently she left work early yesterday and didn't do all her rooms. She thought 511 was checking out yesterday, so she went in early this morning to clean. I'm sure she knocked, but no one answered"—Stanley paused with a nervous little laugh—"of course he didn't, he was dead as sequins in Texas. And presto-bingo, there was the body."

Bobby returned with the charge slip and current statement of account for Room 511.

The name on the carbon was William Lansing.

"You sure a woman checked into the room?" Eddie turned the paper right-side-up for Stanley and Bobby to see. "This is a man's name."

"There should be a letter of authorization if someone used a credit card with someone else's name on it," Stanley snapped, then shook his head, sighing. "I guess you'll have to ask Allie about that."

"What about room service?" Gant asked, looking at the statement of account for Ms. Lansing's room. "Would something ordered last night be on this bill yet?"

"That would depend. If it was taken up after two in the morning, probably not."

"There's nothing on here about a bottle of champagne," Gant said. "Is there any way to check if it's been added?"

"Certainly. Bobby, call Mildred and see if 511 got champagne. *Vite!-Vite!*" Stanley sighed as Bobby hurried off. "Sometimes you have to light a fire under that dear boy."

Gant looked down to hide the smile he couldn't stop, rereading the register, composure regained by the time Bobby returned.

Mildred, Bobby reported, had no charges for 511, but she

recalled that, when processing the overnights, champagne had been sent to 511 that had been billed to another room. She was going through the overnights now to see who had placed the order.

Stanley beamed proudly. "Is that woman not amazing? She has the memory of an elephant—unfortunately, she has the figure of one, too."

An elderly couple came up to the counter beside Gant, and Stanley told Bobby to help them. "Just move down toward the end," Stanley whispered. "We don't want the old folks having coronary city hearing there was a murder in the hotel last night."

Gant went over the list of guests again. Only two rooms adjacent to 511 on any of four sides or four corners had been occupied last night. He decided to leave them for Donald to question, but wrote down the names and home addresses in case Donald overlooked the idea. Then he came to the listing that had puzzled him before. "Is this room in this building? Three-oh-three-dash-six-oh-nine?"

"That means the person switched rooms. Let's see." Stanley cocked his head to the side to better read the printout. "Mr. Aurelio Santiago. Okay, here it is. He checked in Friday and paid cash for two nights in advance. He was in room 303 originally and then moved to 609 sometime yesterday."

"Does it say why he moved?" Gant asked of the computer codes.

"No, but it was probably a stopped-up toilet or someone in another room playing the TV too loudly. We try to accommodate people and often find it's easier to move them to a new room, if possible, rather than having them put up with the wretched-of-the-earth Puerto Rican repairmen we have working here."

"I don't guess you were here when he switched rooms."

"Saturday's my day off. I drove over to Venice for the day. The West Coast is so much nicer. If I wasn't locked into this horrid lease in Hollywood, I'd move in a flash."

"Who would have been here?"

"Let's check the employee code on the printout." Stanley ran his long finger underneath a row of letters and numbers squeezed together without spaces. "Allie Meyers again. It looks like she's the one you want to talk to."

Gant looked at the wall clock behind Stanley. Almost 11:30. He could kill half an hour until noon. Maybe go out by the pool and hope that woman with the diamond-rock ring and backless bathing suit strolled by—without her husband. Or maybe he should try to call Janice again at Pan Am.

The phone by Stanley's hand rang twice quickly. Stanley answered, nodding as he said, "Yes ... Yes ... Yes ... Thank you, Mildred. You *are* a dear." He hung up and turned the computer printout sheet away from Gant. "Oh, it's your Mr. Santiago again. The room switcher."

"How's that?" Gant asked.

"Mr. Santiago is the one who ordered the champagne for Room 511."

"Did he?"

"Yes. And he ordered another bottle for his own room. That would be 609."

"Has he checked out yet this morning?"

Stanley went over his sheet again. "Lucky you. He's still here."

Taking the elevator up to the sixth floor, Gant checked the ankle holster that held his .45 in place under the loose pant bottom of his red-and-black Air Jordan warm-ups.

As the elevator opened on six, Gant turned right down the empty hall and counted off room numbers raised on door plaques, stopping at 611. Listening, he heard only a religious program playing on the TV in 612; all else seemed quiet.

He rapped softly on the door to 609, then waited. Not getting a response, he knocked again, harder.

An interior door opened and a female voice called, "Just a minute." Then footsteps hurried to the door, opening it. "What's the matter, did you lose your key?" Allie Meyers was startled seeing Gant—obviously not whom she expected to find. She tightened the grasp of the damp bath towel that wrapped around her breasts. Her extraordinarily long hair was soaking wet.

"Mr. Santiago here?" Gant asked, looking past the half-naked women into the room. The bed was unmade and a part-full bottle of champagne and two glasses sat on the nightstand.

"No. No, he's not."

"That's who you thought I was, then?" Gant smiled.

The woman looked very uncomfortable. "Was he expecting you?"

"Hard to say. I'm with the police." Gant pulled out his red nylon wallet, opening it, showing his badge. "Can I come in?"

"Is something wrong? Has something happened to Aurelio?"

"Let's talk inside."

Now she was nervous. "Can I change first?"

Gant shouldered his way into the room. "Sure. Use the bathroom."

"Did Mr. Santiago say why he wanted to change rooms when he came to see you at the desk yesterday?" Gant asked.

"He said children swimming in the pool woke him up in the morning." Allie Meyers was seated on the bed, having put on the minidress bought yesterday with Santiago's money, feeling conspicuous in it now, slutty. She knew how this must look to the police detective even though she'd tried to explain it: how she didn't usually do things like this—spend the night with guests—but this one was just special, charming, handsome, and—yes—rich. Her hair was still damp, hanging into her lap, getting the dress wet and feeling cold against her skin. She'd asked Gant to turn off the air conditioning and he had.

Standing, Gant leaned against the sliding glass door, watching people strolling the beach six floors down and lying on floats in the calm azure sea. "You have many kids in the hotel?"

"I don't know," she answered quietly. "Some."

Eddie hadn't seen any. "He didn't tell you he knew anyone else in the hotel?"

"He said he was here alone." Allie had already told him that. She'd also told him that she didn't know where Santiago was now—that he'd been gone when she'd awakened this morning around ten. But last night Santiago had said that he'd gotten a telegram calling him away on business today, to Switzerland. She'd also told him about Santiago's being from Costa Rica, that he had an estate in the mountains, and that he traveled throughout the United States and Europe on business most of the year.

Eddie hadn't found any crumpled telegram in the trash can, nor had he found the envelope the telegram would have been delivered in, figuring that even if a man would save a telegram, why save the envelope? Besides what the woman told him, there were no signs left behind whatsoever that Aurelio Santiago had ever been in this room, that he even existed at all. And that made Gant suspicious as hell. Everyone always left behind something, not necessarily anything of value, but some evidence that they'd been there—unless they purposely didn't want to. '

"Would you mind coming to the station, talking to one of the artists to make a composite of this guy?" Gant asked.

"Detective, I don't see how you can really be this concerned with Aurelio." She was almost pleading with him. "He's one of the sweetest men I've ever known."

"I'm sure there's some logical explanation. It'll all be some mistake. Mr. Santiago's probably on his way to a Swiss bank right now to take out a hunk of money to buy you a diamond the size of goddamned Paris." As he said it, Gant wasn't very surprised to see her nodding like she believed him.

Allie met Gant at the station an hour later. He introduced her to the police artist—a patient, smiling man who arrived with pads of sketch paper and a bevy of pens. The artist wasn't a department employee; he was a retired college professor from New York who taught art courses at UM part-time.

The professor free-lanced for Dade-Metro, the only force in south Florida that still used a live artist. Everyone else had gone to composite books: pages of clear plastic on which were printed nearly every type of individual facial feature created by God, the devil, and all forces in between. Witnesses would pick out the eyes, nose, mouth, chin, forehead, cheekbones, and ears, and put them all together in hopes that the resulting image looked something like the suspect.

Uncle Floyd hated composite books and had ripped up the one delivered to Dade-Metro, saying that people talked to artists, and, while they were talking, they often remembered things that wouldn't come to them while flipping through some goddamned little pamphlet.

While the professor laid out his pens over an empty desk, Allie kept telling Gant how wonderful Aurelio was, and that she was only doing this to prove that he couldn't possibly be involved in any wrongdoing—especially not a murder. He was too gentle a man.

Gant smiled and nodded. After turning her over to the professor, a man with a bendable ear who'd heard many tales of woe—both legitimate and insane—and reacted with passionate concern to all, Gant closed himself in Captain Marler's office.

Uncle Floyd was behind his desk, reading a departmental memo that someone had the nerve to put on his desk on a Sunday. He motioned for Gant to have a seat, then mumbled, "Bullshit, bullshit, bullshit," reading the rest of the memo. Coming to the last line of type, he crumpled the paper in his massive hand and dropped it in the trash can. Looking past Gant, he saw Allie Meyers through the glass partition. "That the girl who slept with our missing Latin last night?"

"Yeah."

"Cute. Those *amigos* know how to pick 'em."

"Talk about a one-night con job. He told her he owns an estate in Costa Rica." Gant shook his head, slouching in the straight-back chair. "You know she's actually here thinking she's helping this Santiago guy out. But who knows? Maybe it *is* just a coincidence. I ran his name through our records, then FBI and Immigration. Came up empty. Guy's clean on paper, anyhow."

Uncle Floyd got up and went over to the cabinet for his bottle of Crown Royal. "I don't know why you're even interested in this case," he said, pouring half a glass. "Donald's probably got it solved by now."

Gant laughed. "Yeah, right. Who did it? The old guard or the black cook?"

"Donald said something about a butler. Heh-heh-heh."

Gant loved to hear Uncle Floyd's deep laugh.

Seven

Aurelio Santiago had a busy Sunday.

Back at Sonesta Beach, Amy Lansing awakened before he could get the methaqualone down her throat. She struggled, thrashing across the bed, making it an effort to keep her from knocking into her dead lover and smearing his blood all over the sheets. But he managed to force the one-gram dose into her, and within a few minutes she was bleary-eyed and calm, as though drifting on a breezy cloud, then nodding off altogether. At first Santiago worried that he might have given her too much, considering the champagne already swimming in her bloodstream; but, unconscious, she breathed steadily, as though sleeping.

He'd bought the ludes in the Elbow Room Bar in Lauderdale. The squirrelly little pusher to whom he'd paid two bucks a pill said that each of them was a full gram and would keep someone pretty well spaced, but anything more might be permanent lights out.

Once Amy Lansing was doused by the drug, Santiago carried her down the enclosed stairwell over his shoulder, managing her weight fairly well, having to stop once to get his breath. He left her hidden under the steps inside the stairwell doors near the parking lot long enough to drive his rented Buick compact close by. He put her in the trunk, then went back to his own room.

Allie Meyers slept soundly as he pulled in the rope from the balcony and packed away all his clothes; he also emptied both trash cans into his suitcase, not knowing whether there was anything incriminating in there and not wanting to take time to find out.

He left Sonesta Beach, taking the Florida Turnpike down to Homestead. He had a trailer there that sat along the swampy overgrowth in the rear of a run-down park off U.S. 1; it was a dive, hidden amidst a clutter of beat-looking Pintos and Novas and other equally deteriorating trailers, but it cost only $200 a month for the summer, and looked like a good hiding place to him.

It was 4:00 A.M. when he arrived there. Making sure none of his neighbors could see, he unloaded Amy Lansing from the trunk. He tied her up and locked her inside the trailer's only bedroom.

Days before, he'd moved all the furniture out of there, jamming it into the cramped living room, setting the mattress on its side against the wall. He'd taped black cardboard over the oblong bedroom windows to keep the light and the curious from peeking in, and reversed the bedroom doorknob so that it locked from the outside.

The only thing left in the room where Amy Lansing lay imprisoned was a pale green carpet remnant. The cheap shag was too long by about a foot, and the excess had been left turned up the wall by the trailer's owners, a middle-aged Pennsylvania farm couple who had been only too glad to rent to Santiago for the summer while they were back north.

With the Lansing girl secured, still unconscious, Santiago fell asleep on the threadbare couch in the living room, only to be awakened by sounds from her around noontime.

She was kicking frantically, eyes wide open, trying to scream through the cloth gag stuffed in her mouth. She struggled with Santiago, but he got another lude in her, pushing it down her throat with his fingers as she gulped for air. The pill put her back under quickly, but, in their thrashing, her T-shirt had twisted up around her waist, revealing the thick brown triangle of her pubis and the nice swell of her ass.

Santiago's joint stiffened looking at her, but he reminded himself that there was a job to do, details to be attended, and forced himself to leave the bedroom.

Just after 6:00 on Sunday evening, Santiago dialed the number of William Lansing up in Opa-Locka. He hadn't rehearsed any sort of kidnapper speech because he didn't figure there was anything much to it.

The call was picked up after one ring by a meek-sounding man he recognized immediately as Amy's father.

"Lansing," Santiago said, his voice plain now, almost nondescript, "I've got your daughter. She was in the Sonesta Beach Hotel getting fucked by some young college boy. You reconsider my offer and you'll see your daughter again. Otherwise, I'm gonna screw her little cunt to death and mail you back the pieces."

Lansing breathed, swallowed. "Who is this?"

"Fuck you, Lansing. You talking makes me feel like screwing your little girl."

"No . . . Wait. What do you want me to do?" Lansing seemed confused. "I . . . I don't understand what's going on."

"Simple. We had a little conversation a while back. I expressed interest in the plans for a weapons system you designed. Remember?"

"Oh, my God!"

"Don't say your prayers. God ain't gonna help you. I want the plans—and I got your daughter. Just a simple exchange. Right? So don't fuck it up." Santiago paused, letting it sink in. "And I'm gonna make it all so fast and easy for you, it'll be done with before you know what day it is. That way you won't have time to do anything but what I tell you to do."

"Please. You must let my daughter go."

"We'll talk about it later—tonight. You be at the phone

booth in the Denny's parking lot near Hialeah Racetrack at
eleven. That's eleven P.M. It's right off the expressway. And
I'll tell you something else: you see cops, you better keep
fucking quiet or your daughter's one dead pussy." Santiago
waited, then said, "You gonna be there, shithead?" He didn't
hear anything but what sounded like sobbing. Getting louder
now, Santiago said, "So you gonna be there, or do I start
slicing up your daughter?"

"No! God, no!" Lansing had trouble breathing air. He was
close to hyperventilating. "I'll be there."

"Good. Remember, you had an easy way out last time we
talked. I offered you big money, but you said no. So take it up
the ass now, motherfucker. And be at that phone at eleven."

Santiago hung up, thinking he'd done a pretty good job of it.
Weird, though; he'd always wondered how somebody would
react at being told their kid'd been grabbed. They really
didn't react much at all. It was more like shock. Well, like
he'd told Lansing, the asshole had his chance to make some
money on the deal, but wouldn't take.

Santiago made a second call. This one to the same number
he'd called the night before from the hotel leaving the one-
word message.

This time, a man answered. "I was getting nervous. The
shooting made the news." The man spoke calmly, emotionlessly,
like a chess player.

Santiago knew better and wondered who the guy was trying
to fool, coming off like a steely hitman in a bad movie, with
that flat monotone voice. "There was nothing I could do about
it," Santiago told him. "*You* said she was going to be alone.
She wasn't. She had a boyfriend."

"She's been keeping him a secret then."

"What's that supposed to mean?" Santiago asked.

"It's not important. I hope he didn't cause any problems for
you."

"Nothing I couldn't handle." There was arrogant pride in
Santiago's voice.

"You've contacted poor William?"

Poor William? Jesus, this guy was into playing some Hollywood role; he hadn't talked like that when Santiago had met him at the backroom poker game at the country club four months ago. "I got to him just now. He sounded kind of numb. Are you sure he won't call the police? I don't want any more complications."

"He is as predictable as a clock. He will do anything for Amy."

"You better be sure."

"Believe me. I know William. But there is a possible complication." The man paused with almost high drama, taking a puff on a cigarette. "Your picture made the Channel Ten News."

"What?" That caught Santiago off guard. How could they even suspect him of anything, much less have a picture?

"It was an artist's rendering. An average likeness, but a definite resemblance. Then, again, maybe it's because I knew who it was supposed to look like."

Santiago couldn't believe it. "Are you sure? What did they say?"

"Only that you were 'wanted for questioning.' It's a term the news media uses to talk about suspects without being sued for slander."

Like I don't know that, asshole, Santiago thought.

"This *does* change things," the man continued. He was starting to annoy Santiago with this attitude of his.

Santiago's head felt tight, as though his blood wasn't flowing properly. He tapped his fingers against the cheap wall paneling as he fought to think. "We have to move a little faster—move up the rendezvous by a day or so. Once I make the switch with Lansing, it's just a plane ride and a buy away."

"A quarter-million, right? One twenty-five each?"

"That's the deal," Santiago answered, thinking, *Screw you, sucker, there's a split only if both partners survive to enjoy it.* "I'm contacting Lansing again later tonight. I'll let you know what happens."

The man said, "I'll be here."

*   *   *

"I want to speak to the news department." Santiago waited while the receptionist who'd answered the phone at Channel 10 put him through.

"News," a businesslike woman answered. There was a lot of activity in the background: voices talking, someone shouting about getting a camera crew to a fire in Coral Gables, a teletype printing.

"I saw your program about the shooting in Key Biscayne."

"Uh-huh?" the woman said, shuffling papers on her desk, half-listening.

"You showed a picture of some man. A drawing, I think."

"Yeah, right. It's called a composite. Is that all you want to know?"

"No. I think I might have seen the man."

"Yeah? Where?" The woman's interest didn't seem to increase; she obviously had dealt with a lot of cranks.

"The guy I know is named Domingo. Is that who the drawing is of?"

"Wait a minute." The woman covered the phone mouthpiece, shouting something Santiago couldn't hear. She came back seconds later. "Guy we have is Aurelio Santiago. Sorry, I guess your friend just looks like him. Thanks for calling." She hung up.

Santiago held the receiver in his hand long after the line had gone dead. He stared at it until the sound like a siren came through, signaling that the phone was off the hook. There really had been a picture—a drawing—of him on the news. How the hell had anyone made a connection that fast? It didn't make sense. They had him pegged as a suspect just because he'd left the hotel this morning? His bill had been paid in advance; there hadn't been any need for him to check out. How could they have known when he'd left? Had someone seen him leaving the building with Amy Lansing's body draped over his shoulder? His palm began to sweat holding the phone, so he hung it up and wiped his hand on the thigh of his ice blue Calvin Klein jeans.

He stood and paced the small living room, feeling a hollow

sensation each time his foot stepped down on the aluminum flooring. Shit, having a picture floating around of him *did* complicate things. It gave cops probable cause to pull him over if they looked in the car and saw him behind the wheel. It was drawing undue attention at a time when he needed to blend with the scenery.

He rethought last night in his head, over and over, then finally realized that only one person would know what he looked like well enough to help the police put together a sketch: the woman he'd slept with last night, Allie Meyers.

The thought of it got him crazy. The bitch had double-crossed him. She was supposed to be his alibi, not his prosecutor. He swung at a lamp, knocking it off the end table. It crashed into the wall, its ceramic base breaking in half. Once it landed on the floor, Santiago kicked the yellowed lampshade, then stepped on it, flattening the wire frame.

How could she have done that to him? Women—Jesus, they were incredible. Everything else was flawless. *He* did not make mistakes. It was always some woman. He paced, banging his fist against the wall.

Eight

Eddie Gant had an address for William Lansing in Opa-Locka. He drove up interstate 95, through moderate Sunday-dinner traffic, to question the man whose name appeared on the American Express card Amy Lansing had used to pay for her two-night stay at Sonesta Beach.

Allie Meyers had described the Lansing girl as a cute twenty-year-old college kid—definitely not a hooker. Allie had been working the desk when she'd checked in. The Lansing girl had explained to Allie that it was her father's American Express card, and he'd given it to her to pay for the weekend as a treat for getting good grades. She didn't say where she went to school.

Since the prostitute theory seemed out, Eddie considered others. The murder was execution style, so maybe it was a drug deal gone sour. Maybe Amy and the boyfriend were campus connections—Gant had seen all sorts of straitlaced kids turn sellers for the easy bucks, a lot of them now doing the mandatory ten for peddling coke.

How and if Santiago fit into all this was still a question;

Gant had delivered the composite to the TV stations to try to stir the guy up. He *would* like to know why Santiago had sent the champagne if he didn't know Amy Lansing. Of course, there was a possible explanation for that, too. Maybe Santiago had been hitting on the young couple to have a foursome— Santiago and Allie Meyers with Amy Lansing and her lover—and the champagne had been his introduction.

There were plenty of possibilities and only one thing for sure: without either Amy Lansing or Aurelio Santiago, the investigation would bog down hopelessly in speculation.

Taking the Opa-Locka exit, Eddie stopped at a pay phone half a mile off the interstate and tried to call Janice.

But again, it was Beth who answered. "She's back in Antigua, Eddie," Beth said, less annoyed than when Gant had awakened her Friday night.

"Did she say anything to you about her transfer?"

"Maybe you'd better ask her yourself. I gotta run. Good-bye, Eddie."

William Lansing's address was in an established neighborhood of small homes, all of which were built in one of three designs. Lansing's was a white rancher in desperate need of fresh paint; it had a flat roof and dark gray hurricane shutters tilted open at every window. The door to the single-car garage was closed, and the slate walk from the driveway to the front door was overgrown with spiked yucca plants and untrimmed evergreens. The hurricane shutters gave the place a stark, closed-in feeling, like a prison or military barracks.

Eddie knocked on the front door, badge in hand. When no one answered, he strolled around the outside of the house and tried unsuccessfully to look in beneath the overhang of the metal shutters. The garage was windowless, so he couldn't tell whether there was a car inside. Eddie checked the mailbox at the curb, finding it empty. He looked up and down the shaded street. None of Lansing's neighbors were outside; there were only a few sprinklers shooting a watery spray across tiny green lawns and a pair of beagles nipping at each other's tails a few houses down.

Eddie put one of his cards in the front door and was back beside the Lotus when he saw a brown Olds Cutlass turn up the street. The driver slowed, seeing Gant standing in the driveway, then stopped in front of the house next door, remaining inside, engine running.

Opening his wallet to expose his badge, Gant approached the car. It had a dull finish, with lots of dings along the side and a rusty dent in the left front fender. The windshield was dirty, except for a slightly clearer path made by the wipers. It looked like a car to go with Lansing's house.

There was a man seated behind the Cutlass's wheel—Gant could see that much—but he didn't seem to be moving at all. He seemed frozen. Had Eddie not been able to see the driver's hands on the steering wheel, he'd have been hard-pressed not to take his .45 from its ankle holster.

Gant rapped on the driver's window. "You wanna roll it down?" He put away his badge and made a cranking motion with his hand.

The driver kept looking straight ahead, finally pushing a button that brought down his window.

Gant bent over and saw a thin rumpled-looking man, about forty-two, with untrimmed black hair swept sideways to cover a bald spot. He wore plain black-framed glasses and an inexpensive white shirt that fit in the neck and shoulders like a sack. The car's air conditioner was running, yet the thin man's face was wet with perspiration.

"Mr. Lansing?"

The man nodded nervously, eyes locked straight ahead.

"My name is Eddie Gant. I'm with the police. I came to talk about your daughter." Eddie paused. "There's been——"

"Officer, please, I cannot talk to you." Lansing was having trouble breathing. "If anyone sees you. . . ," he said weakly, shaking his head. He started to speak again, but began crying; his forehead dropped down hard on the steering wheel.

"Mr. Lansing——"

He jerked upward, as though shocked. *"Please,* you have to

leave right away." The man's face was drawn, sallow looking; there were dark rings under his eyes. "He said"—he began sobbing—"he said if I talked to the police, he would . . . he would kill her." His entire body went limp against the steering wheel, and the car began to drift forward.

Eddie grabbed the gearshift, forcing it up into Park. Once the Olds stopped, he opened the door and had Lansing sit back, trying to steady him by the shoulder. "Someone called about Amy?" Gant asked, kneeling beside the car.

"Yes." Lansing shook violently. "Now go away! He could be here. *Anywhere around here!* Watching right now." He panted, unable to get his breath, even though drawing in deep gulps of air. "You . . . you have to leave." Desperation and panic choked in his throat.

"Look," Gant insisted, "I've got to talk to you. Your daughter was with someone who got murdered."

Lansing's weary eyes were bloodshot. "And now he's going to kill *her* unless I do what he says. And he said *not* to talk to the police."

"There's no guarantee what will happen even if you don't talk."

"No. No!" Lansing pushed Gant with surprising strength, catching him unaware, making Eddie grab the car door to keep from falling over. "Go away. You'll only get her killed." Lansing pulled the car door shut and drove across the curb, turning into his driveway. He stopped just long enough to find the automatic garage opener, then pulled inside when the door raised just high enough to allow the Cutlass to pass beneath it.

So Amy Lansing had been kidnapped out of the Sonesta Beach Hotel. It made Gant wonder. Either criminals were getting dumber or harder up. Whoever kidnapped the girl either hadn't bothered to check that her father didn't look to have dime one to his name, or else they were going to get out of him what they could and forget about it. Of course, Gant remembered, the guy *did* have an American Express card. Shit, maybe he did have some money. Still, the kidnapper was taking one helluva chance. Kidnapping carried a potential twenty-year sentence and turned into an FBI matter if the victim was carried across state lines. Even if he got ten grand out of Lansing, he'd have been better off hitting a couple of grocery stores—that was looking at a possible five-to-ten, probably less if he could pull it off without guns.

Gant put a call into Captain Marler from a pay phone at an Exxon station near the interstate. Wendy, Dade-Metro's resident computer whiz, answered at the squadroom and said Marler had gone for the day. Maybe Eddie should try him at home.

He did, and Uncle Floyd's wife, Alice Ann, picked up the phone on the fifth ring. She sounded tired. "Yes, Detective Gant. I remember you. You were over for dinner last month, weren't you?" Alice Ann Marler was a year or two older than Uncle Floyd, a woman who looked fresh from the beauty parlor everytime Gant saw her. She wore a little too much makeup, but seemed to fit right in with the other "old gals"—as Uncle Floyd referred to them—Gant had seen her shopping with at the Jordan Marsh in Dadeland Mall. "Detective, maybe Captain Marler hasn't told you, but he's not living here now." Her voice faltered slightly saying it. "He has a room at the Airport Hotel on Lejeune Road. I'm not exactly sure where it is, but I have the phone number he gave me in case of an emergency."

The Airport Hotel was a small four-story cement-block relic that looked about to be pushed out into the middle of the busy four-lane road by towering buildings that had been built up around it over the past twenty years. Its front windows were covered with a year's worth of soot and dirt from the seemingly endless flow of traffic that drove along Lejeune Road. The dark blue awning over the entrance was streaked and dry-rotted from exposure to the sun.

At one time, the hotel had well served the limited number of people who laid over at Miami Airport. But that was decades ago, before South Florida's staggering population boom, and now the place had been left for dead, serving $35 whores and felons in hiding.

Gant hadn't been here since he'd used the place to hide a federal witness back in the late seventies. Since then, the lobby had been reduced from a wide sitting area and television room down to barely enough space for the front desk and a newspaper box that was chained to an exposed support beam. What had been the rest of the lobby was now divided off into a greasy hamburger joint with a separate entrance. The same destitutes and whores who used to lounge in the lobby, shouting, fighting, cutting each other with kitchen knives, had moved on to other places where they could get out of the heat for free.

It all left Eddie with an uneasy feeling. Why hadn't Uncle Floyd said anything to him about moving out of the house in Westwood Lakes? Were there problems at home?

The fat Latin working the desk didn't interrupt the chewing of a Big Mac—squishing the sauce-dripping burger in one hand and a styrofoam container in the other—to tell Gant that Marler was in *veinte-tres*.

Gant didn't trust the elevator on a bet, so he took the stairs. The stairwell was dark and hot, as though the air inside had been festering, a slow-cooking stink of excretion that was so strong that it left Eddie fighting the urge to retch by the time he reached the second floor.

Out in the hall, half of the recessed ceiling lights were burned out. The ones that were lit were dim. The brown commercial-grade carpet was completely worn through to the concrete slab in places too numerous to count; one spot even had a wide scorch mark on it that carried up onto the crusty wall—remains of a fire probably set by some addict weirded out on Chinese red that unfortunately hadn't burned the whole damned place down.

Gant knocked on the door to Room 23. He heard the cheer of a crowd on a TV set playing loudly inside, a sports event of some sort. "Captain!" Gant shouted, knocking again. He tried the knob and the door opened.

There were no lights on inside the small room, and the odor

of stale alcohol was potent. A small black-and-white TV set danced shadows over the walls; on the screen, two black lightweights with firm shoulders and lean waists flailed away at one another, urged on by a rowdy crowd. In the center of the room, Uncle Floyd was tilted all the way back in the La-Z-Boy recliner Gant remembered from the Marler's den. There was no bed in the room—only the chair, two TV tables, and a twin-burner hotplate plugged in on the kitchenette counter beside the sink.

"Captain?" Eddie was five feet from the back of the recliner before he realized that Uncle Floyd was asleep. There was a nearly empty bottle of Crown Royal by the leg of Marler's chair. On the counter was a brown paper bag crumpled over at the top that looked about the right size to hold a fresh bottle. "Captain?" Gant gently shook the big man's shoulder, trying to bring him awake.

Uncle Floyd, mouth open, snored quietly. He wasn't wearing his upper plate, and there were wide gaps left between his teeth.

Gant had never seen Marler without his dentures before and thought how much older it made him look. "Captain? Captain, let's go."

Marler didn't stir.

Eddie stood over Uncle Floyd and looked down at him. In the dirty, dimly lit room, Marler appeared even darker-skinned than usual, in need of a shower and shave. White stubble poked across his upper lip above the narrow moustache. His short-sleeved white shirt was wrinkled, stained under the arms with sweat. His shoes and socks were in a pile at the foot of the chair, his bare feet sticking out from the bottom of his pants, toenails untrimmed and split.

Eddie didn't try to awaken him again. He left, locking the door on his way out.

Eddie drank a Coke from a plastic Burger King cup. Sitting in the Lotus, parked in the food-chain's lot, the memory of playing in a high school baseball game kept coming back to him.

He'd made the varsity team as a freshman and by mid-season had worked his way from being used as a pinch runner and late-inning defensive infielder to starting shortstop. Eddie's father, who worked mining phosphates in the fields east of the Everglades, had promised to make Eddie's first game as a starter. But his father never made it to the game, apologizing to Eddie that his boss wouldn't let him leave early. Later, Eddie learned that his father hadn't stayed at work late at all; he'd gone off to a strip joint where there was some new dancer who'd let you stick your hand in her G-string so long as there was a $5 bill in your fingers.

An entire year passed before Eddie confronted him about it. His father hadn't been apologetic at all; he'd just said, "Son, that's the way men is." Even as a kid, Eddie thought that was one lousy fucking answer, and he'd never looked at his father in the same way again.

Nine

He used to use knives all the time. They were easier to get than guns—cheaper, too. At any hardware store, $25 bought a hunting knife with a 10″ blade; it might not have been high-quality steel, but it cut fine.

When Allie Meyers had invited Santiago to get her address from ID in her wallet, he'd done it only in case she asked him about it later. Now he was glad he had.

It was about 7:00 when he drove into the parking courtyard of the small apartment complex where she lived. The sign at the entrance advertised the units as one-bedroom efficiencies, which Santiago interpreted in agreement with his hunch that she would be here alone.

Easing slowly down the *cul-de-sac*, Santiago wished he knew what kind of car she drove—that way he could tell if she was home or not without actually going to the door. She'd gotten off work yesterday around 7:00, but today she might have different hours.

He parked near the end of the lot beside an eight-foot-high section of privacy fence built around twin dumpsters. Getting out, he walked along the cracked sidewalk, stepping over breaches in the concrete where spreading roots of palm trees broke through. He was careful to keep his hands in the pockets of his windbreaker to hide the knife.

A middle-aged man who looked like a banker jogged down the sidewalk toward him. He had on a coordinated red-and-gray running suit and was huffing from the strain, his fleshy bulk sloshing up and down as his feet landed hard on the pavement. His face was red, dripping sweat, and Santiago could actually feel heat radiating off him as he ran slowly by.

Santiago waited until the jogger disappeared down a narrow path between two of the low-level buildings before he approached Allie Meyers's apartment. He wanted to be quick at her door, and he was. Gripping the knob, he wedged his shoulder against the door, then hit it hard. With his full weight behind the impact, he broke the small deadbolt out of the wood frame with a sharp crack. The door swung open and Santiago stepped inside.

He found himself in a small living room. Without taking another step, he waited to see whether anyone responded to the noise of his entry. After a few seconds of silence, he assumed no one was home.

The room was warm with natural light through the sliding door. An arched-back sofa and matching rose-colored armchairs were positioned cozily on the mauve carpet. One wall was lined with paperback books and a high-tech component stereo with two bookshelf speakers. Partitioned by a black-lacquered Oriental screen was an oval marble-top table with four wrought-iron ice-cream-parlor chairs.

Santiago closed the vertical blinds over the sliding glass door and sat in one of the armchairs. He took the knife out of his pocket, slapping the handle against his right palm. He'd wait.

Ten

Now he remembered why only guys working narcotics and vice drove the hot-shit cars: the things were meant to draw attention, and did. Sitting in the Lotus parked under a towering palm tree three houses from Lansing's, Eddie Gant felt conspicuous. Since his arrival an hour ago, two brothers and an *amigo* had strolled by. Eddie had been slouched down in the driver's seat pretending to be asleep, but the one black guy had rapped on the window anyway and asked Gant if he had any nose candy.

Gant started to think he'd be better off calling it a night, maybe coming back after daybreak in a brown Plymouth, but at 10:45 he saw Lansing's garage door open. The Olds backed down the driveway.

"What the hell!" Eddie said to himself, sitting upright. But before he turned the engine over, he noticed headlights lift up on a car across the street about seventy yards away.

As Lansing turned out of his driveway away from Eddie, the other car—a black late-model Trans Am—pulled from the curb, driving toward him.

Low behind the wheel, Eddie tried to get a look at the driver as the black car turned a U in two cuts. Christ, it was Donald Stripes. The Trans Am must have been out of the Dade-Metro impound lot.

Stripes sped down the block to catch up with Lansing, who was now about ten houses away.

Gant revved the Lotus Turbo and followed.

Lansing, then Donald, turned south onto Red Road. Overhead, the landing lights of a 747 making its final approach into Miami International hung low over the street like a lumbering monster in the dark sky. The big plane flew directly over Gant, engines roaring. Eddie glanced up at it, then looked back at Donald.

Ahead of the Trans Am, Gant caught glimpses of the Olds's taillights. Controlled intersections came closer together now, so Eddie tucked up tighter to keep from getting boxed back by other cars. Stopping for the light at West 49th Street, Gant, Stripes, and Lansing were nearly lined up one behind the other.

The Olds went off the light and switched into the right-hand lane without signaling. Stripes stayed on its tail, but Eddie dropped back, allowing another car to slide between him and the Trans Am. When Lansing turned at the next intersection, Stripes was less than three car lengths behind, about to plant himself up Lansing's ass if the Olds stopped suddenly.

Traffic was now very light, yet neither Lansing nor Stripes seemed to realize they were being followed. Eddie wondered if either knew how to use a rear-view mirror.

Lansing passed the overhead signs designating turn lanes onto the Palmetto Expressway, then steered into the parking lot of a Denny's restaurant. He stopped at a phone booth on the grass-planted island between the lot and road.

Donald rode Lansing's bumper through the turn, but had the obvious good sense not to pull up behind him at the phone. Stripes drove around behind the building, reemerging on the other side with his headlights already off as he stopped alongside a parked 18-wheeler.

Gant watched from down the block. Having given the other two cars a long lead, he'd been able to turn onto a dark side road near a carpet warehouse. Now, through a chain-link fence, he saw Lansing get out of his car and close himself into the phone booth.

The dark-haired man had on the same clothes he'd worn that afternoon and looked equally as nervous. He stood there fidgeting, as though he'd pace if only there were room.

Suddenly he picked up the receiver and began to talk without having put in a single coin or punched button one.

Gant thought, *Okay, so someone called him.*

"You've been followed."

"What?" Lansing's voice shook. He heard the words but didn't understand them.

"Did you call the police? You couldn't be that fuckin' dumb . . . or crazy, *are you?*" Santiago raised his voice threateningly.

"My God, no!" Lansing pleaded, pulling on the front of his shirt. "I didn't call the police. One stopped by my house, but I didn't say anything. Please! You've got to believe me. Please!"

Santiago let him worry about it a few moments.

Lansing whimpered. "I didn't tell them anything. *Nothing at all.*"

"All right, you fuck. You better not be lying, because you're only gettin' one more chance. You got it?" Santiago watched Lansing from a phone booth down the street. He wiped his mouth with the back of his hand. The sweat from the warm night was making him itch. "There's a taco place a block from the track. You know where I mean?"

"I don't know—yes, I . . . I think so." Lansing stuttered, struggling to keep himself together.

"Be there in two hours. Make sure you're not followed . . . or your daughter dies."

"I didn't *know* I was followed." Lansing looked around frantically.

"Hold still, goddammit. You just stay at that phone for five minutes after I hang up. Got it? Stay on the phone and pretend you're still talking to me."

"I don't understand what——"

"Just keep talking on the phone. Or pretend to keep talking after I hang up. That's simple, right?"

After a moment and more pulling on his shirt, Lansing said yes.

"Good. Now you keep on the phone for five minutes—*five minutes*. Then get to the other phone booth at one A.M. And don't go home in the meantime."

"What is it"—Lansing began, out of breath, his voice quivering badly—"that you want from me?"

"I'm not sayin' anything now. You might be fuckin' dumb enough to be wearin' a wire."

"Please! I'm doing everything you told me to do. I just want to know——"

"The other phone in two hours. Alone."

Lansing nodded weakly. "Yes"—then abruptly—"is Amy all right?"

Santiago hung up.

That poor sonofabitch, Eddie thought, watching Lansing. The man was bent over as if there were a terrible cramp in his side, and he clawed constantly against the front of his shirt. Eddie had no idea who Lansing was talking to on the phone, but he sure was staying on the line a long time.

The Denny's wasn't crowded; there were only a handful of cars in the lot and two tractor-trailers. An elderly couple walked out the front doors, the man picking his teeth with a toothpick while the woman put away her change purse. *Shit,* Gant thought, *no wonder old people get mugged, walking head down, folding up their money out in public.* The pair past the newspaper vending boxes, turned the corner, and disappeared from sight.

An American-made compact pulled into the lot just as the old couple drove out in their Lincoln. The small dark-colored car circled behind the restaurant, reappearing on the side where Donald sat in the Trans Am. The other car slowed, easing up alongside Stripes.

Gant peered forward, straining to see details under the amber glow of the parking-lot lights.

The gun blasts came one after the other like rapid thunder, joined by snapping bursts of orange flash. The compact car sped forward, wheels spinning. It ran over the sidewalk, bounding down onto the road, heading away from Gant toward the Palmetto Expressway.

"Oh, damn! No!" Gant swore, slamming the Lotus into gear, cutting the wheel hard to make the turn in front of the link fence. He swerved out onto the street, not slowing to make the turn, driving hard for fifty yards, then skidding out the tail end of the Lotus as he knifed into the Denny's lot. He braked to a hard stop beside the Trans Am, started to get out, then stopped. Seeing Stripes's body told him there was no sense checking for a pulse.

He charged the Lotus out of the lot, turning toward the entrance ramps to the Palmetto, feeling the Turbo go airborne when the inclined merge way leveled out. He passed fifteen cars in a half-mile that took twenty seconds to cover.

There was no sign of the small Buick by the 27 or 834 exits, and Gant realized that even if the compact had come down this way, his odds of staying on the right trail now had just become incredibly long.

Without a police radio in the car, he was unable to alert dispatch about the shooting until he found an emergency phone at the cloverleaf onto the East-West Expressway.

The woman who took the information did so with disinterest, almost casually. Eddie wanted to scream at her that a cop had just been killed—didn't she give a damn? Didn't she feel anything at all? He slammed down the phone and stood there, angry, feeling so goddamned helpless. There was nothing he could do for now. Stripes was dead. Fuck. Stripes was goddamned dead.

Racing up the expressway on his way back to Lansing's house, Gant couldn't help but remember Lincoln Jones. Jones was the first cop-killer he'd ever gone after. Lincoln had put a machete up to a uniformed officer's neck on a bet with a friend that he could cut the cop's head clean off.

Gant took two weeks to catch him. It was another fifteen months before the case was scheduled, and, after a two-week trial, the jury hung because one of the twelve-panel group was afraid the guy would fry if convicted. A second trial was scheduled four months later, and that jury had the good sense to convict Lincoln. But the asshole's public defender lawyer appealed, and the case got remanded for a new trial on an evidential technicality.

A third jury also convicted Jones and another appeal was taken, but this one got thrown out. Almost four years to the date from when he was arrested, Lincoln Jones began to serve day one of a twenty-five-year sentence, being given credit for time already spent in jail during his trials.

Lincoln was in only two weeks when he was killed by a stray shot during a mass escape attempt. But the saga of Lincoln Jones did not die with his body. A woman who had not been at any of his three trials suddenly appeared from Washington, D.C., claiming to be his common-law wife. She said Lincoln had not been trying to escape, but had been killed by angry guards who thought her deceased husband should have gotten the death penalty. The ACLU believed the woman and filed suit on her behalf against Dade County, the state of Florida, the warden of the correctional institution where Lincoln was killed, every guard on duty at the time of what was now the "alleged" escape attempt, and a dozen other people and governmental agencies. In short, anyone who had a file on Lincoln Jones more than half a paragraph long got sued.

In all, Gant read newspaper estimates that the criminal trials and appeals of Lincoln Jones had cost the taxpayers of Florida $20 million. Jones's common-law wife/widow was suing the collective defendants for another $50 million. The murdered policeman, whose name no one could ever remember anymore, left behind a wife and three children who got $9,000 a year in death benefits.

Uncle Floyd said that Lincoln Jones was a case in criminal-justice economics if you considered that the cost of trying to convict him was almost forty million times greater than the price of a single .45-caliber bullet. That, Gant realized at the time, was not an especially novel idea, but it sure as hell made sense to him. Then and now, because, goddammit, you just didn't kill cops.

Eleven

Santiago put the Python .357 magnum under the passenger seat. He took the Palmetto Expressway north, staying in the middle lane, keeping his speed within 5 miles per hour of the 55 limit.

He knew he should go back to the trailer, stay out of sight, but he felt too up—not uncontrolled, just into what was happening. There was a sense of emotion in doing this job on his own that hadn't been there working for someone else. He was the boss now. And he liked the way he was performing so far. He was up to the task—even better than necessary.

Doing the kid last night at the hotel hadn't been tough at all, not once he'd gotten inside the room. It didn't take much to hold it together long enough to put a gun alongside someone's head while he was asleep and pull the trigger.

But taking out the dork in the Trans Am was tougher. He'd made it look easy, of course, but there was a talent to it. He hadn't alerted his target at all when he'd come up alongside him; the round-faced guy behind the wheel had looked over at him like he was annoyed—like what the fuck was Santiago

86

doing there? *About to blow your fucking brains out, amigo,* Santiago thought, laughing.

When the guy had seen the gun pointing at him, he'd frozen, staring down the barrel with horrified fascination. Santiago had smiled and pulled off two shots. The first had slammed the man back against the side door; the second looked to have taken his whole head off.

Once he'd done it, Santiago had seen the expression on Lansing's face; the poor asshole stood there in the phone booth, looking like he'd just shit himself. *That,* Santiago thought, *should let the jerk know who he's dealing with.*

Santiago hooked up with the interchange onto Interstate 95 and took it north to Fort Lauderdale. He got off at the second Lauderdale exit, having to ride around a little while before he found what he was looking for.

The last time he was here, the place was called The Lace Garter, and you could see it clearly, sitting back about fifty yards off the highway. Now there was a two-story office/shopping plaza built between the club and the road, and The Lace Garter had become The Naked Flamingo. Santiago figured the previous owners had shed one corporate shell for another when the feds started swooping in about unpaid employment and personal property taxes.

He parked near the door, rolled up his shirtsleeves to show off the Rolex Presidential, and unbuttoned his shirt collar so his heavy gold chain came into view.

Inside the front door was a small alcove where a gorgeous dark-haired girl sat invitingly on a tall stool. Her legs were crossed so that the split up the side of her long white dress exposed bare thigh to the curve of her rump. The dress front was low-cut, with a revealingly deep V, the dark circles of her areolas showing through the thin material.

Beyond her, through another set of doors, flashing lights cast mysterious shadows against the carpeted wall and loud music throbbed from the heart of the club.

Santiago couldn't get up to the young woman in white because of a short man standing between them.

The man was red-faced, flipping through empty sections of his wallet with nervous fingers. "I thought sure I had some cash with me."

"Sir," the hostess smiled cordially, "like I said, I'm sorry, but we only allow credit cards inside. The cover has to be cash."

"Maybe if I could talk to the manager——"

Santiago wedged his shoulder between the older man and the enticing woman. He had out a wad of bills—hundreds as deep into the pile as could be seen—and he peeled one off, adroitly quarter-folded it with two fingers, then presented it to her. Latin-smooth, he said, "For my friend here and myself. And the rest, lovely lady, is for you." He tucked the bill deep into her cleavage, feeling warm, full flesh.

"Thank you!" she squealed, overplaying it like a bad high-school actress trying out for a Christmas-morning scene.

Santiago smiled. Inside he felt absorbed by the flashing lights, the deep bass of the music. Three young, large-breasted women gyrated in various poses of arousal on a trio of light-encircled stages, all of them stripped down to G-strings.

The man he'd put out the ten-buck cover for was on his sleeve. "I can't thank you enough, there, uh, whatever your name is." The man laughed nervously, watching the redhead on center stage slip painted fingernails into the waistband of her metallic-silver G. "Can I buy you a drink?"

"No," Santiago cut back. "Just get as far fucking away from me as you can."

There were plenty of places to sit. Santiago did a quick head count and came up with twenty customers, most of them seated at the bars up against the stages. Santiago moved over to the row of half-circle booths that lined the left wall. He slid into the center of the vinyl-lined seat and watched the nineteen-year-old on the small stage closest to him.

She had silky blonde hair that streamed over her shoulders like a thousand eager fingers. A lean girl, she had surprisingly big breasts for one as small-hipped and -waisted as she was. Her nipples were rose-colored and stiffened into erections as she pulled gently on them, her face expressing ecstasy from self-touches.

Two kids who looked like college freshmen sat near the stage with a view directly up between the blonde's long legs. They were trying like hell to look comfortable watching this mostly naked woman get off on herself for their pleasure. It got even harder when she dropped to her knees in front of them, pulling down her red G-string, fluffing her hands through a thin line of pubic hair, separating her folds to let them glimpse a hint of pink.

But while her fingers played for the boys, the young dancer looked toward the dark booth where Santiago sat, always looking for the new face to seduce. Her eyes meeting his, she licked her lips, opened her mouth just far enough, then peeled her G off. Leaving it around one ankle, she kicked it off expertly, sailing it through the air toward him.

Santiago caught it easily, inches above the table. He raised the panty to his face and kissed it, then smiled. This would be her last song, he knew. The practice was the same at clubs all over the world. Once they stripped bare, they did only one last dance; then the new girls came on wearing sheer teddies or T-shirts and legwarmers to start their act.

A waitress in a short black skirt and white unbuttoned blouse came for his drink order. Santiago figured, *Why not? One drink wouldn't hurt.* When she returned with his Bacardi on ice, he pulled out the thick wad of bills, displaying them openly so the naked blonde still dancing on the stage could see.

The dancer spread her way through a finale, then wriggled off the stage. She reemerged minutes later through a side door, wearing a red string bikini and white lace garter belt. She saw Santiago watching her and played it coyly, first visiting the college boys, bouncing over to them, her breasts barely contained in the bikini top. Putting her garter-tied leg up on the bar stool beside the boys, she bent forward, stroking their smooth faces, kissing them both on the lips once they each pressed a dollar bill inside her garter.

No one else sat near her stage, so she came over to Santiago, putting a little extra in it for him, shoulders thrown back, hard nipples looking ready to poke through the tiny top. "Hello," she said, a young friendly voice—clean-and-pure, innocent-but-fuckable girl next door, none of that milk-toast phoniness like the older dancers who still thought sexy was what it had been in old Dean Martin films. She bent forward, letting her breasts nearly spill into view. "My name's Vanessa."

"Are you . . . much of a gambler, Vanessa?" Santiago asked, his smooth South American accent in full flow. He reached into his money pocket.

"I don't know. That would depend on what you've got in mind." She played along, eyes unable to hide the appetite Santiago's thick wad of bills aroused.

He counted off hundreds—ten of them—and laid them out in front of him across the oval table. The remainder of his bills still made a thick fold—nothing but hundreds showing—as he put them back in his pants. "Here's the bet. For each inch my cock is less than ten inches, you get one of these green pieces of artwork here." He sat back, arm resting on the short shelf behind the booth.

Vanessa's smile broke into an amused throaty laugh. She straightened, crossed her arms, considering him with her hip cocked to the side. Flipping back her hair, she said, "I guess you get something if you win the bet."

"I get you."

She bit her lip gently, then laughed again. "Ten inches, huh?"

Santiago nodded, showing a slight poker-faced smile.

Vanessa slid into the booth beside him. "I don't guess at ten inches I can lose this bet no matter how it turns out." She moved closer, her posture very inconspicuous that she was undoing his pants with one hand, managing it rather easily. "Jesus!" was about all she could manage to gasp.

Vanessa knew the night desk clerk at the Shimmering Shoals Motel, so Santiago purposely passed that one by. He didn't know shit about Vanessa—other than that she had a dynamite figure and her hands felt like warm silk when she reached inside his pants. He wasn't about to chance walking in on some standing rip-off she might have set up with some local goons.

A block from the Shimmering Shoals, Santiago saw a turquoise neon sign for Las Cascades, a sprawling two-story motel with three separate buildings connected by a covered walkway. Las Cascades didn't translate to anything in Spanish and Santiago figured it was just a hopeful way to Latinize an otherwise American place to draw in South American money.

"You ever been there?" he asked Vanessa, driving past Las Cascades.

"It's nice, but expensive," she replied, looking over her shoulder at the elaborate neon sign. Turning at that angle just about brought her left breast out of her string top. She'd dressed up the bikini more appropriately now for the street, having put on a pair of tight black leather pants and tan pointed-toe cowboy boots that had three-inch heels.

"We'll go there, then." Santiago started to make a U-turn against the sign, then remembered he didn't want to alert any cops. He went down to the light and turned there.

"You must have a lot of money," Vanessa said.

"*Dinero,*" Santiago grinned. "*Mucho dinero.*"

"What're you into? Coke? Guns?"

"Oh, no. Nothing like that. Venture capital."

"What's that?" she asked, as if the term were some kind of Mafia code word. "Venture capital?"

"I invest money in projects that should make more money."

"You sure don't spend it on cars," she kidded.

Santiago laughed. "I told you. It's rented. It was the only thing I could get."

"This time of year, I thought nobody came to Florida."

"Well"—he faltered for a moment—"I . . . only know what the woman at the car place told me." He shrugged. "Maybe she doesn't like Latins."

"Maybe she ought to try the ruler test." She leaned over and rubbed her hand against his crotch, kissing him softly on the neck. As he pulled into Las Cascades parking lot, she sat back in her seat. "Did you really give Franco three hundred dollars to let me off early?"

He pulled into a space near the office. "I considered it . . . a bargain."

Vanessa took his face in her hands and put a deep-tongued kiss through his lips. "I'm going to make sure you think it's worth every cent."

Santiago paid cash for the room. The $150 outlay still didn't appear to dent his roll of hundreds. He waved off the starched bellman, saying he'd find his own way. "Nothing personal though, okay?" he said to the young Cuban kid, palming him a ten-spot.

Vanessa was alive on his arm, soaking up the attention Santiago lavished on her, intensely flattered by the amount of money he was spending on her.

She was still new enough at this to be charmed by wealth, Santiago figured.

The room was nice, but not the best Santiago had ever seen. Vanessa loved it. The wall-to-wall carpet was so thick it seemed to envelope a bare foot up to the ankle. The king-sized bed had designer sheets; in the bathroom, rice paper covered the walls and bronze fixtures adorned the sink.

Santiago wondered how young Vanessa really was. He had figured nineteen, but maybe younger. Truly a gorgeous girl, though. She was unscarred by a profession that could get very nasty. Her skin was flawless and bronzed all over with suntan.

"The bathtub! Look at this bathtub!" she cried, turning on the water and discovering Jacuzzi outlets as they squirted hard lines of water across the oversized red fiberglass tub. "Let's get in it," she squealed with excitement, stripping off her top, bending over to feel the temperature of the water.

Santiago loved the way her breasts hung down. Watching her undress the rest of the way had his shaft aching to get out of his pants. He wanted to come up on her from behind, grab her by the hips, and fuck her until she screamed from having all his cock inside her. He loved it when taking all of him made them scream. Allie Meyers had screamed like that; he'd undressed in the dark, and she hadn't realized the size of him until he was in her. Yeah, Allie Meyers had been nice—it was too bad about her. And this one—Vanessa—what a body, and so vital and eager. She could scream even louder, he bet.

"Come on!" she urged, stepping into the water, easing herself down into the filling tub.

He checked his watch. "You go ahead and get in," he spoke over the sound of rushing water. "I have to make a few phone calls."

"At this hour of the night?"

"It is still daylight in Costa Rica."

"Oh," she said, as though she'd just learned something.

"I'll be right back." He threw her a kiss, closing the bathroom door.

Santiago dialed the desk and told them he was going to make some outside calls and if they wanted him to pay for them in advance, he would. The clerk on duty said so long as they weren't long distance, there would be no charge.

Santiago thanked him and called the pay phone in Hialeah, listening carefully in the rings to see if he could detect any listening devices drawing on the signal.

"Hello!" a desperate William Lansing answered.

"What took you so long?" Santiago demanded, keeping his voice down so that Vanessa would not hear him—the girl was in the bathtub happily singing a song Santiago didn't know.

"I just got here. It's only . . . it's only five till."

"Who was in the black car?"

"Oh, Jesus, God, I don't know—I swear. I didn't even know anyone was there. You've got to believe me. *Please!*"

"I don't know if I can trust you. I think you talked to the police."

"I didn't tell them anything. Why would I do that? I don't want anything to happen to Amy . . . Don't hurt her . . . please." Lansing barely kept the words from getting choked in his throat.

Santiago smiled. Lansing had broken. He was his. "Two things. I want the plans—the weapons system. You know what I'm talking about, right?"

"Oh, my God!"

"You'll get them for me."

Lansing sobbed.

"You'll get them, *right?*"

"Yes—yes. What choice do I have?"

"None. Not a goddamned one. Just remember that." Santiago let silence hang between them, giving Lansing a chance to pull himself back together.

"Is . . . is Amy all right?"

"She's fine. But she'll be better once you've got her back. I think she's worried I'm gonna start sticking things between her legs."

"Oh, Jesus, no. Don't. Please, I'm begging you. Don't do anything to her." A tone of powerless frustration weakened Lansing's voice. "I'll get the plans. Just tell me what to do and I'll do it."

"The rest could have been simple, but like I said, I don't know how much I trust you."

"I didn't talk to the police, I——"

"Hey, asshole, I'm talking—got it? That means you fucking listen. Maybe you haven't talked to cops, but maybe you're too dumb to know they're trailing you. So here's what we're gonna have to do. We're gonna make our little exchange—your girl for the plans—somewhere where it's not so hot." Santiago kicked off his tasseled loafers. "Tomorrow you get yourself a plane ticket to Barbados. Get there and get a room at a place called the Barbados Beach Villas. Got that?"

"Barbados? My God! Why can't I just give it to you here? We could meet tonight. I could have them for you in—in an hour."

"Forget it. I told you, there's too much heat around here. You know *heat?* Cops? FBI? Lansing, we get caught switching this stuff, you got as much to lose as me. People go to jail for selling military secrets. You know that, right?" The silence told Santiago that Lansing hadn't had time to rationalize the whole scheme. "Get to Barbados tomorrow, Lansing. And whatever else you do, don't go home. The cops're gonna be all over you."

"But I'll need to get——"

"You don't need to get shit but those plans and your ass to Barbados. You got a credit card in your pocket—use it. Buy whatever you need. You go home, your sweet little honeychild is gonna die."

Lansing breathed unsteadily.

"You got it all?" Santiago demanded. "Barbados. Barbados Beach Villas. The plans for Amy. Right?"

Lansing's voice was very weak. "Yes."

Santiago made another call.

The man who answered calmly asked if everything was on schedule.

Santiago said, "I've made a change. I think the police are watching Lansing. He says he didn't talk to them—maybe he didn't—but I'm not taking any chances."

"So, what is the change?"

"Lansing's meeting me in Barbados. I'll get the plans on the island."

"Is that wise? Our buyer is there."

Jesus, like I don't know that, Santiago thought. "No Miami cop is gonna follow him to the bottom of the Caribbean. We'll be in and out in seventy-two hours."

The man paused. "Yes. I like it."

Good for you, Santiago thought. *If you're so goddamned brilliant, why haven't you bothered to ask how the hell I'm gonna transport a kidnapped twenty-year-old out of Miami into Barbados? Goddamned amateur!* Four months ago, he was an overextended businessman going broke on "free" pussy. Santiago had approached him with the plan—*his* plan—now this guy acted like he had to approve everything. Santiago feigned enthusiasm. "Imagine how those women are gonna fall all over the sixty-foot yacht your share'll buy." Some people were so easy to lead on.

A final call was necessary to make arrangements for a new false passport. Santiago's friend said it would be ready tomorrow at 3:00, but he'd need an extra $100 for the rush job.

Santiago said no problem, just make sure it was perfect. If the computer threw out his passport number, somebody's ass was dead. His friend merely laughed.

Vanessa was still singing in the bathtub. Steam rose up off the swirling water. Her full breasts seemed to float heavily, her big, soft nipples breaking the surface. She'd soaked her hair and it looked dark, finger-combed back off her face. "Oh, I want to see it," she said, arms coming up through the water, reaching out for him.

Santiago removed his shirt and socks, then unbelted his pants, unzipped them. Three inches of his erection stuck out of the waistband of his dark blue underwear.

"God!" Vanessa gasped. She stroked a wet finger along the underside of his shaft head, then pulled down his trim-fitting bottoms. His length jutted straight out from his loins, and when Vanessa wrapped both hands around him, she still didn't have all of it in her grasp. Kneeling in the tub, with Santiago standing in front of her, she took him in her mouth, engulfing him with the warm thickness of her saliva.

Santiago caressed Vanessa's face, watching her cheeks bulge with his size, as he let himself be taken away by the velvet licks of her tongue.

Twelve

He couldn't sit still. Watching from the Lotus, Gant waited for Lansing to come home. He'd been there twenty minutes now, having already looked in every darkened window, seeing no one. In a bit of frustration, Eddie had broken the lock on the garage door and pulled it open to make sure Lansing's Olds wasn't inside.

Now he drummed his hands, starting with fast quiet taps, then slamming his palms hard against the leather-wrapped steering wheel. For every minute he sat here, he felt it was getting farther away from him.

He had to start pushing, but there was nobody to push. Santiago was like a goddamned ghost—he could be anywhere in the world by now, and maybe not involved at all. Now Lansing was gone.

It was 2:30 A.M., and he was going to rattle someone's chain about this. Allie Meyers was the only person left. Maybe Santiago had called her. Maybe Santiago was with her.

Eddie pulled away from Lansing's and sped across the miles of concrete highway that tangle south Florida. He passed tractor-trailers doing 70 as though they were standing still. The rush of humid air through the Lotus's cockpit kept him from going nuts.

As soon as Eddie turned into the narrow parking court at the small complex where Allie Meyers lived, he saw the truck. It was a six-wheeler, a do-it-yourself moving van, backed up to a building down on Eddie's right. The back doors were open, and someone was loading a TV inside.

Gant killed the Lotus's lights and engine, drifting behind a row of parked cars, easing to a stop. He grabbed his Persuader riot gun in the same motion that set the emergency brake. He waited until the guy hauling the TV set had gone back up the short set of steps into an apartment before getting out of the car. Goddamned strange time to be moving, Eddie thought, striding into the shadows along the brick-front buildings.

He moved quickly toward where the truck was parked, stopping when the guy came down the steps again, this time carrying a stereo turntable. Getting a closer look at him now, Gant saw he was about 5'8", maybe twenty-five, thirty years old—hard to tell with the Latins. He had thick black hair, a bushy moustache, and a paunch around his stomach that pulled his dark shirt from the waist of his pants. He was not hurrying; he seemed very casual about what he was doing.

The man walked up the wood plank that extended from the rear of the truck to the curb, disappeared inside, then came back down, lips pursed as though whistling, but not making any sound.

Gant pressed himself against the front of the building, the glare of lights in the eaves overhead helping to conceal him against the darkened wall. Once he heard the man's footsteps go back up into the apartment, Gant stepped away from the wall to read the apartment numbers. The guy was going in Allie Meyers's unit.

Could this be Santiago? Maybe he and Allie were making a midnight run for it. Sonofabitch!

Eddie heard footsteps again—slow-moving this time, like maybe the guy was carrying something heavy.

Gant waited to see the man clear the steps. The guy appeared carrying an overstuffed chair. Gant let him get to the truck, then cocked the Persuader, came right up behind the man, gun barrel stuck in his fleshy back. "Freeze or die, motherfucker. Police." Gant looked over his shoulder, making sure no one else was coming out of the apartment behind him.

The man holding the chair trembled. "Hesus-man, oh, plez don' shoot me. Plez."

"Put it down, then you go down on your knees," Gant ordered.

"Man, iz not whachew thin'. Iz not really. Oh, Hesus—Hesus." The man turned around on his knees, palms flat together, like he was praying. He had a round face and narrow eyes that were forced open wide with fear. "I jus' stealin' this stuff, I swear. I didn' kill the *señorita*. I jus' came here an' the door was open an' I wen' for the truck an'——"

"What?—Stop. What're you talking, killed?"

"Yeah. The *señorita* inside there."

"Oh, Jesus!" Gant turned to the opened apartment door, seeing lights on inside. "Anyone else in there?"

"No."

"You lie—you die."

"Iz the truth, man. I swear." The man crossed himself.

"Then you lead the way. Come on—let's go." He waved the Latin toward the steps with the riot gun.

"You're not gonta kill me. I swear, I didn'——"

Gant grabbed him by the shirt sleeve, pulling him up the steps, pushing him into the living room. Eddie came in close behind, using the squat Latin for cover, riot gun aimed for the center of the room about waist high.

No one was in sight.

"Sit!" Gant ordered, pointing to a chair by the sliding glass door. "Don't move."

Allie Meyers was in the bedroom with a knife wound about four inches deep cut across her throat. Bloodstains were soaked into the front of her white blouse, a strange contrast to the small red bow tie around her collar. Her face was pale; her eyes open, stared blankly at the ceiling, but seemed to focus at a point beyond that. Spooky. Gant touched the edge of her wound, where blood was caked dry. He guessed she'd been dead at least six hours.

Eddie went back into the living room, found the phone, and dialed Dade-Metro. "When'd you first get here?" Gant asked the Latin while the line rang unanswered.

The man sat on his hands, very nervous in the chair, glancing toward the door as though wondering whether or not to take off, but unable to ignore the shotgun in Gant's hand, the way Eddie's finger always seemed to be on the trigger. " 'Twas abou' six-turty o'clock. I was juz' drivin' tru, you mus' believe me," he pleaded. "I didn' hurt that poor *señorita* there. I didn' even take nottin' from that room. Only out here. The TV, stereo, that——"

Hearing dispatch pick up at Dade-Metro, Gant signaled for the man to be quiet. Eddie reported the stabbing, saying he wanted the lab team immediately, no matter whatever else they had on tonight. Captain Marler's orders, he said, then hung up.

"What's your name?" Gant asked the man, walking in front of him, going to the front door, closing and locking it.

"Sanchez."

"You got a first name, Sanchez?"

"Hector."

"How about I.D.?"

Hector shook his head.

"Green card? Driver's license? Social security card? Voter's registration?" He always felt strange asking for the voter's card, but he'd learned from experience that lots of new citizens carried them like badges of freedom.

Hector didn't have any of that. Gant searched him and found two dollars and a crumpled McDonald's napkin. Hector—Sanchez—or whatever the hell his real name was—wasn't going to be worth the trouble of arresting, then trying for two weeks to find out his real name. So Gant got out of Hector what he thought he would be worth: that Hector had first cruised by the apartment complex around 7:00 knocking on doors, pretending to be selling magazines; that he'd really been using the opportunity to look inside places and see if anyone was worth ripping off. The door to Allie Meyers's had been broken open, so he'd helped himself inside, seen the dead girl, freaked a little, but decided it was worth borrowing his cousin's truck to make a haul. He just wouldn't go in the dead woman's room in case her soul happened to be starting its voyage to heaven at that time, because you'd go straight to hell if you ever saw something like that.

His story told, Gant told Hector Sanchez if he could get all the stuff out of the truck back inside before any other cops showed, he could walk.

Red-faced after five heavily burdened trips, Hector panted loudly, using the front of his now-unbuttoned shirt to wipe perspiration from his face. "Officer," he said, leaning against the hallway wall. "Iz all back."

Gant was slouched in the chair he'd assigned Hector to sit in moments earlier. The riot gun was perched across his lap, his eyes were closed. He waved the thief away.

Santiago, Eddie thought. *It's gotta be you.* And the only person who could I.D. him was lying in her own bed with her throat slit open. Eddie took several deep breaths, trying to come down a little, trying to think. He didn't know what the hell was going on, but he was beginning to have strong feelings that, whatever it was, Santiago was going to get away with it.

Thirteen

"I need a uniform to cover Lansing's house." Gant stood in the doorway to Captain Marler's office.

Uncle Floyd, in his usual white shirt, no tie, and black pants, loomed behind his desk, holding a thick file of clipped-together papers. He nodded approval without looking up.

Gant started to say something about last night, about having been to the hotel, but decided not to. He went to his own desk and phoned the duty sergeant downstairs, telling him to put somebody on Lansing's house and notify him immediately of any activity.

None of the other five detectives in the room talked to one another. Wingate stared out the window at yet another cloudless, hot-and-humid June Miami day. Donald Stripes's desk, covered with notes and reports about the murder at the Sonesta Beach Hotel, was noticeably inactive. No one said anything about Stripes, and no one looked at the empty desk.

DeVito, the youngest of Dade-Metro's small detective force, a University of Miami criminologist graduate, was on the phone with his wife, asking questions about how she was feeling, and kidding that everyone in the station said it was going to be a boy. His conversation was unusually stilted, and Gant knew DeVito was just reassuring his expecting wife that everything was okay, *he* was okay. With Stripes the second Dade-Metro officer down in three days, nerves were short. The instinct was to tighten up, to be extra cautious.

"Eddie." Uncle Floyd leaned part way out of his office, gesturing Gant to his office. Once Gant was inside the glass partition, Marler said, "Close the door," then sat behind his desk. The big man looked humorless, but didn't show any agony of having been passed out from drinking twelve hours earlier. He was freshly showered and shaved, his clothes neatly pressed.

Still, to Eddie, he no longer looked like the same man.

Uncle Floyd said, "You sleep last night?"

"No, sir."

"Think that's a good idea? Tired people make mistakes."

"Lots of people do things they shouldn't do."

Marler accepted the comment. He looked down at his desk a moment, silent, then shook his head. "Poor Donald. He never saw the shooter's car coming, huh?"

"I don't think so."

Uncle Floyd got up, walked past the open window that let in the hot morning air. "I shouldn't have put him on this."

Gant started to say something when Marler opened the cabinet and poured himself half a water glass of Crown Royal, but kept quiet.

"If I'd known what was involved here, I wouldn't have. That's for goddamned sure." Uncle Floyd went back behind his desk, settling down in the wide chair. "So," his glass was hidden inside the wrap of his huge hand, "we've got three dead people and one missing. The boy at the hotel—who we still don't have an I.D. on—killed with a .380 slug. The woman—what was her name?—who worked the hotel and spent the night with Santiago."

"Allie Meyers."

"Yeah. Throat slit open. And Donald. Taken out with a

.357. Three dead and all with different weapons." Uncle Floyd drank some Crown Royal. "Three killers? Two? One?"

"They all link to Santiago."

"Sure. Whoever he is. Anything turn up from getting his composite to the TV stations?"

Gant shook his head.

"Doesn't surprise me. Drawing looked like half the people in Miami. But I think you're right about it being one killer." Marler crossed his fingertips over his pencil-thin moustache. "And I figure Santiago's just as liable to be the one as anybody else we got—especially considering we got nobody else. I put all-points out on him. And Wendy's notifying the airlines, Amtrak, bus lines, FBI, customs—the usual." Uncle Floyd paused, considering Gant. "You gonna sit down, Eddie? You look like a greyhound at the starting gate."

Gant took the chair opposite Marler's desk as the captain opened the case file.

Marler said, "Lab boys ran fingerprint crosses on Sonesta Beach and the girl's—Meyers's—apartment. We got two common sets of prints. One set's yours." Uncle Floyd looked overtop the report. "Son, you gotta stop pawing all over everything."

Eddie didn't react, looking straight ahead, not at Uncle Floyd.

"The other set of prints was picked off Amy Lansing's room, the Meyers apartment, *and* Santiago's room at Sonesta Beach. We've run I.D. on the prints and come up with nothing. Wendy was supposed to have Telexed them to the FBI before she went to work on the airline passenger lists; but, even so, we won't get anything back until tomorrow or Wednesday."

"Swell!" Eddie replied sarcastically.

"That's the game, son," Marler said, holding the sheath of papers in his fist. "I do have one new piece of information— something these million-dollar computers have managed to produce—I got a car registration from the license number you took off Lansing's Oldsmobile."

Damn! Eddie thought. That was something he'd meant to do. Maybe he was tired.

Uncle Floyd continued, "It's owned by ML Engineering Com-

pany, Limited. They're up in Miami Shores." Marler gave
Gant a street address that Eddie recognized as a small indus-
trial park not far from where Lansing lived.

"I don't figure Lansing's at work today," Eddie said.

"Me neither. But could be somebody up there's heard something from him. Could be Lansing's confided in someone he
works with and they're scared for him. So if some sweet-
talking detective showed up and convinced them that he was
gonna help Lansing out . . ." Uncle Floyd took a full swallow
of Crown Royal. "But if you got other ideas . . ."

Eddie looked around almost absentmindedly at the FSU
football trophies, at the toe of his Nikes, at a cigarette burn
on the cheap commercial carpet by the leg of his chair . . .
something about seeing Marler take that swallow of whiskey
today . . . after last night . . .

"Eddie, I know this thing with Donald's got everybody a
little upset. It's always bad when somebody who works this
close to you goes down. But you know that. You've been
around longer than most of these kids. Hell, if it wasn't for
that big dose of federal money we got three years ago, half the
so-called detectives around here would still be in uniform.
They look up to you, son. They see you getting beat by this,
they're gonna be hurtin'. But if you're pulling through, they'll
follow your lead. It was a terrible thing that happened to
Donald, but we can't get sucked under by it. Don't let it get to
you, Eddie. Okay?"

Eddie stared blankly. "Maybe if things work out and I get
back together with Janice, you and Alice Ann and Janice and
I could go out for dinner one night." When Uncle Floyd nodded, Eddie headed for the door.

"Eddie——"

Gant stopped.

"——Donald's laid out at the funeral parlor down South
Dixie. I can't remember the name of it—the one the depart-
ment always uses because somebody's brother-in-law owns it.
You know where I mean?"

Eddie turned to look at Marler, but Uncle Floyd had twisted

around in his oversized chair and was looking out the open window, Crown Royal in hand.

"He's just gonna be there today. Then his wife's taking the body back home with her to Ohio. I think it's Ohio. Donald didn't have many friends in the department, so . . . I thought if you stopped by, you know, after you check out this engineering place where Lansing works, it would be a nice gesture."

Eddie walked out.

Eddie had expected the place to be a white-walled clutter of electronic gadgetry, microchips, wires, soldering irons, and components scattered about hard-topped tables with a team of scientific-looking types like William Lansing bent over their work, studying it with intellectual concentration as they prepared their next step.

Instead, the lobby looked like a downtown Miami law firm. The carpeting was a rich magenta that coordinated perfectly with multicolored pastel walls. A sofa and loveseat were positioned near a heavy glass coffee table, and in the corner was a lavender ceramic vase, its wide mouth filled with dozens of silk tiger lilies.

The company's receptionist, looking both efficient and attractive in a black-and-tan striped blazer, sat at a half-circle desk of deeply polished cherrywood. Behind her on the wall, in bronze letters each the size of Gant's hand, was *ML Engineering, Incorporated.*

Beyond the receptionist, through double glass doors, was a hallway with six or eight doorways leading into what Eddie guessed were individual offices.

"May Ah help you?" the woman asked, her accent resounding with echoes of Georgia that didn't match the sophistication of her designer fashions.

"William Lansing? Is he in? I need to speak with him about—— "

"Ah'm sorry, sir. But Mistah Lansing will not be in today."

"Do you know where he is then?"

"Ah'm afraid Ah couldn't release that information." She smiled more than politely.

"Is he sick, or just not here?"

She considered him suspiciously, head tilted back slightly.

Eddie showed his badge.

The receptionist picked up the phone. "Maybe you should speak to Mistah Marsh."

Anthony Marsh's office looked straight from a New England's men club, circa 1915. An oriental rug lavishly adorned the hardwood floor; and on dark-stained walls hung huge oil paintings of cherubic women in frilly dresses with top-hatted gentlemen leering at them, the men's walking sticks often juxtaposed at suggestive positions across the bodies of ladies who were painted into the background.

Heavy floor-length curtains covered the window behind Marsh's desk completely blocking out the afternoon sun, leaving only dim bulbs in a small chandelier and an amber-globed desk lamp to brighten the otherwise-dark office. Handmade wood cabinets lined three walls; and behind their glass doors were odd-looking collectibles and *objets d'art*.

Marsh himself was a handsome, lean man with close-trimmed white hair and the pointed nose and chin of a northern European. He wore aviator prescription glasses with the slightest pink tint to the lenses. His suit was a rich golden brown with hair-thin beige stripes set in the summer-wool fabric at one-inch intervals. The fit was so precise that Gant guessed it had to be tailor-made.

Marsh's handshake was firm, businesslike, his voice smooth and sincere, making Gant feel at ease. "Please, sit down." He gestured to the trio of high-backed glove-leather chairs across from his desk, then sat down himself. "You're with the police," Marsh said, sounding intrigued, hands folded on the forest green insert of his cowhide desk blotter.

"I need to talk to William Lansing." Gant couldn't find a comfortable way to sit as straight as the chair was designed, so he leaned forward.

"No trouble, I hope."

The last thing Eddie felt like doing was being patient with some high-society company president half a generation removed from Beacon Hill, but he didn't see any shortcuts. He laid out the whole story, about the kidnapping, Lansing's refusal to cooperate, then later being at the scene of a detective's murder.

Marsh listened intently, expressionless, his position shifting only to take a cigarette from the silver container at his right hand, putting flame to it with a Dunhill lighter.

Eddie had expected something from Marsh. Surprise. Shock. Despair. Grief. Concern. Anything but silence.

"You tried him at home?" Marsh said once Gant had unfolded the entire scenario.

Gant couldn't believe Marsh would even ask that question; surely the man was logical enough to realize that would be the first place he'd looked. "He's not there. Hasn't been all night."

"I'm sorry, then. I don't know what else I could add."

"Does he have any family around here? Someone he might go to if he was in trouble?"

Marsh thought a moment, deeply enjoying the long pull from his cigarette, then shaking his head. "I *am* sorry, detective. I don't really know that much about his personal life. We have never associated much outside of the business."

I don't goddamned believe it, Eddie thought. *I'm sitting here for the entertainment of some millionaire who'll turn this into some wonderful anecdote for his next Palm Beach cocktail party.* Gant rose, glad to be out of the straight-backed chair. "Thanks for your time"—God how it hurt saying that—"If you hear from him, would you call me? Eddie Gant. Dade-Metro Police. We're, uh—how do you say?—in the book."

The receptionist had been going out the door for lunch just as Eddie came down the hall from Marsh's office, so he followed her to the parking lot, breaking into a slow jog to catch up when she unlocked a classic royal-blue MGB-GT.

"Nice car," he said, feeling sticky in the humidity after the cool dry air conditioning in Marsh's office. "A lot of people I know would kill for wheels like this."

"Yes. Ah know. My ex-husband threatened to kill *me* for it.

But mah lawyah said to have *balls*, and we held out for it as part of the settlement. Ah think it killed Dave to have to let it go." She smoothed the back of her skirt getting behind the wheel.

Eddie leaned on the open driver's door to keep her from pulling it shut.

She smiled, "Ah don't mean to be impolite, but Ah have an engagement foh lunch."

Gant held onto the door. "Tell me, just what kind of stuff does ML Engineering do?"

She shrugged. "They're designahs and plannahs mostly. We handle a lot of private contracts. Some government contracts, too. And they're consultants to othah outside companies."

"That's Marsh's car?" Gant asked, pointing to a bronze Jaguar sedan; the car was parked diagonally across two spaces that were posted *RESERVED: ML Engineering Officers.*

"Yes, it is."

"He must do okay here, huh?" Gant was trying to be friendly, seeing her patience wearing thin.

"Mistah Marsh is a very shrewd businessman. He does *very* well for himself. This company has come a long way in the past three years."

"So what's happened in three years?"

"That's when Mistah Marsh took over. Before that, Bill Lansing ran the company, and he ran it terribly. He was a very good engineah, but not very good with business. Ah rarely got paid on time and when Ah did, the checks very often bounced. Mistah Lansing was close to bankruptcy, Ah think, befoah Mistah Marsh came and took over."

"I was wondering what the L was in ML Engineering. It's Marsh-Lansing, huh?" Eddie thought about Marsh's Jag and Lansing's beat-up Olds Cutlass. "I think Marsh must be getting the better end of the deal."

"Mistah Lansing is lucky not to be in a soup line. Mistah Marsh saved him. He even tried to culture him, Mistah Marsh did. That's what he calls it to try and make someone a better person—to improve them. He calls it 'culturing.' He cultured me, Mistah Marsh did. I had my teeth done over and went to modeling classes. Not to learn about being a model, but to know how to hold mahself better, make a better appearance. And Mistah Marsh had the company pay for it. He said impressions are very important."

Okay, Marsh, Gant thought, *so you're as slick as you look. Good for you.* Eddie stepped back from the MGB. "You have a nice lunch."

She nodded, giving him a posed smile Eddie figured she learned in modeling school.

Fourteen

Santiago cleared customs in Barbados. The name on his white immigration card matched that of his new passport: Diego San Miguel. This passport, like the others, was Costa Rican, so he could keep his story about being a South American businessman with an estate in the mountains where afternoon rains kept the countryside cool and birds flew in through open windows. He liked that particular fiction.

The temperature was mild in the open-air body of the airport. A lazy breeze gently rippled the Barbadan flag that hung from the thirty-foot-high concrete ceiling that seemed magically suspended overhead.

Santiago carried his own suitcase, waving off the beckoning assault of imposing baggage handlers who hustled up to him wheeling squeaking metal dollies.

At the airport's front curb, a scurry of black men hurried back and forth organizing small groups of tourists onto buses, shouting the names of various hotels in accents that the array of white-skinned Americans, all looking disoriented and ill-at-ease, struggled to interpret.

Santiago wedged through the tourists, walking between bumpers of two passenger vans, crossing to the cement island that divided black-topped service lanes. There he found a man slumped asleep behind the wheel of a compact Daihatsu station wagon. He reached into the open driver's window and jostled the man awake. "Cab?"

In Barbados, like most other Caribbean islands, it was difficult to tell which cars were for hire and which were not, since few—if any—carried signs or markings that identified them as taxis.

The older driver snorted a few times, coughing himself awake, mumbling something Santiago didn't understand. But the driver turned the engine over, so Santiago slid his suitcases across the back seat and got in.

"Take me to Bridgetown. Okay?" Santiago said.

The driver nodded, shifting into gear, jerking the car away from the curb.

Being driven across the rolling countryside, between tall fields of spiky sugarcane, Santiago marveled—as he always did in Barbados—that the island was still its pretentious little self: three sand and one rock shores that formed a slightly lipped dot in the sea, where children dressed for school in stiffly starched uniforms, and the land was divided into plots called parishes named after this saint or that; where an undercurrent of violence and unrest existed below polite manners; where the British accents of the natives were found so quaint by flocks of American, English, Canadian, and German tourists. It was true that, on the surface, Barbados was much more civilized than Jamaica, with its endless political unrest and Castro-incensed Kingston shooting sprees, or Haiti, with its voodoo, rampant crime, and unbelievable poverty, but the core of tension was identical.

Like the rest of the Caribbean, Barbados was essentially impoverished. Most of those born here would never leave; they were, for all practical purposes, prisoners of the sea. Trapped here, they did not feel grateful, as many tourists thought they should, for the foreign dollars that poured into their country, for they would see but pennies on the dollar.

The bulk of the monetary trade would be channeled back to the United States and Europe, to corporations that owned the hotels and restaurants. Most of the natives experienced an inner exploitation because they earned less in a year than the price of a week-long stay at the luxury hotel that employed them.

Some openly rebelled. Some accepted it, satisfied never to leave a place they truly considered paradise. While still others swallowed their resentment, satisfied to work their revenge by providing ploddingly slow and uncaring service to the tourist trade.

It was for different reasons, but Santiago was not especially fond of the Caribbean. He considered it as much a modern-day haven for pirates as it had been in past centuries. Geographically, accessible coastline was scattered about an entire chain of islands and thousands of square miles of ocean, all readily available as a route of escape or refuge for the pursued. And since each island was governed by a different ruling body— ranging from colonial monarchies to puppet-dictatorships, all in constantly shifting conflict with one another—there was little if any coordination of law enforcement among the islands, and that was assuming what law enforcement there was wasn't more easily bribed than outrun.

The chaos would have seemed blueprinted for Santiago's plans, but there were drawbacks to systemless societies. In the United States, a land of endless rules, you could learn the loopholes and survive well by squeezing through them. When there were no rules, only instincts remained, and that meant watching constantly over your shoulder. Because here, even rules among thieves were ignored. The chances for success may have been greater in a struggle to outwit the authorities, but the opportunity to remain alive once the deal was down often became elusive.

Santiago had the cabdriver drop him near the harbor downtown. Carrying his small soft-sided luggage by its shoulder strap, Santiago walked across the short bridge that led out of Bridgetown's business district. He stayed close to the railing, avoiding the recklessly ridden bicycles that jumped the curb when cars crossing the bridge blocked their path.

A gentle sea breeze made for less-imposing temperatures but was a mixed blessing, for it brought with it the smell of stale garbage and rotten fish.

Across the bridge, a row of short buildings lined a wide concrete patio along the tiny harbor. There were two art galleries, a shop specializing in German crystal, an expensive dress boutique, and a marine-supply shop that advertised its service of minor repairs for yachts moored in boat slips along the patio's edge.

The only other business bore no name, only a hand-painted sign that read, in scrawled letters: *Custom Jewelry*.

Santiago pulled open the heavy glass door to the nameless shop and walked in. A delicate brass wind chime sounded, brushed by the top of the door. No one sat behind the small glass counter that was the narrow shop's only apparent source of stock. Prints of famous island artists—Gauguin and Homer whom Santiago recognized—hung framed along two-story-high white walls.

Santiago was alone, his leather-soled shoes echoing over the ivory-and-brown tiled floor. He looked to the landing at the rear of the shop, where a half-flight of steps led to a doorway stuck dead-center in the wall like a rectangular bullseye.

The door opened and a woman wearing a flowing pink dress of wrinkled cotton appeared. She gave Santiago a tourist's welcome: a wave and a hearty hello. She was American, flashing a pretty smile of bright white teeth. Her legs were deeply tanned, lots of them showing through high slits in the side of the dress as she walked toward him. She looked like one of those women who handed out perfume samples at cosmetic counters in American department stores. "Feel free to browse," she said, never forgetting her smile. "If I can help you with anything, please let me know."

"Actually," Santiago said, walking by the case of heavy gold rings and bracelets, "I'm looking for Gus."

"Gus?" she smiled.

Trained well, Santiago thought. "Gus. Triacas." *You know,* he was thinking, *the guy who fronts this place to run stolen gold and diamonds that he buys off fences in the States for ten bucks an ounce that's too hot to move anywhere else. That Gus. The guy who was into stolen jewelry and a whole lot of other deeper shit.*

The round black telephone rang on the table behind the counter.

"Will you excuse me?" the woman asked.

Santiago nodded, strolling to the front door, looking outside.

The woman answered the phone with a cheerful hello, then said nothing else before hanging up. "You can go back," she said to Santiago, her smile and welcome-tourist voice gone now.

As he went toward the stairs at the rear of the shop, the woman took a chain of keys from a drawer beneath the display counter and locked the double set of bolts on the front door. Santiago climbed the short stairs, leaving his case on the landing. Going through the door into the back room, he found Gus Triacas standing behind a handcrafted cherry desk.

Triacas's short, compact build made him look like a boxer who'd managed to keep his form twenty years after retirement from the game. There were heavy gold rings on three fingers of the hand extended to Santiago. "How are you doing, my friend?" Triacas's accent was thick with his native Athens.

"Good," Santiago nodded.

Triacas sat down, leaving Santiago to stand. Besides the ornate desk, Triacas's burgundy leather chair, and a few more island paintings, there were no other furnishings—only a ceiling fan with four globe lights that cast a rose tint.

"Do we still have a deal?" Triacas said, his tone more that of statement than inquiry.

Santiago nodded, holding back his eagerness, wanting to see if there was a hard line to play out successfully. "If you say so."

Triacas laughed. "What do you mean 'if I say so'? What's that supposed to mean? If I say we have a deal and you don't, then we don't have a deal and my time is being wasted."

Triacas had jumped him to the punch, keeping the pressure on.

Santiago crossed his arms, uncomfortable standing there, as if he were up for inspection, but he was determined to play tough. "You tell me you have a buyer for my product, but I don't see him. I only see you."

"What can I tell you?" Triacas held open his arms, tilting back in his chair. "I put together this deal for the man. For you. He decides he wants to stay in the background, that's his business. What do you care who he is, so long as he pays your price. And he *is* going to pay your price."

"We might have to talk about that."

"Talk about what? I don't understand all this uncertainty I'm hearing. I expected that when I saw you this time, you'd have the plans and the deal would be made."

"I don't know, Gus." Santiago shook his head. "Complications. The heat came on strong in Miami—four dead people up there. It wasn't as simple as I'd hoped."

"If it was simple, anyone could do it. And I don't deal with just anyone." Triacas sounded aggravated now. "I listened to your offer because of who you knew, who you'd worked for, and what they told me about you. If you'd come in here talking like this two months ago, I wouldn't have wasted the effort to spit in your face. You said you had something I might want. I found you a buyer. We agreed on a price. There was no discussion of how difficult this would be for any of us. That is part of the business. You *make* it part of your business if you want to do business." Triacas opened his arms again. "But I don't know. Maybe you don't want to do business. You tell me." Triacas waited, looking dead into Santiago. "Well? You want to do business or not?"

Santiago had thought Gus was a little prick when he'd first met him; now he thought he was a big prick. Sure the guy was playing with him. Why not? Where else was Santiago going to go with this kind of stuff in a hurry? Anything else would take time—too much time, time Santiago didn't have. Developing the right new contacts would be difficult. He might end up having to deal with the Russians directly, or maybe through the Poles or some embassy, like Mexico City or Guatemala . . . Cloak-and-dagger shit and that meant worrying about the CIA, NSA, FBI, State Department. Fuck. Triacas was a prick, but a damned smart one. He seemed to know Santiago's options better than Santiago did. "Yeah. We got a deal."

Triacas smiled. "Fine. Good. When do you want to make the exchange?"

"Maybe tomorrow. Maybe the next."

Triacas's smile faded quickly. He frowned impatiently. "I need to know exactly. My buyer isn't going to hold a quarter of a million American dollars in his pocket until we get word from you."

Santiago couldn't help thinking: if things hadn't gotten switched in Miami, if the Lansing girl hadn't shown up at the hotel with her boyfriend, if he'd been able to pick up the plans in the States . . . If, if, if . . . But Lansing wasn't even here yet. What if he didn't bring the plans? If he didn't come to the island at all? More ifs—but no, Lansing wouldn't be that dumb. He'd show because he knew he'd wind up dead otherwise. He'd seen him waste that guy in the Trans Am, he'd know he'd come back for him, make it painful, then bury him right beside his daughter under the wall-to-wall carpet in that trailer in Homestead.

"Day after tomorrow," Santiago finally decided. "In the morning. Nine-thirty."

"Where are you staying?" Triacas asked. "In case some change has to be made."

"No changes. We got a deal, right? Like you said. You meet me here nine-thirty in the morning, day after tomorrow. If you're not here, or the money's not here, we got no deal."

Triacas condescended.

Triacas, the fuck. Santiago didn't trust him—shouldn't have from the beginning. Santiago realized now that he'd been too anxious to swing the deal when he'd made a commitment to the Greek. He should have checked around. This stuff was worth way more than a quarter-million, and Triacas knew it.

And Triacas had said the buyer would be there to meet with him. Shit, Santiago had figured on getting the buyer aside, splitting the difference that would have been Triacas's commission as the go-between, and cut Triacas out altogether. But Triacas had been too smart for that.

So, Santiago thought, *I'll just have to be smarter. Maybe Triacas doesn't know all the ways I can turn this deal.*

He took a cab back to the airport and rented a car. From there he drove to the southern coast of the island, the area preferred by rowdy Americans and Germans over the serene quiet of the western shore. It was getting dark, so he turned on his headlights for the final five minutes of the drive.

Unable to see the small side roads for the glare of oncoming cars, he missed the cutoff and had to turn around in a hotel parking lot and double back.

The small tin-roofed house, painted bright pink, sat lopsidedly in a shallow gully hidden from the road. There was no finished driveway, only worn tire tracks through foot-high grass, and, heading down, the rented Toyota's small tires splashed through narrow trenches of runoff water that refused to drain from the low points.

Santiago stopped the car twenty feet from the house, turning off the headlights. He got out slowly, keeping his hands away from his body, knowing that behind closed curtains at one of six darkened windows, someone would be aiming a gun at him.

Fifteen

Gant let the shower water run down hot and hard over his shoulders. Steam filled the confines of the bathroom and he breathed deeply of thick warm air. It was calming and he needed the effect to overcome his frustration.

Santiago had vanished, taking Amy Lansing with him. The APBs hadn't turned up anything—nothing from the airlines, bus stations, or customs either. And Santiago's composite was now being buried amidst more recent murders and drug busts on the local news. Allie Meyers—the only one who had ever seen Santiago—was dead. Donald Stripes had been killed for being at the wrong place at the wrong time.

Eddie pegged Santiago as an arrogant bastard. There was no doubt in his mind that Santiago had done it all: the murder and kidnapping at Sonesta Beach, Donald Stripes, Allie Meyers. Three very clean, very cold-blooded murders, executed professionally except for one thing: Santiago had left his fingerprints all over everything, as if he knew he was going to get away with it, that he would always remain far enough ahead to escape the clutch of his pursuers. Hit, run, hide, then strike again.

And Santiago was good. It haunted Eddie that when Santiago pulled the trigger on Stripes, Eddie had been so close to him—within a hundred yards—and maybe that was the closest he'd ever get.

William Lansing was the only remaining link to Santiago, the only constant. Santiago wanted something from Lansing—money, presumably—in exchange for the return of Lansing's daughter. So, sometime, somewhere, there would have to be an exchange. Gant's only hope was to be there when it went down.

On Monday afternoon, Eddie walked up the marble front steps of the funeral parlor in one of his drug-runner outfits: Perry Ellis silk blazer, bold-striped shirt, loose-fitting pleated white pants, and iguana-skin boots. He wasn't a churchgoer, so these were the only "dress-up" clothes he owned.

Immediately upon entering the foyer, he became aware of the strong smell of flowers, almost sickeningly sweet. Central air conditioning hummed steadily and quietly, as much a part of the background as the somber music that played deeply through speakers built into the walls.

Down a carpeted hallway were six viewing rooms. In front of each was a black placard posted with the surname of the deceased.

A young man wearing a dark suit, with deep acne scars in his cheeks, rose from a lavender velvet love seat. In a quiet, rehearsed voice, he said, "Good afternoon, sir. To whom are you paying respects?"

"Stripes," Eddie replied, looking to see if anyone else from Dade-Metro was here. Outside of one viewing room, he saw three squat older women in almost-identical paisley dresses, one wearing a veil, consoling each other.

"That would be the far door on your right. The end of the hall." He held his hands together, then smiled in feigned understanding. "My condolences."

Eddie walked passed the three older women. One said how

poor John was better off this way. "Oh, yes," another said, "he wouldn't have wanted to live like that. He is better off where he is now."

Yeah, right, Eddie thought, *the guy's better off in a box? He must have been from Gainesville.*

The room where Donald Stripes was laid out was much smaller than the rest.

A closed bronze casket was squeezed back against the wall. It was adorned with a big circular wreath of flowers draped gaudily in black silk that Gant recognized as the standard departmental send-off. Two other arrangements of artificial flowers, undoubtedly recycled and supplied by the funeral home, lay conspicuously alone on a wide white shelf.

A woman wearing an ill-fitting black dress and clutching a wrinkled handkerchief sat uncomfortably in a gray chair. She looked numbly toward Eddie, not blinking, seeming to look behind him.

"Mrs. Stripes?" he asked, barely whispering. "Don't get up. Please." He took the hand she'd extended automatically toward him.

Her face was puffy, and her makeup barely hid the dark circles beneath her eyes. She was not an unattractive woman, but very plain, looking awkward in mourning. The corners of her mouth fought to turn upward, but it was not a smile.

There was an uncomfortable silence, made worse by the fact that no one else was there—only the depressing music and air conditioning made any sound.

"I just came by to tell you that"—he couldn't seem to find the words—"Well, that I'm very sorry about what happened."

"You knew Donald?" she asked, sounding anxious to talk about him, as though someone else's memories would intensify her own, maybe keep him real, more alive.

"Yes. I . . . we worked together." Gant started to say that he'd been with Donald when he was killed, but caught himself.

"You're a policeman?"

Eddie nodded.

"It's a very dangerous job, isn't it?" She sounded so naïve saying it, as though repeating what someone else had told her.

There was another awkward silence. Then Eddie said, "You're going back to Ohio?"

She nodded. "My son and I."

Gant followed her gaze to where a young boy stood near the casket; he was so small and quiet that Gant hadn't seem him.

"Matthew," Mrs. Stripes spoke softly. "There's a man here who was a policeman with Daddy."

The boy didn't respond.

Mrs. Stripes said, "He's had a tough time with it. I think after . . ." She stopped, her thought lost. Tears welled in her eyes, and she wiped them from her cheeks with her handkerchief.

Eddie walked over to the boy, going down on one knee to be at the same height. "Hi."

The boy looked a lot like Donald. His small hands were folded together as he turned toward Gant with big blue watery eyes.

Eddie was going to tell him how brave his daddy had been, what a good detective he was, how he and his daddy had been such good friends, and that Donald always said how much he loved his son, but, looking at the boy—the youth, the innocence of him—Eddie couldn't.

"My daddy's in there," Matthew said, pointing to the shiny casket. "He's real sick and he can't ever come out."

Eddie felt a sense of shock, as though his senses were blocking things out, not letting him feel any of this. But, Jesus, how could this be happening to this little boy? "I'm very sorry about your dad." He held the boy's small, warm hands until Matthew turned back toward the coffin.

"He can't seem to stop looking at it." Gant hadn't realized Mrs. Stripes had walked up behind them.

The silence returned again.

Eddie released the boy's hands and stood beside her. "I hope things go well for you in Ohio. I grew up here, but sometimes Miami really isn't a very nice place."

She managed to nod.

On his way out, Gant stopped to sign the register. All the pages were blank. Not even Uncle Floyd had come. In careful printed letters, he wrote: *From a dear friend, Eddie Gant.*

*   *   *

Amy Lansing's body was found beneath the shag carpet in the bedroom of a trailer down in Homestead; that's what Wingate told Gant when Eddie phoned in to check if there had been any sign of William Lansing.

"When did you get this?" Eddie was annoyed that he hadn't been contacted right away. Standing at a pay phone in front of the Lum's Restaurant in South Coral Gables, the variables came to mind. Amy Lansing was Santiago's leverage. Without her, what did he have on Lansing? And, horrible as it seemed, Eddie couldn't help but see past the tragedy of the death to realize the convenience of it. Now he should be able to bring Lansing in to cooperate. Surely Lansing would want the man responsible for the death of his daughter to be taken down.

Wingate said, "We got word 'bout half-hour ago. Seems some folks down there saw a Latin fellow going in and out at odd hours and got suspicious and called in a complaint. But Homestead cops told the people no crime had been committed and there was nothing they could do. So, earlier this afternoon, a bunch of the locals down there broke into the trailer and found the body."

"Lab run fingerprints yet?"

"The team just went out before you called. We got a bit of a jurisdictional problem between us and Homestead, but they're backin' off since we got a link up here." Wingate said, "This the Santiago fellow you been after?"

"I think so, yeah."

"Dude's cuttin' up pretty good, *homme*. I don't know all what you got, but the man really done this lady in from what I got over the phone."

"He use a knife?" Eddie guessed, sensing a pattern: guns for the men, knives for the women.

"Oh, yeah. Went a little nuts on her, too. She was naked and had what one of the Homestead boys said looked like dried dick juice over her throat and face. And some more in her trim. I think your man got hisself off 'fore he did her."

"Christ! The bastard leaves plenty of evidence of where he's been, what he's done, but none of where he's going."

"Well, you know he's still 'round Miamuh, *homme.* But I don't know if that's good or bad. Shit, most times we just can't get these maniac motherfuckers. They too unpredictable. Just gotta hope they get bored 'round here and move on, you know?"

"Let me talk to the captain." Gant had an idea what he wanted to do, but needed to know that Marler would be there to cover his ass.

"Uncle Floyd's gone home. Said he wasn't feelin' very good."

"Damn!" Of all times—Gant had never known Marler to be sick a day all the years he'd known him.

"Any way I can help?"

Gant thought for a minute. "Yeah. Give me five minutes, then have the duty sergeant pull the uniform off Lansing's house. That's Lan-sing. You got it?"

"L-A-N-S-I-N-G? That it?"

"Yeah. And if you don't mind jerking him, say it's captain's orders, case he wants to know."

"Shit, babe, that won't get me in no hot water. If you want it, Uncle Floyd'll do it. You're his Number One. He'd do anything you say."

Sixteen

Gant stood back from the door, lined the heel of his iguana-skin boot inside the knob, and gave a sharp kick.

The door burst open with a loud snap, slamming into an interior wall. Eddie went inside. There was no foyer. He stepped directly into a small, cluttered living room.

"Lansing! You in here? It's the police!" He went through the unfurnished dining room and checked the kitchen, smelling the mess before he saw it. Pots and dishes were piled countertop-high in the sink, and the stove was caked with hardened residue of burnt food. By the side door was a grocery bag stuffed with trash that had amorphous moist shapes soaked through the brown paper. Greenish-black mildew spots crawled up the window over the sink and on the wall behind the trash.

Eddie backtracked through the dining room, crossing the middle of the floor where there would have normally been a table. "Lansing!" he called again, although sure by now that the man was not here, and hadn't been since yesterday from the closed-up smell of the place.

The small bedroom, the first room down the hall, was dominated by a lopsided sofa covered with a dark brown sheet. In the corner was a small desk, the size a grade-schooler would use, and on it were piles of electronic components: strange little gadgets of metal and copper, some plugged into boards and soldered there, others lying scattered about the way a carpenter would spread out an assortment of nails looking for the right kind. In one desk drawer were plastic boxes partitioned into small compartments that held more component parts. Another drawer was stacked with catalogs from mail-order houses with high-tech names that sold this sort of electronics stuff, none of which made sense to Gant.

The second bedroom was obviously Amy's—or else it had been. It was the only room so far that looked at all organized and clean, although there was a substantial layer of dust over everything that told Gant she probably hadn't lived in here for a while. Even the knobs of a small TV set and her stereo were covered with a uniform coat of dust. Gant remembered Allie Meyers telling him that the Lansing girl said her father paid for her stay at Sonesta Beach as a present for getting good grades, so maybe she lived at school.

Gant went through the last bedroom, the largest of the three. The double bed was turned down on only one side. On a dresser top, cluttered with rubber bands, paper clips, pens, and change, was a framed photograph of Amy. There didn't seem to be a Mrs. Lansing, and, for some reason, Gant had always assumed that there wasn't, although never really putting it in definite terms until now. Lansing just hadn't looked like the sort who would be married. Divorced, yeah. Married, no.

Eddie tore up the bedroom, looking for bankbooks, a place where cash might have been hidden, notes made perhaps during conversations with Santiago—after all, wouldn't he have had to write down any instructions Santiago had given him for making an exchange for Amy?

But there was nothing. Maybe Lansing had refused to deal. Maybe that's why the girl had been killed. *Shit, who knows,* Eddie swore. He turned over the mattress, dumped out all the dresser drawers on the floor, looked behind the ugly painting that hung on the wall. He didn't know exactly *what* he was looking for, only that he'd know it when he found it. And he hadn't found it—yet.

He kicked the pillow that he'd knocked onto the floor; then, as an afterthought, picked it up, feeling its stuffing to see if there was something inside. But there wasn't, and the mere fact that he'd looked made him feel as if he were fishing in still waters with the wrong bait.

He went back into the bedroom that Lansing appeared to use as a workshop. He sat in the small chair and went through all the stuff on top of the desk. He picked up a few items, using tweezers to examine the tinier pieces, knowing how ludicrous this was, as though there were going to be tiny letters on the side of each part describing its function.

When the phone rang in the other room, it startled him. His arm jerked, and the small twisted piece of copper he held in the tweezers dropped onto the desktop, immediately becoming lost in a hundred other odd-shaped units. But the phone rang only once.

Eddie waited for another call to come in. The one-ring-hang-up-then-call-back signal was as old as Alex Bell himself. When there wasn't a second call, Eddie remembered the small laminated-wood box on Lansing's nightstand: a phone answering machine. Apparently it had just answered a call. If Lansing had a remote device with him, he could be receiving messages at home—messages from Santiago—without ever needing to be here. Gant wondered why he hadn't checked the machine in the first place.

It only took a few seconds to wind back the tape in the answering machine. Either Lansing didn't get many calls, or he had a remote device that allowed him to erase messages as he listened to them from somewhere outside the house. Gant switched the dial to *playback*, and the tape started to turn smoothly.

The first two calls were only hangups—Eddie could hear the click of a receiver being put down, followed immediately by the sound of the voice-activated machine switching out of its recording mode.

The third call came through loudly. Eddie turned down the

volume as he listened to the woman's voice. She spoke clearly, not at all inhibited by the mechanical device that answered her call. "Mr. Lansing, hello. This is Debbie at Sun-Florida Travel. We *have finally* gotten through to Eastern to get the confirmation number for your six-thirty flight to Barbados. It's C, as in Charles, Q, as in Queen, nine-five-seven-six. You shouldn't need it, but, just in case, I thought I'd let you know. Have a nice trip and thanks for using Sun-Florida."

Eddie carefully laid two pairs of blue jeans across the bottom of his suitcase. He put the Persuader riot gun on top of them, then felt the underside of his soft-sided luggage. The hard barrel was still too prominent. Some baggage attendant might accidentally brush against it and realize it was something more than a bottle of liquor.

He found two beach towels in the bottom of the bathroom closet and folded them on top the blue jeans, then laid the riot gun down and felt the bottom of his suitcase again. Much better—he had to really press in before feeling the hard length of the shotgun's barrel. And once he packed other clothes on top of that, it should be fine. The extra shells—beside the seven already loaded into the weapon—he stuffed inside a rolled-up sweatshirt jammed into a hard-sided corner.

The phone beside his bed rang and he grabbed it up. "Yeah?"

"It's Wendy, Eddie." She sounded tired and frustrated. "First of all, William Lansing *was* on Eastern's evening flight to Barbados. I got hold of this travel-agent lady you gave me the name of at home, and she said Lansing called her this morning, and that all the arrangements were put through on a rush basis, because, she said, he was very urgent about it all. Said he had to get there today. And he's staying at a place called—wait a minute, I've got so many notes here I can't find it . . . Here it is. He's staying at the Barbados Beach Villas—on the west coast, if that means anything to you." Wendy took a deep breath. "Now, I can't find Uncle Floyd. Anywhere. Did you know he's not living at home? He's at some crappy hotel down on——"

"Don't tell anybody about that," Eddie cut back quickly. He

had the receiver pressed between his shoulder and ear, sloppily folding a tennis shirt into his suitcase.

"Okay." Wendy was taken aback by the tone of his voice. "So you did know about it?"

"Yeah. But I don't want anyone else to know. You understand?"

"Sure, I guess. But what's the big secret? Lots of us have had split-ups with——"

"It's not a split-up. It's . . . I can't go into it now. Just keep it to yourself."

"Eddie, Alice Ann didn't make any secret of it when I said I was looking for Uncle Floyd. If someone else calls, I'm sure she'll tell them, too."

"Look, Wendy, I really don't want to go into it now." Gant made a bad folding job of another shirt and dropped it in his suitcase. "My problem is I've got to get an expense voucher authorized to catch the ten P.M. flight."

"That's another problem. The ten P.M.'s booked solid. I got you on standby. That was the best I could do."

"Shit. You're kidding. This is supposed to be the fucking off-season. Call them back. Maybe you got some Haitian who can't use the computer. Who the hell goes to the Caribbean in the summer?"

Wendy sighed. "I'll try again, but until further notice, you're on standby. I mean I even tried telling them this was a police emergency, but all I could get you was a flight out tomorrow morning at seven."

"Goddammit," he snapped, then exhaled deeply. "Shit, sorry, I'm not mad at you, Wendy."

"How do you think I feel? Who do you think's been making all these calls."

"I know—I appreciate it. I owe you one."

"You owe me *two*."

"Yeah, okay. What about the hotel?"

"That was no problem. You're set at the same place Lansing's going to."

"What's the name again?"

"The Barbados Beach . . . Villas," she answered, pausing to

check her notes. "Now, there was also something else you said you wanted me to check on last time you called, but you couldn't remember what it was."

"Yeah, thanks for reminding me." Gant counted out five pairs of underwear. "I need you to keep calling ML Engineering in case Lansing shows up at work. Talk to a guy named Marsh. He runs the place. Tell him you're a cop and he'll probably cooperate. Don't waste your time with the receptionist; she'll be too busy studying notes from her modeling class."

"What?"

"Never mind. Just give Marsh a call every day, okay?"

Wendy didn't answer, but Gant could hear her writing something down. "Eddie," she said, "we did already have a conversation about this whole thing being against regulations. That Barbados is maybe a thousand miles outside our jurisdiction. And you know once you're down there, you're not a cop anymore, you're just another foreigner. A tourist."

"Yeah. You were a good mother. You told me all about that." Passport, he suddenly realized. He'd forgotten to look for his passport.

"I mean this time . . . well . . . I think you're carrying it too far. I don't think you're considering the risks. The exposure. Why don't you let this one go, Eddie?"

"No way. I want this bastard."

"Just like all the other 'bastards.' If *you* can't get away with shit like this, neither can they. Isn't that what you always say?"

"Not word for word, maybe, but you're close." Where the hell was that passport? "You see, if someone isn't out there putting these motherfuckers to the test, pretty soon they'll all think it's worth the risk because no one's willing to go on a limb to haul their ass in."

"Oh, Jesus! Spare me. Is this a comic book or real life?"

"If there's a page number under your feet and a Marvel Books logo over your head, it's the strips. Otherwise . . ."

"What?" Wendy asked, then, "Oh, I get it. Hah-hah, Eddie." She sighed, "Well, I see my advice is being considered *seriously*, so let me check the plane tickets again. I'll call you back. But you know something? I think Wingate's right about you."

"How's that?"

"He says the reason you hate big-time crooks so much is cause you're jealous of them. That that they're what you'd really rather be . . . but you're not—how did he put it?—a gambling man."

Eddie hung up without saying good-bye. He stared at his suitcase a few minutes, then closed the top, snapping it shut. He'd find the passport later. There was some real apprehension in his stomach, a little adrenaline making him slightly fuzzy with nerves. He didn't think much of Wingate's idea. All he knew was that Santiago had to fall. The asshole'd been pirating around south Florida on a seventy-two-hour gang-bang shoot-'em-up. That kid at Sonesta Beach. The Lansing girl. Allie Meyers. And Donald, too. Shit, he'd almost forgotten Donald. Yeah, Santiago had to fall.

Wendy was right, though, about his being just another tourist in Barbados. But that was okay. Being a tourist meant he wasn't a cop, and there were disadvantages to hauling around that badge; it could get to be a heavy procedural weight. Laws put the good guys against the bad guys in the same game, but gave different rules to each side.

Chuck the shield, though, and suddenly that changed. Once he hit foot in Barbados, that he was a Dade-Metro detective meant nothing. It would just be him and Santiago. Same game. Same rules.

Eddie liked it.

Seventeen

The Barbados Beach Villas was a half-circle of small buildings scattered across a rising slope of golden seashore. Half the guest accommodations were town houses, and half were motel rooms. Architecturally, there wasn't much difference between the exterior design of the two; both were two stories high and four units wide, finished with smooth stucco and dark wood trim. Inside, the layout differed in that the town houses used both levels of living space for a single guest, while the motel rooms were built with separate upper and lower entrances. The individual buildings were connected by macadam walkways that ambled through neatly trimmed grass and a forest of tropical trees and shrubs, with an occasional footbridge providing access over trickling waterways.

At the resort, Santiago blended into the manager's midnight cocktail party. The forty or so people cluttering the poolside patio, holding plastic cups of red rum punch, were for the most part British or Canadian, with a few Americans mixed in. Some dressed for the islands—baggy shirts and dresses of tropical fabrics and patterns—while others outfitted themselves more as though this were the country club back home, wearing bright salmon or blue sports jackets and long dresses with plunging necklines.

A single strand of oversized red and green Christmas lights was strung between palm trees around the patio, adding color to the evening's festivities, reflecting magically across the still surface of the crystal blue swimming pool. A three-piece steel band played hauntingly clear sounds that echoed into the hills, while, overhead, a full moon shone in a star-filled sky. It was a made-to-order Caribbean evening, as though staged for photographing the cover of next year's brochures.

Santiago spoke politely to anyone who met his eyes. This was supposed to be a get-to-know-everyone gathering, and while he didn't want to know them all, he was looking for someone in particular.

He shook the hotel manager's thin hand, telling him what a wonderful time he was having, then moved on to a corner of the patio, to a spot where he could look up the hill to William Lansing's room.

An hour ago, Santiago had been sitting in his rented Toyota two-door across from the entrance to the Barbados Beach Villas. He'd spotted Lansing arriving by cab around 11:00. The thin engineer looked drawn, tired as he'd stepped from the cab, carrying with him only a small suitcase and a long cardboard tube. The plans would be in the tube, Santiago knew, having felt satisfaction and relief upon seeing it, his fears that Lansing might lose his nerve and back out of the deal easing.

Santiago had kept a distance while Lansing registered. The lobby was tiny, a doorless 10' x 20' room, and Lansing had looked over his shoulder repeatedly, his head motions jerky, as though expecting someone to be sneaking up behind him. When the bellman had offered to carry Lansing's bag, Lansing jumped, startled by the approach. He'd backed away, like a small child frightened by a strange insect, then walked off quickly through the sprawling grounds, constantly comparing the number on the key ring he'd been given to room numbers that he squinted to see.

Lansing had appeared near panic when unable to find his room right away. He'd broken into a half-run at one point, clutching his suitcase and the cardboard tube, unaware of the odd looks he drew from other guests as he scurried by them like a mouse locked in a maze.

Finally he'd located his room up the slight hill near the top of the complex. Once there, Lansing had struggled to get his key into the lock. In the process, the tube had fallen from beneath his arm and gone rolling sideways down the walk, leaving Lansing to hurry after it.

Once inside, Lansing had drawn the curtain over the double sliding glass doors that led to a private porch. He'd turned on what looked like every light and stayed in.

After having watched Lansing's room for ten minutes, being passed twice by the same hotel guard, Santiago had decided to follow the crowd to the late-night party, where he was now.

Tomorrow, he decided, he would have to find a suitable place—somewhere remote but easy to find—to meet with Lansing. For the rest of the night, Santiago was going to stay nearby. It was a little extra insurance—maybe too much caution—but he wanted to make positively sure that Lansing was here alone, that he hadn't gone to the police, to the CIA, or the State Department. Santiago hadn't been in contact with Lansing for almost twenty-four hours now, and in a pressure situation, minutes could make a difference.

Since it wouldn't be smart to be registered in the same hotel, what he needed was an available woman, someone interested in a stranger for a little Caribbean romance—a woman staying here that he could be with through the night and into tomorrow morning. That way, he could keep watch on Lansing with his new lover as the perfect unsuspecting cover. He could even tell her the story about his estate in the hills of Costa Rica.

The manager's cocktail party broke up around 1:00 A.M. After all, the booze was free, and the hotel was in the business to make money, not give it away. As soon as the big bowls of rum punch stopped appearing from the poolside prep kitchen, the partygoers took the hint and began heading back to their rooms.

Santiago looked everyone over one last time. Strangely enough, there didn't seem to be any unattached women; they all were paired off either with a husband, boyfriend, or another woman. He followed the departing crowd up the macadam walk toward the lobby, watching in case he'd missed someone, or that someone who appeared taken was actually alone. But, for the most part, the people separated into the groups he'd figured them for, so he kept going up the hill. It looked as though he would have to go to his hotel, request an early wake-up call, then drive back down here to spend the day on the beach, watching Lansing from there.

Nearing the parking lot, Santiago heard loud music: heavy bass tones, pumping through walls of the building just ahead, the one that jutted out from a slope in the hill. Looking up, he saw a wide bay window, inside of which red and white lights flashed, along with shadow forms of people dancing.

The islands still hadn't caught up with the American trend that disco was dead.

He found the entrance to the hotel discotheque and walked under the awning. As soon as he entered the foyer, the impact of the loud sounds pressed into him. Cold air conditioning poured out so strongly that he could feel his pores tightening.

"Room key?" the muscular black doorman asked.

Santiago hadn't seen him standing there in the dark corner. He reached into his left pants pocket, seeming surprised that no key was there. "I'll be right back." Turning to walk away, he stopped. "The hell with it, eh?" he said, back in front of the doorman again. "I don't feel like making the trip. These hills . . ." He took out his wallet, fingering the thick wad of bills, feeling the doorman staring. "What's the cover?"

The black was expressionless, his head seeming small atop broad shoulders and a thick wrestler's neck. "S'okay, mon. You can go in." He gestured Santiago past with a burly arm.

Santiago handed him a $5 bill anyway. "For you, then."

The doorman didn't smile; he just took the bill, nodding once.

Santiago passed inside where flashing lights turned complete darkness into bright patches of red, green, and blue, then back to black again. Twisting bodies on the dance floor looked so arousing this way—brief glimpses of men and women caught in provocative poses by the strobe lights, then disappearing into the dark, only to reemerge in yet another alluring pose.

Santiago leaned against the wall that was carpeted with a thick shag rug. Trying to get his bearings, he could feel eyes considering him as they did any newcomer.

It was difficult to tell for the flashing of lights, but the small disco looked only about one-third full. Maybe disco was dead in the Caribbean, too, but management, like the workers they oversaw, was moving too slowly to realize it. In the Caribbean, dust often had to settle on the bones before a burial was ordered.

There were about forty people in the room. Half danced, the others lounged on comfortable-looking seats and at the bar. Men outnumbered women by nearly two to one, and it seemed as though lots of male fantasies about finding a wild island woman would go unfed tonight . . . again.

The song ended and the flashing of lights stopped. The entire room became evenly lit in a dim red. A reed-thin black deejay, working a console of knobs and turntables near the bay window, continued dancing with himself as though music still played. He put on another record—this one more mellow, an American pop love song Santiago recognized as three or four years old, but he didn't know the title or artist.

At the end of the bar, Santiago saw a wide-shouldered, middle-aged man pressing himself close to a bored-looking young woman. The man had a cigarette and drink in one hand, no doubt breathing odors of stale tobacco and whiskey on her as he whispered hopeful words of attempted seduction.

The woman sat facing the bar, wearing a pink sleeveless top and short white skirt. Santiago couldn't see her face, but from the layered-cut black hair and the leanness of her waist and legs, he guessed her to be no older than twenty-five.

The man wouldn't last much longer with her. His ego appeared locked in her sights, being shot down by her disinterest.

Santiago circled around the room, getting closer to them. He could hear the man mumbling to her, his hands as close to her as possible without actually touching. His Hawaiian shirt was opened crookedly halfway to his gut, exposing gray chest hairs and a heavy necklace of shark's teeth hanging around his neck.

Silently, the woman got up, leaving her drink.

"Hey, honey!" the man called, grabbing her arm. "Where you think you're goin' after I bought you this drink?"

Unable to get her arm free, the woman picked up her glass and splashed the remains of her drink in his face.

"Sonofabitch!" he shouted, releasing her as he squeezed shut his burning eyes. He wiped his face roughly with the front of his shirt, then lunged drunkenly off the bar stool after her. He tripped over his own feet, hitting the ground with a hard thud. He crawled forward, grabbing the woman's ankle, twisting it.

Startled, she went down—yelping, screaming loudly when the man started clawing his way up her legs, getting one meaty hand inside her skirt.

Santiago needed three steps to get to them. He grabbed the man by the hair and pulled back hard, jerking his neck. With the guy looking up at him in surprise, Santiago slammed his fist dead center into his face. He felt blood spurt over his hand as soon as he made impact, and knew he'd broken the asshole's nose and knocked out at least one tooth.

The man screamed and collapsed into a ball, both hands clutching his face, unable to stop the flow of blood through his fingers.

A fascinated crowd encircled Santiago and the man on the floor.

Looking through the bodies, Santiago saw the woman making her way for the door, taking short running steps in highheeled shoes, favoring one ankle.

The big doorman pushed aside the spectators and glared, finding Santiago in the center of things. "What de fok goin' on heah, mon?" he demanded, putting his shoulders back in an aggressive posture, chest muscles looking about ready to rip out of his shirt.

Santiago started an explanation, but got cut off by the very vocal crowd, all of whom came to his defense. From the differing versions of events shouted at the bouncer, it was obvious no one had really seen much of anything, yet all were determined the result was deserved.

The doorman wasn't pleased. He picked up the hurt man, who now seemed close to unconsciousness, then scowled at Santiago. "Ah don' wanna see your face, mon. Get out."

Santiago headed for the door through a ripple of applause.

It had been a stupid goddamned thing to do—Santiago realized that now. His intention had been to blend into the background, not to do anything to make himself stand out. But it had been so instinctive, a reaction, like a knee-jerk.

The hotel security guards, for the most part older men, were absorbed in getting the man with the bloody face into the lobby. The bouncer went with them, carrying the man by the legs and arms without the help of a stretcher, and in a mix of voices and island accents, Santiago picked out the word "ambulance."

He observed this from inside a cluster of trees, hidden from view by hanging branches. There was no sense even pretending any more that he belonged; if the bouncer saw him again, he might call the police.

Damn it! He'd blown his chance to keep watch on Lansing. Maybe he should just do it now. Break into Lansing's room, kill him, take the plans, and be done with it.

He thought quickly, weighing options. No, that wouldn't work. It was too hot around here; he'd made it too hot. There was no sense rushing things, because he had time. All the pieces were in place, ready to be put together. Lansing had the plans. Triacas had a buyer with a quarter-million. And in the trunk of Santiago's car was his backup: an Israeli Uzi automatic and a small handgun, both bought from his old friend at the house at the southern end of the island.

Acquiring the weapons had finalized preparation. All that remained now was the execution. Being too anxious could screw the whole deal, cause him to make a mistake.

Eighteen

It had been over a year since Gant had seen John Martin, and, during that time, his friend had put on some weight.

Martin walked across the terminal at Miami International, bellowing loudly, "Yeah, yeah, I know it," as though he and Eddie were the only ones around, "I've got a little friend around the middle." He slapped Gant on the back, as if he were trying to dislodge something caught in Eddie's throat. "But let me tell you, Ed, I married this little Eye-talyun slut, and she cooks better than she fucks and three times as often."

Martin was an Alabama redneck through and through and never made the slightest effort to hide the fact. His stubs of white-blond hair were kept short in a military-style crew cut, and the backs of his ears and neck actually were red from overexposure to the sun. For a man who'd been born, raised, and—with the exception of a year in Vietnam—never spent a day in his life north of Montgomery or south of Key West, his body had never acclimated itself to the southern sun.

"I'm sorry it took me a while to get up here to you, Ed, but security's a real bitch around here these days. Gov'ment like

140

to have you believe all these dopers is runnin' in through Texas and Georgia now, but it ain't so. But that's about me. How you been hittin' 'em?"

Eddie tried as best he could to steer his barrel-shaped friend off to the side, away from the tired-looking group of passengers who headed down the international departure ramp dragging flight bags behind them like rag dolls.

"I need a favor," Gant said quietly.

"Sure." Martin's voice boomed. "Name it."

Eddie didn't think this was the place for what he was about to say, but he'd already wasted half an hour waiting for Martin, and his 7:00 flight was due to board in twenty minutes. "I'm going to Barbados——"

"Great place. You'll love it. I was down there—"

Eddie held up his hand to quiet him. "I'm going on business. Sort of unofficially. I haven't had time to clear things through channels, and I've got a .45 around my ankle and a riot gun with some extra rounds in my suitcase. I want you to make sure I can get on the plane without any hassles."

The joviality disappeared from Martin's expression. He wiped his thick hand across his mouth, making a quiet sucking sound. When he spoke, the words came out as far under his breath as he could get them. "Metal detector's no problem, but sometimes the airlines X-ray the luggage going on board. If they spot something, I can't tell them not to take it off. It's their policy."

"Anything you can do?" Gant said, hands in his pockets. Moving out of the flow of travelers, he leaned back against the cement wall, catching the eye of a stewardess going down toward his gate. For a moment, he thought it was Janice; but then, for the hour he'd been in the airport, every brunette stewardess he'd seen had looked like Janice—even the ones who looked nothing like her at all.

Martin said, "You *are* still on the force?"

Eddie started to reach for his wallet, but Martin had him keep the badge away.

"I'm only asking. I don't want any proof. I'll take your word, for chrissake." Martin thought for a moment. "You flying down on what . . . ? Eastern? Pan Am?"

"Pan Am."

"All right, tell you what I'll do. I'll get you boarded, then see if this guy I know's going through on-flight luggage. What's your bag look like?"

Eddie described it, then said, "I leave in twenty minutes. If they've gone through it already, they've gone through it."

"Hey, that ain't all there's to it, pal. You're talking federal crime here. Some of those hard-assed marshals come runnin' down here, your ass'll have lots of explaining to do." Martin headed toward the gate. "Come on, let's get you on the plane."

Gant kept up easily with the shorter man, needing only one step to Martin's two.

Martin was huffing and puffing, the extra weight having its effect on him. "Tell you something else," he said, nodding to the Florida State cop as he walked Eddie around a line of passengers waiting to clear the metal detector. "Once you leave the U.S.A. soil of dear, sweet Miami, you're on your own. Those island bastards catch you totin' a weapon you're liable to go bye-byes. My advice to you is not to grab your luggage too fast when you get off the plane. Wait and see if they're goin' through incoming bags. Sometimes they do, some- times they don't. You see them searching luggage, go through without yours. Take your carry-on there and nothing else. Buy whatever you need. Matter of fact, I'm gonna go down and rip your name tag off your bag just in case."

The Pan Am attendant standing alongside Gate 17 an- nounced final boarding on Gant's flight to Barbados.

Eddie, carry bag in hand, looked back down the corridor, past the small crowd of people still grouped around security, hoping to see John Martin, hoping he'd be able to tell him there wasn't a problem with his baggage. But John wasn't there.

"Sir," the male attendant said, his hand covering the micro- phone, "you *are* on this flight, aren't you?"

Eddie nodded, heading down the aluminum-walled gangway.

His seat was on the aisle almost dead center in tourist. No way Dade-Metro would spring for a first-class ticket. Then again, Dade-Metro hadn't officially authorized this ticket. Wendy never had been able to locate Uncle Floyd, so Eddie had gone into the station before dawn and done a practiced job of forging the captain's signature. No problem, though—he'd done it before and knew Uncle Floyd would back him up if there was ever a question.

In the window seat, an older woman needlepointed casually. Eddie wondered whether the activity was to keep her mind off the fact that it had never been explained to her satisfaction exactly how a massive hunk of metal could roar into the air and hold itself there.

No one sat between the grandmother and Eddie, so he raised the armrest and propped his leg on the middle seat.

Once airborne, through the sharp banking portion of their ascent into the cloudless morning, the flight attendants appeared wheeling carts stocked with miniatures, mixers, and canned sodas.

Eddie ordered a Coke. While the stewardess poured it, he asked if she knew Janice. She said no, but she was new and didn't know too many of the other people yet.

Eddie drank a little of the Coke, then settled himself down in his seat, trying to relax. He hadn't gotten much sleep since this thing with Santiago had begun, and chances were that wouldn't change much until it was over.

The needlepointer in the window seat lit up a cigarette that looked a half-mile long. "My son," she told Eddie, "married a Baptist. Now he says I shouldn't smoke. My doctors say so, too, but so far I've outlived *three* of them." She grinned victoriously. "It's a bad habit, but it's genetics whether it's going to kill you or not. The luck of the draw. And I was born holding a full house."

Eddie smiled. For a brief moment he saw a value to old age—something that didn't normally come to him—namely, there was something to be said for mere survival. Perhaps beyond all else, it was the ultimate test.

*   *   *

The flight landed on time at 9:15.

Eddie emerged from the plane out into the hot Barbados sun and walked down metal stairs to the runway. Seeing the terminal, he was surprised at how modern it looked.

The long building had a clean, crisp design: white concrete walls faced with smoked-glass windows that were clean and well maintained. The pedestrianway leading inside was a covered gardenlike path, framed by healthy-looking palm trees and shrubs blossoming with wide-open pink flowers.

Blending in with the other passengers as they walked toward the terminal, Eddie felt the uneasiness of being without his home-field advantage. Barbados was definitely the visitor's stadium. It was like when he'd been in state baseball tournaments on a field he'd never played on before. The distance between all the bases was the same; but, on your own field, you knew every little rock and bump that caused the bad hops; in strange parks, you had to learn them, and that could be during warmups or in the bottom of the ninth with two outs, a tie score, and a hard grounder coming right at you.

Inside, the line through immigration was short, needing only to accommodate the hundred or so passengers from Eddie's flight.

Eddie handed over the file-card-size citizenship form he'd filled out on the plane and had his passport stamped. That done, the woman behind the desk smiled politely, motioning him through.

Trying to take in as much as he could of what was happening around him, Eddie moved to the baggage-claim section. There, a conveyor belt was already in motion, slowly turning a line of luggage before anxious passengers, most of whom wore faces of dread, worried that, this time, *their* luggage would be the one lost.

Eddie saw his suitcase come around the belt. He noticed the name tag had been torn off; evidently John Martin had gotten to it in time. As advised, he let it go past, waiting to see what the customs agents did with other bags before he picked up his.

About thirty people—mostly families—passed customs without having to open a single suitcase. Everyone was being allowed through with tired nods from the uniformed men.

Eddie's bag came around a second time. He lifted it off the belt and walked unhesitatingly toward the checkpoint. Brushing the suitcase against his leg, he checked to make sure he couldn't feel the hard barrel of the riot gun.

There were three lines being used by customs. Eddie walked directly to the shortest one, hefted his bag onto the counter, greeting the inspection agent with an impatient hello.

The ebony-skinned man took Eddie's passport, opened it. He examined the photograph of Eddie. "When was this picture taken?"

"Last year."

The man raised his eyebrows, looked more closely at the photo, then returned Eddie's passport and waved him through wordlessly.

Nineteen

The taxi sped through the intersection without slowing for the red light. The chassis bottomed out over the crossroad, forcing Eddie to brace his hand against the roof to keep from banging his head.

The drive west from the airport began through open fields of sugarcane that waved like soft daggers. Beyond that, ramshackle houses were built along steep hills, with brightly colored curtains blowing at opened windows. Then came Bridgetown.

Access into Barbados's only city was by a series of slightly arched bridges, while in the town itself, streets were busy with traffic: diesel-engine buses, cars, bicycles, and hundreds of people on foot.

Construction ranged from squat wood-front shacks to six-story offices of concrete and glass. Eddie didn't see anyplace as new as the airport; most structures looked about ten to fifteen years old, as though a spurt of revitalization had come and gone like a tropical storm. There were the usual offices for doctors, lawyers, and exporters, as well as banks, department stores, and smaller specialty shops. Behind plain doors would also be countless other businesses here of dubious nature, where profiteers found safe harbor for laundering cash through a variety of ingenious methods.

The cabdriver turned sharply down a shaded back street, passing a dance club that had a garish neon sign of blinking pink and blue. The light flashed over a handful of locals who leaned against the wall and sat on the curb with their legs stretched into the street. With the cab windows rolled down, Eddie smelled the sweet scent of marijuana—*ganja*.

They raced through another red light at the western edge of Bridgetown, timing it perfectly to fit between a Volkswagen beetle and a Jaguar sedan.

The western road out of town was open and dual-laned for about two miles, then twisted and turned around corners where tree branches hung low enough to graze the roofs of higher cars. Stone walls held back the hillside wherever the road weaved through sloped terrain, but did so in a space barely the width of two small cars.

Just beyond a narrow-walled quarter-mile of road, the taxi passed a wide bus.

"You got a lot of buses around here?" Eddie asked.

"Oh, yah," the driver said, nodding.

"What happens when you pass each other on a road like back there?"

"Oh, dat never hoppen, mon. Not to worry."

In the tiny open-air lobby of the Barbados Beach Villas, Eddie registered with the middle-aged woman at the desk. She wore a bright-flowered dress and rattled on a practiced speech that Eddie presumed was his orientation to the place: Breakfast was served from 7:00 until 10:30; lunch from 11:00 to 3:00; and dinner from 6:00 to 9:00. On some nights there were special parties, and too bad he hadn't been here last night, because he'd missed the manager's cocktail party—but they'd have one again next Monday. He should always check the bulletin board for what was happening every day. And, he should take care not to go swimming to the right-hand side of the buoys because there were sea urchins—little unmoving "underwater porcupines"—living in the rocks there, and the only way to get their barbs out of your feet was to have them cut out—very painfully.

Eddie thanked her for the information, then asked if his friend had checked in yet.

"What's his name, suh?"

"Bill Lansing."

She consulted a sheath of papers on a clipboard. "Yes. Mista Lansing is in fawty-eight-A." She took back the key she'd placed on the counter. "You should have tol' me dat you had a friend heuh," she said pleasantly, "Ayh put you in a room closer to him."

Gant thanked her again. Registered in 52-C, he carried his suitcase and carry bag out the front entrance of the doorless lobby, stepping over what looked like bloodstains at the foot of three tiled steps. Walking across the grounds, staying in the shade of bushy trees, Eddie passed bathers going to or from the beach. A topless girl about eighteen or nineteen smiled as she walked by.

"Nice place," Eddie said, looking over his shoulder after her. After the taxi ride, it was nice to experience something pleasant.

Eddie's room was on the upper level in a building identical to three dozen others at the resort. From his balcony, he could look conveniently over a small mango tree to Lansing's unit. Eddie hoped Lansing was there, that Santiago hadn't gotten to him first. The .45 strapped around his ankle, he decided to find out.

At Lansing's room, the curtains were drawn over the sliding-glass balcony door and side windows. Eddie listened, but heard nothing except the whirl of the wall air conditioner.

He knocked gently. When there was no response, he knocked again, louder. "Bill? You in there?"

Still nothing.

"Come on, Bill. I need to talk to you about our *plans*." Eddie thought he heard a foot scrape against the tile floor just inside the door. "Hey, Bill, Amy wants to know what we're going to do today."

"Who is it?" spoke the wary voice from inside the room.

Gant recognized it as Lansing. He'd found him—easy enough so far. "Under the door," Eddie said quietly. He slid a dog-eared Dade-Metro card with his name on it under the kickplate.

"I can't let you arrest me," Lansing said, nearly sobbing. "I have to get my daughter back."

"Come on, Bill," Eddie urged, still talking like a friend checking on the day's itinerary. "Open the door. Let's talk."

Lansing didn't respond at first, but then unlocked the bolt and opened the door.

Eddie glanced quickly inside, looking over the small room without entering. "Alone?" he asked, prepared to drop to the ground, grab his gun if Lansing hesitated.

Lansing nodded, pushing his glasses up his nose. "You were at my house," he said, recognizing Eddie.

Eddie went in, locking the door behind him. "Where's Santiago?"

Lansing sat on the bed. He put his glasses on the night-stand and held his head in his hands. "I don't know."

A soft-sided case lay open on one of two matching chairs that sat face-to-face in front of the sliding-glass doors. Propped against the same chair was an oblong tube of heavy cardboard about two feet long.

"What's supposed to happen here?" Eddie asked.

"He said he'd contact me once I was here . . . but I haven't heard . . ." Lansing left his thought unfinished. He looked exhausted, his hair dirty and uncombed, dark circles under his eyes.

"Did you bring the money?"

Lansing seemed puzzled. "Money?"

"The ransom."

"He doesn't want money. He wants those." Lansing pointed to the cardboard tube.

"What's in there?"

"Open it," Lansing invited, sounding oddly as though he was confessing.

Eddie undid one end of the cylinder and unrolled smooth sheets of rag paper, laying them out on the floor when he found them too bulky to hold. There were numerous same-sized pages filled with complicated-looking engineering symbols. The only unscientific notation was the logo and address of ML Engineering that appeared in the lower right corner of each page. "Schematics," Eddie said. "What are they for?"

Lansing kept his head down. "A portable weapons system. For commando troops, antiterrorist squads. It's a government contract." Lansing stood, tucking his shirt into the waist of his pants.

"Where are you going?"

"Aren't I under arrest?"

Gant motioned for him to sit. "I don't want you, I want Santiago."

Lansing shook his head, "What about my daughter?" He waited for Eddie to answer, then said, "I don't want anything to happen to her ..." He sounded defeated as he spoke, as though his will had been drained from him. The past two days had taken their toll. Lansing stared absently at his hand. "I know I'll go to jail now ... I just don't want anything to happen to her. She's the only thing I have in my life." He looked at Eddie. "Can you understand that?" He sat on the bed, posture slumped as though the muscles that held him upright had atrophied and were no longer of use.

Eddie folded the plans into a thick square, not putting them back in the tube.

"You're going to keep them?" Lansing asked.

"I told you, Mr. Lansing, I'm not here for you. So far you haven't committed any crime. You came close to giving away what I'm guessing are military secrets—but you didn't. So all you have to do is get off the island as soon as you can." Eddie made a final fold in the plans. "Santiago will kill you. He's *going* to kill you."

"But my daughter ..."

"Amy's dead."

Lansing didn't respond at all. It was as if Eddie hadn't

spoken. He stared blankly at the floor. Then his shoulders jerked once, and he made an odd little sound. "I don't believe it," he said, his throat tight. "I *can't* cry now."

"Go home, Mr. Lansing," Eddie said. "If Santiago calls before you leave, I'm in room 52-C. He calls you, you call me right away."

Twenty

Santiago unlocked the door to his hotel room and motioned the uniformed young woman inside. She wheeled the room-service cart smoothly to the round table by the patio doors. Outside, the Caribbean Sea glimmered brightly.

Wearing only a pair of briefs, Santiago had her wait while he went through the bills folded in his wallet. Doing so, he stood facing her, and liked the fact that the obvious bulge of his shaft in his underwear made her uncomfortable. She couldn't seem to find a place for her eyes to rest.

Santiago smiled, handing her a $10 bill, holding her hand momentarily before releasing his touch.

The dark-skinned woman, eyes averted from his, took the money with a soft-spoken thanks.

When she left, Santiago tossed his wallet onto the dresser. He opened the glass patio door and took deep breaths of late-morning air, filling his lungs. The day was already sticky with humidity. Branches of the palm tree that shaded his patio hung limply, unmoving. *Today would be a hot one,* Santiago thought, settling down to his breakfast.

As he removed the cover on his eggs and sausage, he watched a solitary jogger pad at a steady pace along the water's edge, feet splashing in waves that lapped gently onto the sloping shore. Strange how some people were so prescribed to certain routines that they couldn't alter them even for a vacation. It could probably be 100°, 90-percent humidity, and that man would still be out there jogging, running until he dropped.

Santiago cut his sausage in half, poked it with his fork, then broke the soft pocket of egg yolk with it. He dabbed the warm meat until it was coated with the runny yellow substance, then ate hungrily.

He drank a large glass of orange juice as well as a tumbler of water. He was likely to do a great deal of sweating today if the temperature climbed as high as it was promising.

Once finished with his meal, he dressed in shorts, T-shirt, and docksiders without socks. He didn't bother shaving because people on vacation often didn't shave. Nor did he wash his hair or even comb it. He was merely a vacationer on his way out to take a few photographs before the sun imposed itself fully on the day. He hung his camera around his neck and went out, hearing the door lock automatically behind him.

He had allowed himself another luxury in staying here. Heywood's was one of the island's more expensive resorts. Built in varying motifs that spread across a mile of white sand beachfront, it was the last developed section of Barbados' northwest coast. Beyond, in hilly St. Lucy's Parish, were only stone and dirt roads that wound haphazardly through colorful lines of crackerbox homes built up on cement blocks.

It was this more primitive route that Santiago took around the northern tip of the island, guided by a map that he soon discovered showed less than one-half of the streets. He had been out here before, though, but only briefly; and, at that, it had been some time ago. All the tiny cutoffs and winding trails could be committed to memory only if driven every day for years.

He passed a dirty white-painted church. Its front doors were open, and inside Santiago glanced sight of a black-suited preacher standing behind a pulpit, screaming praises of the Lord through a bullhorn. Loud choruses of *Amen* responded to him.

Just down the dusty street, a heavyset Barbadan woman in a frilly white dress mercilessly scolded her elderly husband. She tugged at the baggy sleeve of his oversized suit jacket, as though dragging him on a leash.

Santiago drove on, only to pass the church again a few turns later. He realized he was going in circles and doubled back toward the main highway.

He wanted a remote place to meet Lansing, but it had to be somewhere Lansing could find without difficulty.

Santiago sped the Toyota along curving paved roads until coming up behind a wide bus. The oversized vehicle pulled itself painfully up an incline, belching dirty-gray smoke from its tailpipe. Santiago swerved into the other lane to pass, only to be chased back by the beeping horn of an oncoming car. He waited until he reached an empty straightaway, then cruised alongside the bus, looking up at its dirty windows.

Inside, Santiago saw schoolgirls dressed in white blouses and blue plaid jumpers. Their eyes looked dull staring out at him, not so much expressions of drowsiness as uselessness. What a pity. They were being educated in a society where most jobs didn't require any learning. How much intellect did it take to push a room-service cart to the right door? These kids needed to know so much, and so little was going to be taught to them in a classroom. The only useful thing Santiago learned in school was how to count. They'd wanted him to be able to add past a million, but he'd said a million was far enough. He wasn't greedy.

In a secluded section of Barbadan countryside, Santiago found what he was looking for. Built alongside a steep hill was an abandoned stone building. The circular structure had been gutted, and it was damp inside cool walls, where a dirt floor was littered with hay and empty film boxes crushed flat. The interior diameter was about 30 feet, and half that distance up one side was a solitary window. A plaque mounted at eye level claimed this was once part of a sugar mill.

By late afternoon, Santiago calculated, with the sun coming from behind the building, it should be almost completely dark inside. Yeah, this was the place.

Standing in the shattered doorframe, Santiago looked out across a lush valley of unspoiled green pasture where a thin layer of haze hung like a blanket. A mountain rose along the opposing slope where anonymous clusters of houses were grouped near small waterways that trickled to the sea. Even at this distance, some homes were obviously the large estates of wealthy businessmen who sought refuge or retirement in their idea of paradise.

He stood quietly, listening. After a few moments, he heard the whine of a car engine straining to overtake the steep upgrade of the road behind the mill. The sound increased, then loud-revving rpms slowed coming around the bend only to accelerate on again.

It was an obvious spot to stop for pictures. Tourists were likely to be awed by the view; they'd get out of their cars and stroll around, no doubt being curious enough to overcome the dank smell of the mill and peek inside. But Santiago liked the idea of being this close to the sharp incline just outside the mill entrance. It looked as though a body could roll for quite some time without stopping down there. And, he'd just proven to himself that he'd be able to hear any approaching cars. Lansing would just have to be taken care of quickly—that was all.

It was almost 1:00 by the time Santiago found his way back to Heywood's. He'd discovered a simpler route to the sugar mill, making mental notes of landmarks he could describe to Lansing when directing him to their meeting.

Now, back on the porch outside his room, Santiago watched two young women strip off their bikinis and lay face up on colorful thick towels. They were well tanned with the exception of their breasts—as though they'd had a few days here already, but this was the first time they'd found the nerve to stroll off to this more remote section of beach and go naked. Santiago especially liked the blonde one. Her pubic hair was trimmed into a fluffy narrow slit, and she had wonderful long legs.

Unfortunately, he could not join the ladies. There was work to be done—the final steps. By tomorrow he would have the plans and would be meeting with Triacas. That bastard. Something fitting would have to be done with him—no way he deserved to reap rewards for Santiago's efforts. Santiago had been the one to make an initial contact with Lansing months ago, to learn enough about the man and his company to decide he was vulnerable, and to devise and execute this plan.

Jesus, *this* plan. It didn't do any good now, but Santiago couldn't avoid thinking how complicated it had gotten. The transaction—the actual switching of the plans for Amy Lansing—should have been completed two days ago. But the boyfriend's showing up at Sonesta Beach had fouled everything. It had brought the police into the matter. The local morning news made a big stink about it; there was an interview with the cops' "community relations liaison man," whatever the hell that was, who said they'd do everything possible to bring the killer to justice. Sure—Santiago was here now and the police were still in Miami. So much for worrying about them— the fools. They were the reason Amy Lansing was dead. They'd made things too hot for him in Miami, put his goddamned picture on the TV. He'd had to off the girl because there was no way he could get her from Miami to Barbados without taking unnecessary chances. It had been simpler to kill her.

He glanced at his Rolex: 1:15. It was time to call Lansing and set the gears in motion. The little man would have to rent himself a car—and down here that could take a few hours in itself. Lansing would have to find a rental agency with something available, then fill out the paper work and be driven to the police station in Holetown to apply and pay for a temporary license. Only after all that could he start off for the abandoned sugar mill.

Santiago took one last look at the topless girls, then went inside his room, drawing shut the blinds. He picked up the phone, starting to dial, but there was a knock at his door. Three efficient raps.

Santiago eased down the receiver, rising slowly from the bed. He went into the closet and took the pistol from his suitcase, screwing the silencer onto the barrel's end.

The knocking came again. "Are you home?" the voice asked clearly.

Jesus, Santiago thought, *what the fuck was he doing here?* He wasn't due till Wednesday, once the plans had been sold. Santiago put away the pistol and opened the door.

In walked Anthony Marsh, wearing a blue-striped seersucker suit that was without a single wrinkle. "I thought you might need some help." He smiled professionally, walking around the small room as though considering it for critique in a decorating magazine.

Santiago shut the door.

"Have you contacted poor William yet?" Marsh opened the curtains, letting sunlight flood into the room. He picked yesterday's newspaper from the small writing table, unfolding the tabloid-sized pages as he sat by the sliding doors and began to read. "I imagine he's half-hysterical by now."

Jesus, Santiago thought. *Is this guy for real?*

When he'd first hooked into Marsh, the guy had been drowning himself in a sea of available Florida pussy, throwing money away, swimming in a toilet with his own hand on the flusher and yanking steadily on it in some self-destructive binge. Marsh was the president of ML Engineering, but in his celebration of the company's initial success under his tutelage, he'd strayed.

ML Engineering's supposed claim to fame and fortune was a portable nuclear-weapons system—an atom-bomb backpack—that Lansing had been designing for five years. But Marsh, for all his wining, dining, and screwing, had blown the defense department contract. The project ML had invested over $500,000 to develop had no place to go. There was no one else to sell it to—not legally, anyway.

Through the carefully sewn confidence Santiago established with Marsh, Santiago had suggested putting it on the black market, telling Marsh he knew exactly how it could be done. Seeing bankruptcy about to bury his flashy style of living, Marsh had been interested, but hadn't wanted to turn over the plans himself. He'd wanted an alibi—a scapegoat. And the plan to blackmail Lansing, the system's designer, had been born.

Marsh had supplied Santiago with the knowledge that since Lansing's wife had left him, he had become obsessed with his daughter, that he would do anything for her, fearing that otherwise, like her mother, she might leave him. Kidnapping her was the obvious step.

Shortly after they'd decided to go through with it, Santiago had sensed Marsh's becoming anxious, suddenly in a hurry to get the deal over and done with. Marsh claimed to be in dire financial trouble.

Fearing that Anthony Marsh might try the sale on his own, Santiago had rushed things. He'd come to Barbados to meet with the most hopeful connection he knew: Gus Triacas. A price had been arranged hastily. Initially, Santiago had been satisfied to have finalized a deal. Since then, however, he'd grown more and more dissatisfied. The value of what he was selling far exceeded what Triacas had agreed to pay. And once he split 50–50 with Marsh, it was even worse. Maybe Marsh would be happy with enough money for some new venture—maybe letting ML go into reorganization—but this was going to be Santiago's retirement. His last deal.

Twenty-one

At 1:30 on Tuesday afternoon, Eddie Gant saw William Lansing leave his room. Lansing carried his suitcase along with the empty tube that had once contained the weapons-system plans. The engineer walked slowly across the grounds, as though his small suitcase was all the weight he could possibly carry. All the way to the lobby, he never looked up.

Eddie waited twenty minutes—as long as he figured it would take Lansing to check out and get a cab to the airport. Then he walked to the front desk.

Other than the efficient-looking Barbadan man in a white starched shirt and blue pants who worked behind the desk, the lobby was empty. Lansing would be on his way to the airport—at least Eddie had accomplished that much. He hadn't been able to get to Amy in time, but at least Lansing would be spared.

Eddie waited patiently at the counter while the man stapled together a short stack of bills and stuffed them into one of the cubbyhole compartments fixed to the wall.

"May I help you?" the man asked.

Eddie was momentarily taken aback by the black man's English accent. "If a Mr. Santiago calls or stops by for William Lansing, give him this message, okay?" Eddie handed him a folded piece of hotel stationery.

"Certainly. This is for a Mr. Santiago?" The man neatly penned Santiago's name on the back of the paper, spelling it correctly.

"Yeah. Thanks."

"Is there any other message, sir?"

"No."

Eddie walked back to his room. Even as he stayed in the shade cast by rows of tall tropical trees, Eddie felt the sun break out a sweat across his shoulders. There wasn't a cloud in the sky, and he could feel the heat of the walkway through the rubber soles of his Nikes. A breeze would help—the hint of a breeze, even.

Just down the hill, he heard the clattering of dishes being cleared from lunch in the open-air dining room. Cutting between a row of townhouse buildings, he circled around the back edge of the Barbados Villas property, letting his fingers run idly across the loops of chain-link fence as he went slowly up the slight incline.

There wasn't much to do now but wait. Santiago was on the island looking for Lansing and the plans. No doubt he knew that Lansing was staying here and would get to him. That was why Eddie had left the message at the desk. The note said: "Change in *plans*. Bill had to go home. Sudden death in the family. Leave a phone number or place where I can reach you." He'd left it unsigned.

Eddie walked into the small grocery store near the entrance to the Villas' parking lot. A chime hung to the doorframe rang as he entered.

From the rear of the store, an older Englishman emerged from a storage room. The thin proprietor gave Eddie half a nod as he walked past. Shoulders hunched over, he settled himself on a worn stool behind the cash register.

A handwritten sign taped to the refrigerator case noted

that all prices were quoted in BDS, which meant the liter bottle of 7-Up was only $1 U.S. and not $2, as Eddie first thought. He took it from the case, then went to the five-foot-wide section of dry goods for a box of saltines and a small unlabeled block of white cheese. Going up to the counter, he changed his mind about the cheese and put it back, taking a jar of peanut butter instead.

"Here on holiday?" the Englishman asked, adding the prices with pencil and paper, then ringing the total on the register.

"Yes."

"Well, delightful weather we're having." The man's skin was creamy white and hairless, as though he never left his little air-conditioned store. He counted out Eddie's change in Barbados coins. "We're not allowed to give change in U.S. Gov'ment, you know."

Walking back to his room with his bagged purchases, a scrawny caramel cat fell in step behind Eddie. The cat followed him up the stairs to his second-level room, then waited politely for an invitation inside.

Eddie started to shut the animal out, then said, "Come on in, boy . . . girl . . . or whatever you are."

The cat sauntered in, immediately finding something of interest under the bed and disappeared after it.

Eddie didn't want to know what it was that had the cat's intrigue; he'd seen all kinds of monster bugs in Miami and imagined them only ten times worse down here. He started toward the small kitchenette, then realized the sliding glass door to the balcony was open.

He'd left it shut.

He froze, clutching his grocery bag in one arm, slowly starting to edge his way to the drawer where he'd left the .45. Who knew he was here? Santiago?

"Eddie, is that you?" The voice called to him from out on the balcony.

The curtains were drawn back by a woman's hand. It was Janice.

"I can't believe you're down here." Janice took off his shirt, then wrapped her arms playfully around his shoulders. She pressed her lips against his. Her tongue went sweetly into his mouth. "Mmmm," she sighed, "I took some time off as soon as I found out. I heard you were looking for me." Her one hand slid down his back, resting on his ass, feeling him through his jeans. "You've got such a nice rump, Eddie." She rubbed against him, the loose swell of her braless breasts warm against his chest. "Why didn't you call me first? I'd have met you on the plane. We could have made it in the bathroom." She laughed deeply.

Eddie's hands rested on her hips, caressing easily. "I didn't figure you'd be interested . . . not after the other day."

"Shhh. Don't talk about that. I don't want to think about that now."

She'd been doing grass; Eddie could tell from the faraway look of pleasure in her eyes and the happy-aggressive way she was coming onto him. They'd done some good Thai sticks a few times together in Miami. Eddie had snatched the stuff from the property room at Dade-Metro. Janice liked it as an occasional unwinder, and Eddie had no objections, even though he never smoked alone. He usually saved it for the young party girls up in Lauderdale; they always liked smoke or coke, so he'd done plenty of recreational time with them.

Straight, Janice was always more reserved, quiet, practical. Eddie had never pinned it down exactly, but she only seemed into marijuana when she wanted to sidestep reality for a while. Hers was almost an educated therapy; she wasn't looking to avoid reality, only to escape it for a while.

"Are you going to get me out of my clothes," Janice grinned, her almond eyes sparkling with intoxication and passion, "or do I have to do it myself?"

When Eddie didn't respond immediately, Janice took half a step back and peeled her baggy red T-shirt off over her head. She shook out her auburn hair, then caressed her own breasts as her hands slid down toward her shorts, unsnapping them. "I really want you, Eddie." Bending over to step out of her panties, she kissed the outline of his erection through his pants.

Naked, she came back into his arms, and the hesitation he'd felt being caught so off guard by her showing up here was gone. He got lost in the sense of touching her, of being back against the body he'd felt was pulling away from him for good. It was nice being able to touch her again, to feel her so intimately.

He eased her down on the bed, kissing her breasts, sucking a nipple into his mouth, making it hard, biting it gently with his lips.

Janice sighed as he licked the side of her neck. "I'm wet for you, Eddie." Her hands went down the back of his pants. Turning him onto his side, she undid his jeans, peeled them down his legs, stripping him. She laid on his thighs, stroking his erection in her fingers, putting the head of it against her lips, pushing her mouth down around him. "Mmmm." She licked his shaft from her mouth. "I miss being in bed with you so much." Janice rolled onto her back, having Eddie settle his weight on top of her. She parted her legs, guiding him inside her slick channel. "Oh, God, Eddie. That's it! Do me!" She wrapped her legs around his, arms squeezing him, letting him push full thrusts into her vagina.

Eddie felt his head starting to spiral. He hadn't been with anyone since the last time with Janice. It all started to catch up to him. The pleasure was strong, and he felt himself quickly ready to come. He started to slow things down, to take it more patiently. Then Janice cried out loudly, starting to climax. There was no holding back.

Slowly, Eddie awakened, coming out of sleep as though floating calmly back from an ocean's depths of dreams. His entire body felt so relaxed. He wasn't sure where he was at first, needing a moment to adjust to the unfamiliar white walls around him, the view of motionless palm branches through the sliding glass door. His first recollection was of having been awakened by a knock at the door some time ago. How long ago? he wondered. It had been the maid coming to do the room. He'd sent her away with apologies, but she'd snarled anyway. Then he'd said she wouldn't have to come back later—

that was why there were bath towels stacked by the door; she'd left them for him.

Eddie stretched. Turning over, he saw Janice still sleeping naked beside him.

Her breathing was steady and slow. Behind closed eyelids, her pupils danced, no doubt deep in dreams of her own. Eddie hoped they were of him, then at once realized what a corny thought that was.

He looked at his travel alarm on the bedstand. Jesus! It was after four. He'd been asleep for over two hours. God, what if Santiago had called for Lansing? That possibility sat him upright, fully awakening his senses in a hurry. It should be all right, though, even if he had called. Eddie's message would have been relayed to him, and by now there should be some reply from Santiago. The sudden urgency he'd felt relaxed.

He sat on the cool tile floor beside the bed, bringing the phone down beside him. He dialed the front desk and asked if anyone had picked up the message he'd left for Mr. Santiago. The woman who answered set the phone down. Eddie heard her talking to someone else, trying to find out what message he was talking about. When she came back on the line she said, no, the note was still there.

Eddie thanked her and set the phone down quietly. He stood, reached for the University of Miami gym shorts he'd left draped over the chair, and slipped them on.

Outside, the sun shone bright white through dead-still palm branches, casting a harsh glare. It was so cool in the room that it was hard to believe how hot it was outside. The wall air-conditioner had kept up a good fight, churning out freon-charged comfort, but Eddie knew that as soon as he stepped onto the balcony, heat would envelop him.

From inside the sliding balcony door, he looked over the top of the mango tree to Lansing's old room. The curtains there were open now, but presumably the maid had done that in anticipation of the unit's next guests. Other than that, there were no other signs of change or activity.

Across the grounds, couples were dragging beach bags and towels back up to their rooms, looking lobster red and exhausted from overexposure to the heat. It always seemed to take people a few days to adjust to marked temperature changes; Eddie had seen that back in his regional-baseball-tournament days. Teams from up north would come down to Miami, and by the sixth inning they'd be limp out in the field, stamina dripping from their uniforms.

In bed, Janice rolled over, exhaling deeply.

Eddie turned to look at her.

She opened her eyes, blinking a few times, finally getting him in focus. "Jesus," she half-laughed. "I really *am* here." Yawning, she sat up in bed, pulling the covers up to her waist. "Barbados, right?"

Eddie grinned. "I could tell you were out there somewhere—orbiting—but I wasn't sure how far."

"Oh, God." She rubbed her eyes, then switched to her temples. "We aren't on a cruise ship, are we?"

"Unh-unh."

"So it's me that's going around." She looked down at herself, then under the sheets, realizing she was naked. "Mmmm," she sighed, closing her eyes again, tilting her head back against the wall. "Did we have a good time?"

"Fantastic. You came ten times."

"Really? You weren't as good as usual then." They both laughed.

Eddie said, "You want something to drink?"

"No. Good God, no. Just water. Coke if you got it."

"All I was really offering is 7-Up."

"I'll take it. And lots of ice."

Eddie crossed the room, stopping suddenly. "Did you see a cat in here?"

Janice gave him a what-the-hell-are-you-talking-about look.

"It followed me in from the store." Eddie looked under the bed, then checked the bathroom. "Must have snuck out." He went into the kitchenette and opened the tiny refrigerator. Laid on its side, the plastic bottle of 7-Up was already cold, but he still added plenty of ice to Janice's glass.

"What are you doing down here, Eddie?"

"I'm here on a job . . . sort of."

"Sort of?"

He took her her drink, making her move over so he could sit on the bed beside her. "Can I steal a sip?"

She tilted the glass to his lips, then playfully pulled it away mid-swallow. "Get your own," she laughed.

Eddie snapped his fingers. "Room service." Then he collapsed over her waist. "I can't make the trip back to the kitchen. You've sapped my legs." He stroked her thighs through the thin sheet, staring fondly at the contours of her body.

Janice ran her hands through his hair, scratching, playing. "So, you're 'sort of' down here on business. Cop business?"

"I'm looking for a guy."

"And he's here?"

He nodded. "I'm pretty sure."

"Mmm." She took a swallow of 7-Up. "I hope you find him," she said matter-of-factly.

"I do too." Eddie kept stroking her leg, taking down the sheet a little to touch bare skin. Her flesh was so smooth, silky feeling. He tried to distract himself from the question on his mind, but couldn't. "Why did you come here?"

"Didn't you want me to?"

"Yeah . . . but *why* did you come?"

Janice said, "Honest answer?"

Eddie hesitated. "Yes."

"Okay—" Janice finger-combed her hair back off her forehead "—last night, I was in a hotel room—alone. Tammi was out with some skin diver—the usual kind of guy she always goes for." She sipped her soda. "I was feeling a little sorry for myself and decided to get a little drunk . . . a little stoned. So I did. Then, around two, I started sleeping off and on, and whenever I'd wake up, I'd do another hit of Jamaican or some rum. That kept up till this morning, when one of the attendants from your flight—some new girl I didn't know—said you had asked about me. She'd gotten a peek at your name and hotel off your immigration card in case I'd wanted to know." Janice shrugged. "There was a seat on a shuttle over from Antigua, so . . . I came."

"Would you have come if you hadn't been stoned?"

Janice put down her drink. Sweat from the icy glass made her hand wet, so she dried it on the sheets. "Probably not."

Eddie got off the bed abruptly.

"Damn it," Janice swore. "Don't look at me like that. You hurt me back home, Eddie. I mean it really hurt. We were living together and it felt good—real close. Then I go out of town and call you, and some high-school girl who's probably still got your dick inside her answers and says you can't come to the phone." Her eyes squinted, but were moist. "That really hurts, Eddie. Why can't you understand that?"

"I told you I was sorry."

"It wasn't just once. When I was home, other women—girls—called all the time."

"But it wasn't the same as with you."

"Oh, Eddie." She shook her head. "I don't want to go through this again. I came here because I missed you." Janice got up. She took her red T-shirt off the dresser and slipped it on. Looking around the room, she pulled at the snarls sex and sleep had twisted in her hair. "Do you see my shorts?"

Eddie lifted up the bedspread where it lay piled on the floor and pulled her bottoms from the folded-over fabric. He handed them to her. "I don't want you to go. Not like this."

Janice wouldn't look at him. She zipped her shorts, then looked for her shoes, finding them near the door.

"Come on, Janice. *Please.* Talk with me."

"There is nothing to talk about. Okay? You're the way you are, and I'm the way I am." She snapped the strap of her shoe around her ankle. "I don't want the man I'm in love with in bed with someone else. I'm sorry if that's too old-fashioned for you."

"It was the way I lived for . . . for as long as I can remember. I never had a . . . a steady lover . . . a live-in—whatever you want to call it. You were the first person I ever gave a damn about—who I wanted to do more with than fuck once and say good-bye."

"Well," she said sarcastically, putting on her other shoe, "at least I made it past one fuck."

Eddie's fist hit the mattress. "Damn, that's not fair. You

never let me explain it. You're always putting in ... little digs."

Janice stood, fully dressed now, arms crossed, pretending to be patient. "Okay, Eddie. Explain it."

The words were all cluttered inside his head. He couldn't seem to put them in the right order. Why couldn't she see that he'd spent his entire adult life being single, seeing lots of different women, that he hadn't expected her to be any different? But she had been. She truly was something special. Before she'd left him, he hadn't seen it—not yet, there hadn't been time. He'd known her only a few months, and it had all happened so fast. He hadn't realized how much he loved her, needed her, until it was too late.

"Are you going to answer that?" Janice asked.

Eddie realized he'd heard the phone ringing, but for trying to explain things to Janice, hadn't thought to pick it up.

An overseas operator came on the line asking in a difficult accent if he was Eddie Gant. Once he said he was, the call was put through.

"Eddie?" Static nearly buried the voice in the wires.

"I can't hear you," he called loudly. "Who is this?" Then he covered the mouthpiece. "Janice. Please," he pleaded, "don't leave now. *Please?*"

She took her hand off the doorknob.

"What?" Eddie shouted into the phone. "I'm sorry. I couldn't hear you before."

"Eddie. It's Wendy. Damn, Eddie, everything's going wrong." Her voice was shaky, as though she'd been crying.

"What? Wendy? What's happened?"

"Uncle Floyd's had a stroke. They don't think he's going to make it."

Shock seized his chest. Cold filled his stomach and Eddie felt his mind going blank—not accepting it, fighting the words he'd just heard. He had to force himself to breath and the air came in harsh gasps that he had trouble pulling in. "I'll ..."—Oh, God, what should he do? Uncle Floyd— "... I'll come back on the next plane."

"No. Don't! I mean you can't. There's some Internal Affairs

lieutenant here now. He's taken over the section temporarily. Lieutenant Simpson. He's got something out for you, Eddie. I didn't tell him anything about where you are. I just said you were on vacation. But he's pissed off about something. He's already put in a call to someone else over at IA, and they're talking about some sort of investigation on you."

Eddie couldn't feel anything. He stared at the floor numbly.

"Eddie? Are you there?"

He nodded.

"Eddie?" Wendy called louder. "Can you hear me?"

"Yes." He was barely able to answer.

"Stay down there. You've got the vacation time coming. So maybe this guy'll get replaced by someone else." Wendy paused. "By whoever our"—she tried to laugh—"God, I can't say it—whoever our new captain will be." She started to cry.

But Eddie didn't hear it. He was crying, too. He dropped the phone and curled into a ball on top of the sheets, hugging his arms around his knees, rocking back and forth.

Janice came over to him, stroking his forehead.

"He's dying," Eddie said, tears streaming down his cheeks, looking up at her. "Uncle Floyd's dying."

Twenty-two

The goddamned air conditioner wouldn't work. Keeping the Toyota dead center on the curving road, Santiago hit the dashboard hard just above the cooling controls. Still, nothing but warm air churned noisily from the small vents.

"Fuck it!" he swore, banging the dash once more before turning off the unit with a hard snap.

He reached across the passenger seat and rolled down the window. It didn't make any difference; the air coming through the car didn't make it any cooler.

Santiago's shirt stuck to his back and neck, itching. He scratched his irritated skin and felt himself going toward the edge. The tensions were creeping through his muscles, tightening them. His head throbbed with each strong pulse of his heart.

He reminded himself to stay cool. He needed to be calm now, to be able to act and react with reason, not emotion. Nothing should happen to alert Lansing that anything was wrong—that his daughter wasn't here. He just had to play it out, casually but businesslike, with his usual efficiency. Yes, that was the way. It would go well.

He hadn't passed a single car in the past ten minutes. But when he came around the inclined bend to the old sugar mill, he saw the Moke; the canvas-topped four-seater jeep was parked directly across the road from the mill. Incredible—someone was here? But where?

Santiago pulled off the road just beyond the Moke, filling the air with dust as he braked slowly, tires churning up dry ground. From inside the Toyota, he looked around the green countryside. Scanning the hills above him, the paved narrow road, the steep valley that stretched halfway over the island, there was no hint of who might belong to the jeep. Maybe they were inside the mill or exploring the small forest of trees up the hill. Maybe some young couple had gone off somewhere in seclusion to screw.

Santiago glanced at his Rolex. It was only 4:15. Surely Lansing wouldn't be here yet. Santiago had set the rendezvous for 5:00.

He decided to sit in the car and wait to see who came back to the Moke. He checked the Uzi under the passenger seat in case it had been jostled during the ride. He felt the warm gun metal, then slid the weapon forward to make sure he could pull it out cleanly. The Uzi was fine—the least of his worries.

He sat back and looked around again. Maybe someone had left the little jeep here and gone on without it. If it had broken down within a few miles, this was the first place to keep it that wouldn't block the road. But that wouldn't be it. Driving hazards were a way of life around here, something no one was concerned about. The rule seemed to be: if the mule died, leave him and the cart right where they fell—even if it was just around some treacherous bend—until you saved up money for an ox big enough to haul them both away. *Jesus, the way people thought around here,* Santiago mused. *No wonder they never had anything.*

He decided that if someone didn't come back to the Moke in fifteen minutes, he'd get out and look for them, figure out some way to chase them off. The problem with that, though, was if Lansing showed up early, before Santiago would have a chance to get the other people out . . . Goddammit, he might as well do it now—no sense chancing something else going wrong.

Santiago slammed the Toyota's door shut, still angry about the air conditioning. He listened for voices, feet crunching through fallen branches. It was silent, other than a group of birds flying between trees just up the hill that let out an occasional chirp.

He walked from the shade of the hillside into the sun, immediately feeling the heat pressing over his shoulders. In the middle of the road, he stopped, thinking he heard an approaching car engine. He looked as far as he could around the tree-lined bend, listening, but he didn't see or hear anything, anyone.

Sharp little pebbles pushed up through the thin bottoms of his canvas shoes as he crunched over roadside gravel. He walked to the ledge just beyond the mill. No way anyone would be down there. There was only one way over, and that was straight down. You could fall over, sure, but the only way your ass would come back up was in a body bag.

Santiago looked inside the small sugar mill. His eyes took a few seconds to adjust to the dark, then saw no one was there— just a few more discarded film boxes than there had been this morning.

Maybe he'd just have to chance that whoever had come here in the Moke wouldn't return before he could take care of Lansing. But then, what if they'd just happen to be at the edge of the trees when he killed Lansing? They'd see his face, likely give a description to the police, and he still needed at least another twenty-four hours on this island. It wasn't like Miami here, either—not as easy to hide.

Shit, what else could go wrong?

He left the mill, squinting at the sunlight that shone down over the hill. It wasn't as shaded now as he'd thought it would be; but, in half an hour, by the time Lansing got here, the sun should be all the way down behind the rolling hill.

Santiago walked over to the Moke. There was a sudden rustling just inside the tree line—something big. An animal? Person?

Santiago froze, startled. "Hello?" he called. "Anyone there?" He shaded his eyes, looking from side to side, trying to distinguish shapes inside the tall grass and low-hanging trees. The texture of branches and overgrowth blended in a confusing pattern of sunlight and shade, dark and light greens; it was nearly impossible to pick out a single form.

Santiago eased left, closer to his car. When the sun came directly through the trees it was nearly blinding. He had to put his hand down over his eyes so far that he could only see about twenty feet up the hill. Then, just as he moved into another bright white stream of sunlight, something darted inside the brush again, keeping parallel to him, but coming closer.

Sonofabitch! He could see a more defined form. It was definitely a person, someone going hunched over through the weeds. Someone was stalking him, maybe some goddamned weed-fiend out to steal himself a wallet of traveler's checks.

Santiago broke into a run for his car.

There was a mad thrashing through the brush behind him, twigs snapping, branches thrown aside, weeds being trampled.

Santiago grabbed the Toyota's right-hand door and yanked it open. He dropped to his knees, reaching in under the seat. The handle of the Uzi moved perfectly into his grip. He yanked it out, one-handing it, spinning, blasting a wide sweep of automatic fire out in front of him.

Slugs ripped through the Moke, bit into dusty ground, then went sailing into the lush hillside, closing in on the noise in the brush, finding the body there just as it charged madly into the clearing less than thirty yards away.

It was Lansing, eyes wide, holding a huge kitchen knife high in the air, his shirt ripped at the shoulder, blood scratched across his face and smeared over his leg. Blasts from the Uzi caught Lansing's arm, jerked him back, then cut diagonally downward across his chest to his thigh. More shots came back left to right, straight across the engineer's thin belly, fifteen to twenty rounds ripping through him, thrashing his body, standing him on his toes like a marionette, before throwing him into a high patch of pale green grass, a twisted, bloody configuration.

Santiago was outraged. The asshole! The fucking asshole!

What did he think he was going to do? Take him out? With a knife?

Holding the smoking Uzi, Santiago hurried over to the body. He picked up the butcher's knife and threw it across the road, over the ledge beyond the mill. He stood over Lansing, the dead man's eyes locked open, as blood seeped from his chest.

"You stupid fuck," Santiago swore. "You stupid, stupid fuck." He kicked the side of Lansing's head, making it twist violently on a limp neck. Grabbing a fistful of the engineer's shirt, Santiago dragged Lansing across the road, leaving streaks of bright red blood that steamed on the hot macadam surface.

Stopping at the ledge, he stood Lansing up, steadied the body, then pushed it far enough over so that it would fall deep into the valley, as close to the bottom as possible. Lansing's body floated downward strangely, slowly at first, almost hanging there suspended. Then it gathered speed, bouncing off a protruding rock with a sharp jolt, turning over limply in an extended somersault, finally disappearing from sight.

Santiago hurried. If someone had heard the shots, he wanted to get as far away as he could before they had time to determine just where the sound had come from. He ran to the Toyota, kicking spent Uzi shells into the grass. Suddenly he stopped: the plans. The goddamned plans Lansing was supposed to have brought.

He ran over to the Moke. All the bullet holes in it. Goddammit! He banged his fist against the side of the jeep. This could put heat on if someone started checking this out.

What if he pushed the car over the edge? It probably wouldn't explode. But what if it did? Someone would go down there and look around, maybe find Lansing. Did Lansing have I.D. on him? Shit, he should have looked before he threw him over the edge. What if the car-rental people checked their records?; they'd know who rented the car. Then there would be the blood on the road. Would they put it together—or think it was a bad car wreck?

But what about the plans? The plans—worry about them first. He laid the Uzi on the ground, opened the small side door, and crouched into the driver's seat. He felt around the floorboards, between the seats. There was a temporary driver's license and car-rental agreement in the tiny dash compartment, but nothing else in the front or back seats.

He checked the storage area behind the rear seats. There was only an overnight bag; but, when he lifted it up, he saw the cardboard tube. That was it—the plans would be in there. Santiago threw the piece of luggage out of the Moke and ripped open the folded-over end of the tube. Empty. The goddamned thing was empty. He ripped it open, fighting the stiff material, thinking maybe something was hidden inside. But there was nothing.

"Goddammit!" He threw the torn pieces of cardboard to the ground, staring straight forward, trying to get his head straight. His head was pounding again. He had to slow down, think this out. But there wasn't time.

Fuck it! He released the brake on the Moke, put his shoulder against the window frame, and pushed. The small vehicle moved slowly, gaining a little speed once Santiago had it on the smooth road surface. He set the wheel at an angle that would steer the jeep clear of the mill, then stepped back. The Moke turned slightly, coasting easily; it bumped over the slight step at the edge, then went over.

Santiago heard the loud crash of metal once, then a second impact seconds later deeper down in the valley. But there was no explosion.

He picked up Lansing's luggage, feeling the pressure of time closing in on him. His ears pinched back, listening as he ripped through the bag, going through rumpled clothes, some personal effects. He considered stealing Lansing's passport, then decided against it. He put everything back in the bag and hurled it over the ledge.

Twenty-three

"I've got to go, Eddie . . . Really." Janice stood by the door.

Eddie stared numbly at the sun through arched branches of unmoving palm trees. The big orange ball slid closer to the sea, its descent as slow and steady as a minute hand turning around the face of a clock.

"I know you and your captain were close, Eddie. I'm sorry. But you'll work things out." She smiled hopefully. "One thing I saw in you from the very beginning was that you're a survivor."

He closed his eyes.

Janice stopped trying to smile. "Good-bye, Eddie."

Twenty-four

Where the hell was he? Santiago banged on the door to Marsh's room a third time, but there was no answer.

He turned and walked quickly down the cement patio to the center of the Heywood's complex. He circled the swimming pool, ducking the overhang of aluminum umbrellas that shaded small tables, excusing himself when he bumped into one of the few bathers who lounged on in the fading sun.

Marsh wasn't at the pool bar, nor was he inside the cherrywood-paneled restaurant where white-jacketed waiters made preparations for the evening's buffet.

Santiago ground his teeth together. No way. Never again was he hooking up with a bunch of amateurs like this. Stick to pros. Your own kind. He swore under his breath, turning the corner to the plaza of hotel shops.

There, peeping into a store window, designer sunglasses perched dramatically beneath his panama hat, was Marsh. The president of ML Engineering appeared quite at ease browsing, hands comfortably in the pockets of white linen pants. Marsh's peach-colored Polo shirt looked fresh from the laundry.

"You buying a dozen?" Santiago asked, slipping into his suave Latin accent for the occasion, pointing to the antique vase on display that Marsh was admiring.

"Maybe some other time." Marsh turned gracefully from the window, strolling in the general direction of his room, waiting until they were away from other shoppers before speaking. "So . . . did you make the pickup?"

"There were problems." Santiago had a tough time keeping his voice under control. He wanted to kick the shit out of Marsh—it was all this asshole's fault. If he'd known about the girl's boyfriend staying with her at the hotel on Key Biscayne, there would have been no killing—no killings—the police would have never been alerted, and this whole deal would have been down yesterday. In Miami, Lansing had buckled under, going along with everything. However, the delay had obviously changed that. "He came after me. He actually attacked me. With a goddamned knife."

Marsh stopped, surprised as he considered Santiago, who nodded, confirming Marsh's disbelief. "Something happened," Marsh said. "William would not have——" He paused, realizing. "Then you had to kill him?"

Santiago's eyes widened, thinking perhaps Marsh would like to say that again—a little louder this time—to see how many people he could announce it to.

"Poor William." Marsh shook his head. "It wasn't wrong to involve him . . . or use him. It's just a shame it had to end this way for him." Marsh shrugged, tugging on the brim of his panama hat, "But, with William, this sort of ending was almost inevitable. Some people destine themselves to be used—and used very successfully."

Santiago could see his reflection in Marsh's sunglasses and felt he'd have been better off talking to himself. Was Marsh going to spend the rest of the afternoon philosophizing about fate? Maybe they could wander the hills in search of some ancient temple to pray to.

Marsh began walking again. "At least we have the plans now."

"Oh, yeah. Do we? Then you picked them up while I was out, because 'poor William' didn't bring them." Every trace of

Santiago's smooth, sophisticated South American persona vanished. He sounded like the street Cuban he'd played when first contacting Lansing about having kidnapped his daughter.

Marsh was stunned. "Did you check carefully?" Marsh asked. Then, seeing the look on Santiago's face, he said, "Of course you did." They walked on. "I don't understand it. Something must have happened." Marsh shook his head. "William would never do anything to jeopardize Amy. *Never*. Do you think——?"

"Think what?" Santiago asked sharply.

"That *perhaps* William found out about Amy? That she was dead?"

"No way. Nobody knows about her. How could they?"

"What did you say you did with her body after——"

"*Nobody knows*. That's not it. Your friend just went off because this whole thing has taken too long. Once we *had* to leave Miami, it turned to shit."

As they neared his room, Marsh removed his sunglasses. He pulled his room key from the pocket of his linen pants and unlocked the door.

A young couple stood talking on the walk a few doors away, so the two men remained silent until they were inside.

Marsh's room was warm, as if it had been closed up for hours; Marsh turned the thermostat down to get more cool air circulating, then switched on the standing lamp that stood between two double beds. He kept the curtains closed.

Santiago couldn't sit. He went over to the sliding doors, pulled aside the heavy drape, and looked outside.

The last of the afternoon's sunbathers, having nurtured the final tanning rays from the sun, were leaving the pool area. Santiago watched a shapely middle-aged woman, maybe forty-five years old, pull a sheer top over her otherwise-nude body.

Marsh set his hat on the writing table against the far wall, taking a seat there. "What do you suggest now?"

The woman by the pool was folding her beach towel, laying it over her arm. Santiago wished he'd noticed her sooner.

He exhaled deeply. This—Marsh—was getting to be a ripe pain in the ass. How could such a perfect plan have gotten so fucked up? He could always bail out—but, shit, he had so much time—and money—invested in this. Not to mention what he stood to gain.

Santiago rubbed the back of his neck. "Lansing probably brought the plans with him—I guess. Who the fuck knows? Maybe he stashed them someplace until he knew his kid was okay. Then again, maybe he never took the plans at all." Santiago thought out possible options, speaking them as they came to mind. "Then again, maybe they're still in your office. And if they'd disappear now—if you wouldn't happen to realize they were missing until Lansing didn't show to work for a few days . . ." Santiago turned toward Marsh, figuring, yeah, hell, this would work. "Look, all you have to do is go back to Miami, get the plans, and bring them back here as soon as possible. I'll do what I can to hold off Tria—our buyer. And if he doesn't like the wait, shit on him. We'll sell to someone else. Maybe for more."

Looking right into Santiago's eyes, Marsh said, "That won't work."

"Why the hell not?"

"There are certain internal office security measures. Government regulations. There's no possible way I can get those plans out without being discovered. No way whatsoever. Remember? That's why we had to bring William in in the first place."

"But he's in it. He's deep fucking in it. It'll look like he was the one who took them. He already did once, right? To get them down here."

"A minute ago you said you weren't sure he *did* bring the plans."

"Forget what the shit I said, goddammit." Santiago made a fist, held it a few seconds, then relaxed. He stared outside, thinking Marsh didn't know how close he was coming to getting himself wasted. The asshole had cost him—cost him a lot—and now he wouldn't even hop a fucking plane up to Miami to steal something from his own company that had already been stolen. There must be ways to make copies of the plans—to get by whatever *security* there was at ML Engineering. But if Marsh didn't want to do it, it would be tough to make him. Maybe there was another way. "All right," Santiago sighed. "All right. Maybe he did bring the plans with him."

Marsh nodded his agreement. "You're suggesting we look for them?"

"Since you're telling me there's no other way—is that right? Unless we get them from Lansing, we don't get them?"

Marsh thought a moment, taking a cigarette from the gold case that sat atop the writing table. "I would say that's correct. Security is very crucial, very tight at work." He lit the cigarette with his Dunhill lighter. "But," he said, exhaling a breath of smoke, "what if we don't find them?"

Santiago closed his eyes. Why was this asshole always so goddamned concerned with their next move? After all, Marsh was just here for the ride, waiting it out until the deal was down and it was time to collect his share. Why did he want to know all this? Santiago wondered. Marsh had always been annoying, monitoring each step along the way as though he were contributing to it. Santiago had written that off as Marsh's living out some James Bond fantasy. But what if he'd underestimated Marsh? Maybe Marsh wasn't what he seemed. Maybe he had some plans of his own? Maybe just seeming like he was playing along, as some sucker, when he was really looking to run a double cross on Santiago.

"Tell you what," Santiago said. "Tonight . . . in about"—he paused, looking at the distance between the falling sun and horizon—"three hours, we'll go to Lansing's hotel room. Together. You and me. And we'll look for the plans."

"You want me to go?"

"Why not? You came down here to help me out, right?"

Twenty-five

The more he thought about it, the worse it seemed. The worse it seemed, the more he drank. The more he drank, the more he thought about it.

"Vicious goddamned circle," Gant mumbled to himself.

There was a quart bottle of Jamaican rum on the table beside him. His original intention had been to drink it all as fast as he could swallow, but, he'd taken a long time before managing the first taste. Staring at that sealed bottle, he'd seen images of Uncle Floyd passed out drunk in that cheap-ass airport hotel, Crown Royal empties all over the place. But then, the more he'd thought about it, the worse it had gotten; and as it kept getting worse, he kept getting closer to the bottle, finally going in it.

Now a third of the rum was gone.

It had been a long time since he'd had this much to drink. He was surprised how well he was handling it—handling it too well, in fact, because things weren't getting any better.

Eddie ran the corner of a saltine into the jar of peanut butter that sat open in his lap, then stuck the whole thing in his mouth. The sound of the cracker crunching between his teeth seemed deafening.

Of all the goddamned luck. Lieutenant Simpson, that Internal Affairs asshole who'd drilled him after shooting that Cuban last Friday night, had taken over for Uncle Floyd. There must have been fifty other people in Dade-Matro who were qualified, and Simpson ends up as the new captain.

Anyway it had turned, though, it wouldn't have worked out for Eddie; he knew that much. He wasn't interested in being a cop if Uncle Floyd wasn't there to run things his way. Uncle Floyd was old school; he had balls you could fire from a slingshot and kill an elephant.

Eddie had often wondered what would happen around Dade-Metro once Uncle Floyd left, but he'd always blocked out the variables because none of them were any good.

Shit . . .

Maybe he could go up into the city with the Miami boys and hassle Bolivian dopers. They'd probably take him in a minute. Or DEA. Yeah, a fed job might not be bad. Good benefits. Salary—God knows he could use the money. Christ, money . . .

The more he thought, the worse it got.

He loaded another cracker with peanut butter and swigged some more rum. Think about something else, he told himself.

He tried concentrating on the yellow moon hanging high in the dark black Barbadan sky, the thousands of stars twinkling red, blue, and green around it. *Pretty,* Eddie thought. It was still warm out. The escape of the sun had done little to drop the temperature. The subtlest of breezes tampered with the palm trees, but even as the branches rippled, Eddie never felt any cooler, as though the breeze were hiding in the palms.

The Barbados Beach Villas was quiet tonight. He saw lights strung around the pool area, but they weren't on now. There were only a few people in the outdoor dining room. All evening there hadn't been more than a trickle of customers through there, and one couple had walked up the path below Eddie's balcony complaining about the service and food, saying they wouldn't make that mistake again. So maybe that's why it wasn't very crowded.

Just about to sink another cracker into the peanut-butter jar, Eddie heard scratching sounds down on the ground. He lowered his feet from the railing, tilted his chair forward, and looked over the edge.

At the base of the nearest palm tree, his kitty-cat friend was working his way up the slick bark. The cat struggled at first, then established a foothold and made it to the height of Eddie's balcony.

"Hey," Eddie said, leaning back. "Where'd you go, huh? You left me, you rat."

The cat meowed, cinnamon eyes spying the crackers.

"Want one?" Eddie asked, taking a saltine from the cellophane wrapper.

The cat meowed again, starting to move out along the branch, but the spine of the palm leaf was too frail to hold him. The limb gave, starting to break. With instant reflexes, the cat turned adroitly in place and scurried back to the center of the tree.

"I know how you feel," Eddie said. "You can't get here from there." He stood and went inside his room, switching on a light to find his way to the door. He stepped out onto the landing, whistling quietly to the cat, having to go halfway down the stairs before the tabby finally got the idea he was being invited in.

The two of them went back out onto the balcony, each taking a chair. The cat sat patiently while Eddie broke two saltines into small enough bits for him to handle. The peanut butter didn't interest the cat at all.

"Sorry," Eddie apologized. "Guess I should've got cheese after all." He watched the cat twist the cracker around in his mouth, softening it, taking tiny little bites. "Know any good jobs around here?" Eddie asked, petting the little fellow's head.

The cat wagged its tail once, then, as though remembering his breed's legacy of fickleness, stopped.

Eddie slouched down in the chair, ran his hands through the tangles in his hair. God . . . Uncle Floyd was dying. Man, it wasn't fair. Especially considering that the IA lieutenant was probably back at Dade-Metro this very second, drooling at the mouth, waiting for Eddie's return. At least Wendy had covered for him, saying he was on vacation. Regulations required that he go inactive after a shooting until an investigation was completed, so that was taken care of—something he'd done right—unless Simpson would happen to examine the voucher book and see that Eddie was in Barbados on Dade-Metro funds.

Shit! The more he thought . . .

Simpson would probably either have him arrested for embezzlement—forgery, too, if he realized Eddie had signed Marler's name on the voucher—or would run him up on departmental charges. One thing about Simpson, Eddie bet he was a whiz on regs. The asshole wasn't a cop, he was a goddamned bureaucrat—a pencil-pusher with a badge and gun—the sort who would wear himself out rubbing two sticks together to start a fire when he wasn't interested in the blaze at all; he just wanted smoke.

That wasn't what being a cop was about. "Shit, no," Eddie told the cat. "Me and Uncle Floyd. We were it. The last two real cops in South Florida. Maybe the whole goddamned world."

Gant reached for the crackers, then noticed two people checking into Lansing's old room. Two guys, probably fags, he thought. They sure were having a helluva time with the lock though. They couldn't even get the key in.

Suddenly Eddie stood up. The one guy looked familiar. He leaned over the railing, squinting. Christ! It was Marsh, the society head of ML Engineering—Lansing's company. And he was with some Latin-looking guy.

"Sonofabitch!" Eddie whispered to himself, moving against the side wall of his balcony, hiding there. "Santiago." The Latin was Santiago. It had to be. He and Marsh were in on something together. Eddie's heart started to speed up. "All right, goddammit. All right." He breathed deeply, running the options through his head, trying to clear the haze of the rum. "It might all be goin' to hell," he said, "but we're gonna have one last piece of real police work here." Eddie went inside the room, holstered on his .45, and stuffed his Persuader riot gun into his carry bag.

Twenty-six

"Don't strain yourself," Santiago said sarcastically, watching Marsh gently pull open a dresser drawer and look inside.

Santiago had gotten them into Lansing's room. The door hadn't been bolted; the knob lock was fairly straightforward.

As Marsh eased open another dresser, Santiago grabbed a pillow off the double bed, mashed it in his hands, then, feeling nothing, ripped the case open, pulling through fluffy synthetic stuffing with enough vigor to have found a hidden dime. "Shit!" Santiago swore, taking hold of the other pillow.

"There are only a few places the plans could be," Marsh said with his usual calm. "The pages are rather large. Each about this big." He measured out his hands in a rectangle about three feet by two. "It's not something you could hide in a shaving kit."

Santiago didn't think Marsh looked too nervous at all for a corporate president who was in the process of breaking and entering in a foreign country, a locale where he probably didn't know a single lawyer who could get his case scheduled in front of the judge he played golf with on Thursdays. But then, Marsh had never seemed nervous all along. Sure, he'd been leery when Santiago had first approached him with this idea. Marsh had hesitated, but never had shown a hint of nerves. That had annoyed Santiago before—as though Marsh didn't really know what he was getting into—but now it concerned him, and it was a growing concern.

Maybe Marsh wasn't rattled because he didn't have much of anything at stake. Marsh hadn't killed all those people back in Miami—or Lansing here—and it sure as shit would take a hungry district attorney to prove that Marsh was Santiago's accomplice to the extent that he could hang an accessory noose around his neck. But there was still plenty to worry about. Unless . . .

. . . Unless Marsh didn't think there was anything to be worried about. Maybe for Marsh there *wasn't* any reason to be concerned because maybe Marsh knew something Santiago didn't. Maybe Marsh had his own plans.

"Do you want me to check behind this painting?" Marsh asked, pointing to the framed print on the wall. "I think it's too small, but I saw the way you were staring—I thought you wanted me to look at it."

Santiago hadn't been looking at the artwork, he'd been looking at Marsh. "Go ahead; open it up. Just in case."

Santiago bent down next to the bed, lifting up the mattress, turning it sideways to look between it and the box spring. A noise outside alerted him. "Shh!" he whispered urgently to Marsh.

"What is it?" Marsh asked, his voice hushed, but not overly concerned.

Santiago motioned for him to keep quiet. He slid his feet silently across the tile floor, lifting up the sport coat he'd left covering the Uzi on the chair by the door. He grabbed the weapon, then slid back against the wall facing the door, and crouched down.

"Who's deh?" a voice demanded outside the room. The beam of a flashlight crossed over the drawn curtains. Someone was very close by.

* * *

Damn. One of the guards. Eddie hadn't seen him coming, but he saw him now.

Eddie was behind a six-foot-tall hedge just outside the door to Lansing's room. He'd been listening there, hearing mumbled voices inside while drawers and closets were opened. No doubt Santiago and Marsh were looking for the plans.

The guard shone his flashlight across the hedge again. Eddie had a thin line of sight through the thickly packed branches. He could see an older man, sixty or so, squinting into the pale yellow beam cast by his hand-held light. As it passed over him, Eddie averted his eyes to the side, so his pupils wouldn't sparkle and reflect back the light.

"Come out!" the guard insisted. "Come out now! I seen you in deh." The guard took a hesitant step forward toward the hedge, but shone his flashlight to Eddie's left, across the short clearing between Lansing's building and the one next door.

Eddie looked around without moving. He had nowhere to go to his right; there was only the wall there. To his left, across the ten-foot open space, was the next series of two-story units. In front of him was the hedge and the guard—neither of them physical threats, but the guard would surely get a look at him. To his rear, though, that was his only way out. If he sprinted the fifty-foot distance fast enough, before the guard could react and get around the hedge for a look at him, Eddie could turn the corner behind the buildings. Once there, he could use the walkway that ran just inside the barbed-wire fence that surrounded the Barbados Villas.

"Come out heh, *now!*" the guard insisted, approaching slowly.

Persistent for an old fart, Eddie thought, watching the guard continue to shine his flashlight in an ever-widening beam, still unable to see Eddie for the thick foliage of the hedge. As soon as the flashlight aimed far to his left, Eddie took off.

"Stop! You deh!" the guard yelled, struggling after him.

Eddie gripped the carry bag that held his riot gun, going hard for the back wall of the buildings, turning right, moving fast down the narrow path, slapping away branches that hung in his way. It was dark, but he kept running full tilt, making a second turn between buildings further down the row, hiding under a set of wood stairs. He pinned himself flat against the wall, feeling his heart pounding, trying to keep his breathing as quiet as possible.

Moments later, he heard the guard come down the path, footsteps heavy, plodding, slowing to a walk a few yards beyond where Eddie hid.

The old man knew he'd lost him, Eddie figured. He probably wouldn't even report this incident—or just say it was a stray dog—because if he admitted he'd lost some prowler, the hotel might consider his age at fault and fire him. At least that's how Eddie read it.

"What is it?" Marsh asked, unmoving; the framed art print still in his hands.

Santiago had moved closer to the curtain when he'd realized the voice outside hadn't been concerned with who was inside the room. Now he smoothed the part he'd made in the fabric to peek outside. "Hotel security. Apparently someone was hiding in the bush over there."

"Who?"

"I told you, hotel security. A guard."

"No. Who was hiding?"

"I couldn't tell," Santiago answered, thinking that a damned odd question to ask. What difference did it make who was out there hiding? Unless it was someone Marsh didn't want him to see . . . shit, that was it. Marsh had someone else here with him. Someone outside who was going to take him out once Marsh had the plans. Marsh *was* working some kind of rip-off. The bastard. That was probably why Marsh hadn't been in his room when he'd come back from the rendezvous with Lansing; there had probably been some kind of setup there, only Santiago had prevented it from going down by not returning with the plans.

Marsh had the wire hanger unscrewed from the back of the picture frame and was pulling out the small nails that wedged the artwork in place. He worked with a solitary concentration, his attention focused as though performing a delicate operation.

"I just happened to think of something," Santiago said, leaning against the wall, letting the Uzi dangle in his grasp.

Marsh looked up from the partially disassembled frame. "What is it?"

"You're taking a helluva risk down here. Immigration's got a list of everyone that goes through. If anyone investigates this thing and sees you and Lansing were on the island at the same time ... that would look real suspicious, don't you think?"

"Except that I should be out of United States jurisdiction when this is over. I have a buyer for ML Engineering. A large corporation has been courting the prospects of a takeover for some time." Marsh pushed his glasses up his thin nose. "They'd shown some interest last year, but never made an offer. I'd assumed it was because of the problems with this project's not being sold. But they seem very willing now. I've already left powers of attorney with the firm handling the transaction."

Weird, Santiago thought. Marsh had never said anything about this before. And if there was a buyout offer, that would surely have kept Marsh from going in on this. Why take a big risk for a share of something illegal when he would surely be getting five or ten times that much legitimately from the buyout? "You're not going back to the States?"

"I don't think that would be wise ... considering this."

"Where are you going?"

Marsh lifted out the print, felt between the backing paper and the art, then replaced it in the frame. "I hope you won't mind, but I don't think it wise to discuss my future plans."

Santiago nodded. "Okay." He tossed the Uzi on the bed and went back to reaching in between the mattress and box spring. He watched Marsh rehang the picture. "You want to see about the bathroom?"

"Yes. Inside the toilet, perhaps." Marsh's tone made it clear he thought this was a waste of time. He turned on the bathroom light, opened the medicine cabinet, looked behind the shower curtain, saw there were no closets to check, flushed the toilet, then looked behind the door. "Nothing," he called.

The impact of the bullet in the center of his chest threw him back over the sink. Probably he was dead before the back of his head had cracked the mirrored medicine cabinet.

Santiago unwrapped what was left of the pillow from the Uzi's barrel. It hadn't made for a bad silencer; turning sharp cracks into hollow thuds, like someone throwing ripe melon against the wall.

There was an acrid gunpowder scent in the air and also the odor of burning plastic from singed fibers of pillow stuffing. Santiago turned on the air conditioner to keep the smell from lingering. He went into the bathroom, using his feet to push Marsh's sprawled legs back onto the tile floor. He wound shut the louvered windows, drew closed the curtains, then locked the bathroom door, turning off the light before closing Marsh in there.

He stood in the middle of the room and looked around. The plans weren't here. It didn't make sense. Why would Lansing have come all this way and not even brought the plans?

Santiago kept on the light beside the bed. He folded up the Uzi's stock, draping his sport coat over his arm to hide the weapon. He let himself out of Lansing's room, locking the door, hanging the *Do Not Disturb* sign on the knob.

He knew he was running out of time for the exchange with Triacas. It was set for tomorrow. Triacas would be sitting there with all that money—*shit!*—and Santiago didn't have anything to sell him. He didn't even have enough of an idea what these goddamned plans looked like to fake a set. No, that was no good either. This thing wasn't big enough to put out the word he'd conned Triacas; he didn't plan to have to work again after this, but you never knew . . .

Santiago ambled leisurely across the crossing pathways of the Barbados Beach Villas, not wanting to seem anxious, but, still, he kept watch for whoever could have been waiting outside for Marsh. Whoever it was, surely they wouldn't make any move without knowing what Marsh was doing first—where

Marsh was. Probably not, anyway. Then there was the doorman from the disco, the one who'd thrown him out after the
fight: Santiago didn't want to run into him, either. So, he kept
his finger on the Uzi's trigger beneath the sport coat hung
oddly over his arm.

Eddie hadn't had time to rent a car, but he knew how cars
ran; he knew what wires made what go.

The Suzuki-made compact—a tiny two-door hatchback—had
been sitting in a corner of the parking lot, away from the
other cars, under a burned-out street lamp. Eddie had never
seen this kind of car before, but knew it would run like lots of
other cars, and he'd had no trouble popping the ignition and
hot-wiring it.

The bad part had been the wait—hoping like hell one of
those guards didn't come strolling this way and that the
rightful owner wouldn't happen to want to go for a late-night
drive.

Now, though, the wait was over. Santiago walked out from
between two buildings and got into a dark blue Toyota.

Eddie waited for Marsh, but the American never showed.
Christ, Marsh! Eddie had read him all wrong. Never in a
million goddamned years would he have suspected Marsh's
involvement in this. Marsh seemed too clean to run with someone like Santiago. Maybe Santiago had something on Marsh,
too.

The Toyota's lights came on. It pulled from its parking
space. Santiago was leaving.

Eddie didn't wait any longer for Marsh. He didn't want
Marsh.

Twenty-seven

Santiago turned north onto Highway 1 from the Barbados Villas.

Eddie waited for a Moke to pass, then pulled out after him. The Suzuki's headlights spread across the paved roadbed, showing it barely wide enough for two cars to pass; remembering that wide Mercedes bus on the way from the airport, Eddie hoped if one of those happened to come at him, the Suzuki could find someplace to hide in the side of the hill.

It was easy following Santiago through the developed section of Saint James's Parish. Traffic was light enough for him to stay close, but there were enough other cars turning in and out of the assorted restaurants, hotels, and bars to keep Eddie camouflaged. The farther he drove, though, the more desolate it got. No cars came down from the north and there was only a bright yellow Moke between Eddie and Santiago. Once the canvas-topped jeep turned down the winding drive to the No Name Bar, it was as if Eddie had driven beyond the last outpost—just him and Santiago now, and Eddie was pretty sure that Santiago knew how to use a rear-view mirror.

Street lights that had been placed sporadically disappeared entirely. Where restaurants, hotels, and shopping plazas had lined the road were now small unlit private homes that sat up on a sloping ridge; some of the houses looked cockeyed, settled at a wayward angle in the soft dirt. Highway 1 became a long, straight, solitary stretch of black asphalt with dozens of pencil-thin turns onto dirt side roads.

Eddie knew he was too visible. Even when he dropped a quarter mile behind Santiago, it didn't help. The road was just too empty, too straight.

He reached beside him and unzipped his canvas bag. He brought out the riot gun and laid it on the seat. He could do it now—take Santiago out right here.

It would be risky, but he could speed up alongside him, fire one shot through the window. That should do it. But if he missed or if Santiago reacted in time, maybe cutting Eddie off or ramming him sideways, maybe even outrunning the little Suzuki, then Santiago would be alerted that someone was after him. And an aware target was a much tougher shot.

There was also the matter of a badge. Eddie didn't have one here. If he did Santiago here, was it clean enough? Could he get away with it? Was there a flaw that this spontaneous opportunity hadn't given him time to realize?

Then, too, what if this wasn't Santiago? No, hell, it had to be. It all fit . . . Somehow.

Eddie's thoughts were interrupted.

Santiago turned off onto a side and stopped. The lights on the dark-colored Toyota went off, but Eddie could still make out its silhouette, sitting there.

"Shit!" Eddie swore. Santiago had seen him and was obviously interested enough to know if he was being followed or if this was a mere coincidence. Eddie grabbed his short-barreled shotgun. He could do it *right now*. Santiago was a sitting duck.

He looked around: not other cars; a few scattered houses, most of them dark; no one walking the street.

Eddie started to slow to make the turn, then saw headlights coming from the other direction. "Goddammit!" He slapped down the riotgun and kept going, looking straight ahead, driving past the turn off where Santiago sat.

The little car drove by.

Santiago tried to see if the driver was white or black—tourist or local—but it was too dark to tell. If it had been a white, it could have been someone tailing him—maybe the person outside Lansing's room, someone with Marsh. A black he wouldn't have worried much about; he doubted Marsh would have anyone local in on this with him. For Marsh, it would be another Anglo.

Santiago sighed, taking a few deep breaths. He slid his Uzi back beneath the passenger seat, then, thinking better of it, brought it back out. He might pass that white car again.

Had the little vehicle followed him up the narrow drive, Santiago had planned to shoot without bothering whether the driver was white or black, male or female. There was no reason to turn up this rocky little drive unless you were after whoever had turned there ahead of you.

He'd first spotted the white car in traffic back near The Coach House restaurant. It had been lost from his sight to other cars that pulled onto the road; yet when all the others had turned off, the white car had still been there. It could have been someone else staying at Heywood's, he realized; there were a few hundred guests there, but things were getting too tight—at this point, benefit of the doubt was an extinct commodity.

Santiago waited a few more moments, then switched on his headlights and backed out onto Highway 1. The rest of the drive to Heywood's was as solitary as it should have been. He passed three other cars over the two-mile stretch—none of them small white compacts.

At Heywood's, he showed his room key to the guard stationed in the wooden kiosk by the entrance. The guard waved him past, and Santiago followed the wide driveway into the left parking lot.

He circled the area and the adjoining lot as well. There were a few small white cars, but only one looked like what had been behind him on the highway. Santiago stopped behind that vehicle. Leaving the engine to idle, he set the Toyota's emergency brake and walked over to the car. He placed his hand against the hood. The metal was cool; so was the exhaust pipe. Satisfied, he parked in the other lot and returned to his room.

Cautious bastard, Eddie thought. He observed Santiago circle the parking lots, then stop to feel the hood of a small white car—one just like Eddie's—to see whether it was hot.

Having come as far north as Heywood's, finding it the only sign of developed tourist civilization for miles, Eddie had gambled that Santiago would come here. He'd driven past the entrance and turned around, pulling off to the side of the road, hiding in a cluster of thick-trunked royal palm trees planted away from the hotel lights.

As soon as Santiago got out of his car, Eddie crawled under an unambitious barbed-wire fence for a better view of the sprawling grounds.

It was dark across the fifty yards of sand and dry grass that separated Eddie from the long line of buildings that comprised the resort. Lying flat against the ground, brittle edges of grass itching his arms, Eddie scanned the area.

The only guard he saw was the man at the entrance. There was a small window that looked from the rear of the guard stand to Eddie's direction, but it was impossible to tell if anyone was watching from there or not. There seemed to be a lot of other activity, though, concentrated toward the heart of the resort. Many more people milled around, a large group under a lighted portion of beach in the distance. It was a less sedate atmosphere here—more party oriented than the Barbados Beach Villas. What would one of the tourists think if they saw him making a break for it, charging in out of the darkness? Probably that he was just another drunk American.

He decided to chance it. He drew himself into a squat position, then ran forward like a sprinter coming out of the blocks. He stayed low and covered the uneven ground quickly. Halfway there, a sway in the sandy grass caused his foot to strike down oddly, jarring his spine. Eddie winced, but kept running, undistracted.

Eddie slowed when he came into the bright circle cast by a floodlight perched high in a palm tree and took on the pace of someone walking off energy on a nighttime stroll. Rounding the corner, he found himself on a wide patio between two bending lines of double-tiered guest quarters.

Like the Barbados Beach Villas, Heywood's was sprawled out in a series of separate buildings, although here, each section was designed in a different motif.

He continued down the patio, hearing playful splashes and cries of people in a swimming pool just ahead. God, the place was huge. There were more doorways and turns than he could count. A steel band played in the distance. Lights were on in almost every third room, and people sat on balconies drinking and laughing, burning citronella candles to keep away the mosquitoes. Eddie didn't see Santiago anywhere; then again, in this place, he could have been *anywhere*.

Going around the swimming pool, Eddie saw three couples in the water, splashing each other. One man dumped a plastic bucket of water over a woman's head, then lifted up her bikini top as she laughed loudly.

He found his way into a small bar decorated like a bamboo hut, quickly taking inventory of the patrons: mostly couples, except for two men at the bar who drank whiskey and eyed a pair of women over in wicker seats by the window drinking fruity daiquiris. But no Santiago.

Eddie approached the ebony black bartender who was fighting with some concoction in a whirling blender. "Where's the front desk?"

The bartender shook the blender a few times, then switched it off. "What say, mon?" he asked, removing the blender's cap, looking inside it as he dug through the frozen mixture with a long twisted-handled spoon.

"Front desk?" Eddie asked. "Office?"

"Up dat way." He pointed with the spoon, dripping what smelled like piña colada onto the bar.

* * *

It didn't surprise Eddie, but no one at Heywood's was registered with the first or last name of Santiago.

Eddie went back to the bamboo-hut bar and bought a planter's punch in a plastic cup. He took his drink out onto the long patio and strolled from one end of the hotel grounds to the other. The rum tasted fruity and cool, a relief from the warm night.

He kept to no particular pattern, but made four or five circuits of the place. Sometimes he walked down the center patio, other times along the parking-lot side, or between the oceanfront units and the beach. The whole while, he kept his pace casual, just strolling, but the calm he showed on the outside was a fraud.

The alcohol helped some, but couldn't totally subdue the panic he was feeling. This was his last grasp, his last shot at Santiago—he could feel it. The threads that connected the Latin to Miami were slowly being cut away. Once Santiago got off Barbados, Eddie wouldn't know where to look next, or whom else to look for for help, for clues. The bastard had left a trail, but it was like shallow footprints in hard sand very close to the sea—and the tide was rising.

This was as close as Eddie had been to him. Goddammit, he was here. *Right here!* The adrenaline shot through his veins, ready, but there was nothing he could do but wait, stalk. The .45 strapped around his ankle, covered by the loose leg of his cotton pants, felt heavier all the time.

As he started another circuit from the north end, he noticed fewer and fewer lights on in the rooms. The swimming pool was empty, its surface smooth as a dish, and the bars were emptying. He couldn't stay here much longer.

He walked halfway down the center patio one last time, inconspicuously looking in open windows as best he could without getting too close. No sight of Santiago. He'd have to wait until morning, when he could blend back in with the vacationing crowd and use his only advantage: the fact that he knew what Santiago looked like, but Santiago didn't know him.

Eddie threw away his empty cup and went back around the

north row of buildings. He stopped. There was someoné out near the highway shining a flashlight inside the group of palm trees where he'd left his small car. Great! He hadn't locked it, and the shotgun was still in there.

Santiago stood by his porch door. He wore only his underwear, scratching along the sides of his phallus. He didn't like staying in a small room with the curtains and drapes closed. He liked knowing what was going on outside. Still, there was security in remaining hidden, which was why he'd switched off all the lights and had the curtains open only far enough to see out.

There were a lot of good-looking women here, Santiago noticed, seeing them stroll between his porch and the beach. Some were alone, obviously looking for company. There was one man who passed his room twice, carrying a drink of some kind, and Santiago figured for sure the man would come on to one of the women, but he passed by a third time and was still alone. *Maybe he was looking for another man,* Santiago thought.

When an especially attractive young woman walked by in a strapless sundress, Santiago considered approaching her himself—no sense letting it go to waste—but he fought the temptation. It was only about seven hours until he had to make the exchange with Triacas: the plans for the quarter-million. And he didn't have the plans.

He'd thought about stalling Triacas, making him wait another day. But if Triacas balked, or came down in his offer, Santiago would be in a bad position. So he wasn't going to attempt any renegotiation; he had a much simpler plan. He was going to steal the goddamned money from the Greek.

Ripping off Triacas wouldn't be something he'd have to look over his shoulder for. Triacas wasn't connected; he was out there on his own, wheeling and dealing without making too many enemies.

Now it was a simple matter of logistics: how to do it. The jewelry shop where they'd planned to make the exchange was good, but what if Triacas had backup there: goons who probably would be well armed? That was no good. He'd have to do it before Triacas got to the shop.

He'd ambush him on the way. Triacas would probably pick up the money in the morning; he wouldn't chance walking around with a quarter-million on him any longer than necessary. So he'd either meet his principal or make a pickup at the bank. But Santiago didn't know where any of those possible locations were, and there were a dozen roads into Bridgetown and Triacas's shop. It would be a long shot to pick which one the Greek would use. Santiago didn't even know what kind of car Triacas would be driving. But he did know where Triacas lived, or knew where he used to live.

Triacas had a boat. What the hell was it called? Something to do with Greece. Damn it! What was the name of the thing? Santiago banged his fist against the glass door. *Oro?* Was it *Oro* something? The name of a city or town. Athens? That was it: *Athens Oro.* And he docked at a small marina on the southern tip of the island.

Eddie ran along the desolate north boundary of the resort property toward the road. In the darkness, he used his left hand to feel the contours of the fence, guiding him along.

Someone had found the hot-wired car he'd left hidden in the palm trees, but who? Kids? Car thieves? Police?

The ground under his feet turned to powdery sand, causing him to lose his footing across an uneven knoll. His legs went out from under him; but, rather than fighting it, he rolled forward, onto his shoulder, taking the fall in a sideways half-somersault that ended with his being down on all fours in the sand. He stayed there, breathing hard.

None of the hotel lights shone this far. It was about 50 yards to the road, then another 70, maybe 80 yards to the car. Bob Hayes could have covered that distance in less than ten seconds, then leaped over the goal line to make a fingertip catch of a wobbly Meredith pass during his early years at Dallas. Jesus, what made him think of that now?

He stayed down on the sand, fighting for air. It had been a long time between runs around the track at Palmetto High. The Miami spring had been too hot this year.

Eddie unholstered his .45. He started to pull himself up, then stopped. He couldn't show the gun, not yet. He was still thinking like a cop—down here, he wasn't one. He restrapped the combat automatic to his ankle, then started for the road.

His feet padded almost silently over the sand, not nearly as loud as his breathing. Just before the road was a slight five-foot incline; Eddie took it easily, sliding down the loose surface, almost skiing it. He slipped inside a row of palm trees that had ben planted as a natural barrier between the hotel and road. Looking down the line of bending palm trunks, he saw the tail end of the Suzuki he'd stolen. Just ahead of that was another vehicle, something even smaller—not a car and not a motorcycle . . . What the hell was it?

Eddie weaved through the trees, then crawled forward on his hands and knees when he got close.

The other vehicle was a golf cart. Someone sat in its driver's seat, leaning back, not appearing too concerned; he wasn't using the flashlight now, and only the cart's dim red taillights reflected any light along the dark highway.

The sound of static crackled into the air.

The guy in the cart picked up a walkie talkie. "Yah, Pettie Broll. You sendin' someone else out heah, mon? I ain' waitin' all night foh you."

His question received a garbled reply Eddie couldn't make out.

"No can heah you, Pettie. Say again."

The guy must have been hotel security. Eddie inched forward, stopping when another response came over the hand-held receiver. Again, Eddie couldn't pull words from the mix of static and Caribbean phrasing.

"Whacchew mean wait foh dah police? Whacchew call police foh, Pettie? They ain' gonna know whatta do. Jus' come out heah and scratch dher asses, mon? Dis car still be sittin' heah a week from today and we be eatin' shit foh it."

Pettie's reply was inaudible, but the tone was clearly that of authority pulling rank.

The guy in the cart sighed, dropping the walkie-talkie. A moment later, there was more static and the guard grabbed up the receiver again. "Yah, yah, mon. I be waitin'." He dropped the unit again. "Waitin' all fohkin' night, I be waitin'. Dat asshole call dah police."

Eddie came up on the Suzuki's right rear, in the security man's blind spot. He slowly raised himself up, peering inside the car. His canvas bag was still on the passenger seat, but it was twisted into a strange shape, like a crumpled ball. Hell, the riot gun wasn't in it. The guard must have taken it out.

Eddie eased back below the window line of the car. There was only one way to do this. He slowly raised his pants leg up his calf, keeping both hands pressed over the snap of his holster to cover the click of unfastening it. He pulled out the .45, checked that the safety was off.

In one swift move, he ran to the right-hand side of the security cart, gripping the pistol with both hands, holding it two feet from the black man's temple. "Don't even breathe!"

The guard, wearing an olive-drab jumpsuit uniform, looked out the corner of his eye down the gun barrel. He didn't flinch.

"Get out," Eddie instructed quietly. "Get out real slow. I want you to go face down——"

The guard smacked his fist into the underside of Eddie's forearms. The force knocked Eddie back and he almost pulled off a shot. The guard reached down on the floorboards and came up with the pistol-grip stock of the riot gun. As the huge barrel swung toward him, Eddie lunged at the security man. He punched hard smacking his pistol against the guard's forehead, then kneed the riot gun loose.

The guard was stunned, but by no means out. He struggled, grabbing for Eddie's arms, trying to twist them—twist them, hell—trying to snap them off, outweighing Eddie by about forty very solid pounds.

But Eddie stayed close, keeping a death grip on his .45. He managed to get on top of the guard, using what leverage he could, wrapping his arm around the big man's throat, jerking his head back, feeling hard lines of shoulder muscles resisting him.

The guard grunted as Eddie's knee slammed under his chin.

Eddie repeated the move a second time, now feeling warm blood over his hands and arms that ran from the guard's mouth. Eddie brought back his knee for a third shot, but got caught in the ribs by a sharp, powerful jab-punch that went all the way through him. He couldn't breathe. He just tried to hold on, then got hit again, even harder.

The guard pawed one hand on Eddie's legs, going for his balls. Eddie kicked his knee forward, fending off that attack, but caught a hard punch in the side that bent him over. The guy was too goddamned strong—there was no way. Eddie took one more punch to the side followed by another to the stomach that nearly folded him in half. The .45 knocked from his hand, he was thrown out of the cart and the guard jumped on top of him, battering his midsection with hard fists, rolling him onto his side, bear-hugging him, squeezing air from his lungs.

Eddie couldn't see for the pain. His arms were free, but there was no leverage to throw a punch. Jesus, he was suffocating. Feeling the guard's breath hot on his face, Eddie grabbed the powerful man by his ears and held on tight. He tensed his neck, drawing back, and used all the strength in his arms and shoulders to head-butt him.

The guard screamed as the front of Eddie's skull split open his nose. Hands covering his face, he released Eddie and dropped to the ground, legs kicking up dust.

Stunned, gasping for air, knifelike pain piercing his ribs, Eddie stumbled to the security man's cart and grabbed the riot gun. Turning away, he tripped, falling against the front of the stolen Suzuki. He held onto the car for support, wincing, clutching his side as he struggled into the driver's seat.

Help would be coming soon. But not help for him, help for the guard: more security people, the police. Eddie had to get out, but his eyes wouldn't focus. He was on a familiar edge, close to blacking out.

Twenty-eight

At first, the siren seemed like part of his dream; but when the sound became louder, more urgent, more real, Santiago bolted upright in bed.

Quickly, he opened his suitcase, putting the Uzi inside, throwing clothes over it to conceal it.

Hurriedly, he dressed, putting the pistol—a small Turkish .380 with silencer—in his pants pocket. He left his room by way of the sliding glass door, suitcase in hand, and walked quickly along the beachside patio. He turned toward the parking lot and stopped, able to see the twisting flash of red emergency lights reflecting against the front of the hotel.

Santiago moved inside the cover of a service doorway to get a better view. He could see activity out along the highway. It appeared to be a car accident of some sort. There was a tangle of parked police cars and ambulances with lights and sirens going wildly, as if they hadn't gotten where they were going yet, while a dozen people dashed about in complete confusion, everyone shouting orders to which no one paid attention.

Santiago shook his head. He should have known better. Caribbean emergency response. He went back to his room.

He slept until 6:00, not needing the travel alarm he'd set. Already dressed in black slacks and a dark red golf shirt, Santiago watched the last hours of darkness yield to the pink glow of dawn. It was time.

Before going out the door, he checked the belongings he was leaving behind one last time to make sure there was nothing he needed; also that there was no evidence as to why he had been here or where he was going.

The central patio was nearly empty—only hotel employees were awake at this hour—as Santiago walked toward the parking lot.

A sleepy cleaning woman smiled wearily as he walked by. "Hope your stay was nice," she said.

Santiago nodded. He continued onto the car, putting his suitcase on the passenger seat, unzipping it, knowing just how deep into the pile of clothes he'd have to reach for the Uzi.

Pulling onto Highway 1, he immediately looked for other headlights. This was why he wanted to begin so early in the day: it was much easier to see whether he was being followed when traveling empty roads in the dark.

He didn't sight any other vehicles until just north of Holetown. There, a transit bus bringing workers from Bridgetown out to the hotels unloaded passengers at the curb, blocking the northbound lane. Those getting off wore uniforms of bright-colored dresses or bronze-buttoned blazers, some styles coordinating with the theme of where they worked, while others dressed in the plain white called for by their duties as maids and kitchen help.

To his left, above the rolling hillside, dawn was breaking faster than he'd anticipated. The sky overhead was an even white-pink now and some approaching cars drove with only dimmers or no lights at all.

Traffic increased as he passed Sandy Lane, reaching a more populated section of the island. He watched his rear-view mirror for any small white car that might happen to pull onto the road behind him. He drove slowly, allowing impatient motorists to pull into the left lane and speed past him. By the time he turned onto the Spring Garden Highway toward Bridgetown, Santiago was confident that no one was tailing him. All he had to worry about now was Triacas.

The jarring motion awakened Eddie. He was groggy, hurting. His ribs ached deeply, paining even worse as he was thrown around in the dark compartment. He searched for something to hold onto, bracing his legs and arms for leverage. Each time his back hit the metal floor, knifelike twinges pierced his spine. Without light, strangely shaped spots appeared in front of his eyes, twisting, spiraling, making him dizzy. He felt as if he might go out, but held on. Primeval instincts never failed to amaze him; anyone who said humans were that far removed from the jungle had never been out on an adrenaline limb before.

Breaking into the trunk had been easy: a matter of picking the chamber and forcing it with that certain acquired touch. What had concerned him was being able to keep the trunk closed without locking himself inside. To accomplish that, Eddie slipped the belt from his trousers and strung it through a U-hook on the inner trunk lid. He put the belt back through one loop of his pants and rolled over on it. Now Santiago wouldn't be able to see that the trunk wasn't latched, and when he tried to open it, Eddie would have plenty of notice— more time than he'd need—to use the shotgun that was right there in his hand.

The marina looked different to Santiago than the last time he'd seen it. It was smaller, and he remembered two piers— not just one. Had he come to the wrong place?

He pulled off onto the uneven road shoulder before reaching the turn and tried to think. The marina sat at the bottom of a steep private road, nestled inside a curving horseshoe of sand and black rock designed to block approaching storms. There was a white-painted house for the dockmaster—Santiago recognized that—and the double fuel pumps with the faded old Esso logo were familiar. This had to be the same place; maybe his memory was playing tricks on him.

Santiago took the turn slowly, but the Toyota still scraped bottom on the worn stone roadbed down to the marina. He parked near a van from the Crane Beach Hotel, where six Canadian tourists—all men—received instructions from a stocky South American boat captain.

Besides the deep-sea fishing party, there was no other activity. The dockmaster's house was dark, and the nine small yachts Santiago counted tied to the pier bobbed peacefully with the gentle sway of the sea. Overhead, a few relentless gulls squawked at the bait carried in buckets by the South African captain's mate.

At the end of the gangway, Santiago saw a square green flag hanging limply from the stern of a yacht. Immediately, he remembered that Triacas displayed such a flag. This *was* the right marina; perhaps a storm had made its way into the horseshoe-shaped harbor and torn away the second dock.

Santiago glanced at his Rolex. It was 7:30. His stomach growled in protest that he hadn't eaten since lunch yesterday, but eating could wait. Turning around in the driver's seat, he looked at other cars around him. He didn't see any that he remembered as Triacas's, but if forced to bet, he'd put his money on the silver gray Volvo.

He watched the Canadians step awkwardly aboard the South African's charter; one of them nearly toppled backwards onto the dock, but the young mate secured him by the shirt collar. His party loaded, the captain churned twin diesels noisily to life and eased his way expertly from the pier.

Santiago waited until the boat was a few hundred yards to sea, visible only as a black silhouette against brilliant blue ocean, then got out of the car. He walked down the dock with his hands in his pockets, right finger around the trigger of the small MKE, silencer already in place.

Bent slightly at the waist, he looked through galley windows into the yachts he passed. Most appeared unoccupied;

only in the *Marlin-Grabber,* two slips from Triacas, were heavily lined drapes left open behind bay windows.

No one was astern on Triacas's *Athens Oro,* either outside on the deck or inside the galley.

Santiago gripped the hand rail and went on board quietly, not knowing where Triacas might be below, and not wanting his footsteps to advertise his presence. Cautiously, he tested the screen door that led to the galley. It was unlocked. He opened it the width of his shoulders and went in.

The galley was decorated plushly with thick carpet and oversized velour chairs, looking more like the furnished model of a condo than a boat. Across the living area and down six oak steps was a double set of doors with brass handles; cabins would be on the other side of those doors. Triacas would be down there.

Santiago reached behind the curtains and found the pull cord to draw them closed. Once they were shut, near-total darkness embalmed the galley.

Eddie heard the car door, then listened as the sound of Santiago's feet crunching over stones became more distant. Only then did he ease up the trunk—and then only a half-inch.

Bright sunlight hurt his eyes. Squinting, it took him a few moments to focus. What he saw across a short stone-laid parking lot was a hill rising up to a road over which traveled a steady flow of cars. But, closed in the trunk, he had heard other sounds: sea gulls, a diesel engine, the gentle lapping of waves against bulkheads. Smells had permeated the trunk, too: the slightly rotten odor of dead fish and creosote used to treat wood constantly exposed to water. It all told him he was in a harbor or boatyard of some kind. Years spent growing up around various Florida waterways had left impressions.

Eddie raised the trunk about two feet and crawled out, wincing when his ribs pressed against hard metal. He left the riot gun inside, easing onto his hands and knees, staying down on the stone-chip ground.

He was in a small marina. There were a fair number of

boats, but the only person he saw was Santiago walking down the dock.

The Latin hunched forward every now and then, as though he were looking for something. Then he stealthily boarded the cruiser at the end of the pier.

Eddie didn't know what Santiago was doing, but from the way he acted, it was something he wasn't supposed to.

Not seeing any option, Eddie closed the trunk, locking his riot gun inside. The .45 would have to do. He looked down the dock again. Santiago went into the cabin of the yacht at the pier's end. It wasn't ideal, but he might not ever get a clean opportunity. The marina was quiet, relatively secluded, with no witnesses in sight. He had to make the best with what he was given. So far, this was it.

The woman walked up the six steps from below decks, looking puzzled at the darkness. Instead of turning on a lamp, she made her way without difficulty through the unlit galley and pulled open the drapes.

"Far enough," Santiago said quietly.

She stopped, leaving only a foot-wide gap between the curtains. Seeing the gun, she did not look especially afraid.

Santiago recognized her as the pretty woman from Triacas's shop, the one who looked as though she could have been a model ten years ago. She wore the same type of bright-colored cotton dress, only this one was more casual than the other. The tropical print material barely reached her knee and was held up by thin straps over her dark-tanned shoulders.

"Where's Gus?" Santiago asked quietly, moving toward the steps leading below.

"He's——"

"Shhh. Keep your voice down."

"He's not here."

"You tried that last time." Santiago smiled, holding the gun casually, but clearly aiming it for the center of her body. "Remember me? From the shop?"

"Yes. Mr. Santiago." She looked right at him.

"Where's Gus?"

"I told you. He's not here."

"Tell you what, honey. You call his name. Not like something's wrong, but just like you need him for something. Okay?" He drew back the hammer of the MKE for effect.

She considered the weapon expressionlessly; but, as she did, rubbed her fingers as though trying to get something wet off them. "Gus," she called plainly, her voice even.

"Louder," Santiago urged.

"Gus!"

Eddie walked along the edge of the boards nailed crosswise into the pier. Experience had taught him that walkways always carried more traffic in the center, sagging the wood at its least supported place, while the board edges, nailed into frames, held faster and carried a man's weight without creaking to reveal his presence.

The yacht was named *Athens Oro*. From the lack of hinged fishing chairs on the stern and the presence of drapes at every window and porthole, Eddie figured the craft for pleasure— not sport.

Eddie carefully placed the toe of his tennis shoe onto the running boards, grabbed the metal side railing, and hoisted himself into position at the galley's stern corner. He didn't cross any of the windows in case enough light shone through to show shadows inside. Instead, he stayed at the corner, between windows, and listened.

Someone else was in there with Santiago. Eddie didn't want to have to kill anyone besides the Latin; but if the boat started out to sea, there might not be any option.

From somewhere near the fore cabins, a door opened, then slammed shut. "What is it you want?" the voice growled. It was Triacas.

The woman looked at Santiago.

"Tell him to come up here," he whispered.

"Alena!" Gus shouted. "What do you want?" The stocky Greek neared the bottom of the steps.

Santiago heard him, sensed him there.

"What do you want, Alena?" he called again, his voice gruff and impatient.

Santiago pivoted into position at the top of the wood steps, MKE aimed for the middle of Triacas's forehead. "Come up, Gus. Join us."

Triacas tensed, looking for a way out, a path of retreat or counterattack, but the element of surprise had him checked. Standing in the narrow corridor, dressed in a summer-weight white robe, he was defenseless.

Triacas waited before starting up the steps. "I should have known better than to deal with you, Santiago. You're nothing but a worthless hustler. *Aurelio Santiago.*" Triacas spat the name with contempt.

Santiago stepped back to let Triacas pass.

"Are you all right, Alena?" Gus asked.

She nodded, arms crossed over her breasts, considering them not so much with fear, but interest, as though accustomed to this sort of game between these kinds of men.

Santiago motioned for them both to sit on matching velour chairs that backed to the starboard wall. "It's not a rip-off, Gus. This is just a . . . security precaution. I decided it wasn't a very good idea to meet at your shop. Who knows what I might have walked into. But, as you would say, I still want to do 'business.' " Santiago accented the word in Triacas's manner.

Triacas said, "Then you can put away the gun."

"Another security precaution." Santiago glanced at his watch. "Almost eight, Gus. When were you planning to leave? Or am I right? There's someone else at the shop waiting for me?"

"You fool!" Triacas said angrily, much louder than Santiago's level tone of voice. "There is no one else. We were supposed to meet at nine-thirty. *Nine-thirty.* Not eight. The shop is a twenty-minute drive."

"So you already have the money. Right?"

"Put away the goddamned gun," Triacas ordered from his chair. "Do it now and I'll forget this—call it the idiotic ploy of a suspicious man."

"I'm changing the plan," Santiago insisted. "I want the money brought here. In one hour."

"We meet at the shop at nine-thirty. You bring the plans, I'll have the money."

"Don't jerk me around, Gus. I want the money here." Santiago looked at the woman, Alena. "Send her for it. You and I will stay here. And . . . she better come back alone."

"No," Gus shouted, his face reddening. "I won't permit it."

"You got no choice. I've got the gun." He gestured Alena toward the door. "Go. Get the money."

She looked at Triacas. "Gus?"

Triacas stared at Santiago. "You're a dead man if you go through with this, Aurelio."

"There's nothing to talk about. Send her for the money."

"This is absurd." Triacas broke his stare from Santiago and looked over to Alena. "Go. Do what he says. The bastard is a big enough fool to use that gun."

Alena nodded.

Waiting for the woman to appear from the yacht, Eddie looked into the small square windows of the dockmaster's house. Hanging there was an odd assortment of fishing tackle—some, strangely enough, labeled in French. From the south window, Eddie saw the reflection of the *Athens Oro*.

Alena emerged from the galley moments later. She hiked her strapless dress up her thighs to better maneuver the step from stern to dock, making the move with practiced ease. She shook back her thick dark hair and started down the pier like a runway model posing for photographers: head held high; posture perfect without being stiff; a very stylish thirty-five-year-old.

Eddie watched, waited.

"You don't trust her, either?" Triacas said bitterly.

Santiago held back the curtain and watched Alena walk down the pier. "She's got a nice ass." Santiago said, then let the curtain go.

As the thick fabric covered the window, light coming into the yacht's plush galley was reduced by half.

Pacing slowly, Santiago said, "Where'd you find her, Gus?"

"What's it to you, dead man?"

"Come on, Gus." Santiago smiled. "Be sociable."

The Greek shook his head. "You are such a crazy shit."

"And you're an ugly old man." Santiago leaned against the wall and took a few deep breaths. "So . . . where'd you nab her, Gus?"

Triacas said nothing, then, "At a club near Garrison Savannah. She was due back in the States for a hearing. Her fiancé was being investigated on smuggling charges." Triacas leaned back, relaxing slightly, but not surrendering, like a man who knew that revenge would be sweet. "She didn't want to go back, but she needed a hiding place."

"And you accomodated her?"

Triacas shrugged. "She said she liked dangerous men."

"Maybe she'd like me."

"You *may* be dangerous, Aurelio, but only to yourself."

Santiago didn't want to hear his bullshit. "She wasn't with you last time."

Triacas laughed. "There have been, what?—I don't know—fifty probably since then. A boat in the islands does wonderful things for a man who also has a lot of money and a jewelry store." Triacas crossed his legs, the skirt of his robe lifting to expose his genitals surrounded by coarse dark hair. "Women are attracted to *class,* Aurelio. Remember that. It may not be too late for you—then, again, I imagine it is."

"It's closed," Eddie said, turning away from the dockmaster's quarters as Alena neared him. He stepped back so that she would have to step around him.

She looked at the scratch alongside Eddie's face, then at the blood on his shirt sleeve. "Excuse me," she said, walking between him and the railing.

"I got a cab here, and now I've missed the charter. Do you happen to know of a phone nearby?"

She walked on, headed toward a Volvo parked not far from Santiago's car. "No, I don't," she said over her shoulder.

"Too much to drink last night, I guess." Eddie followed her.

"Does it to me every time. Then there was a little scuffle in the bar . . . the police came."

Alena got in the Volvo and rolled down the window. "Sounds like quite a night," she said in a blasé voice. She put the key in the ignition, but didn't start the car. She looked at him again, the scratch on his face, and smiled, amused. "You really are a mess."

Eddie realized that she was right. His clothes looked as if he'd been in them for days. One sleeve was torn, his shirt had a grease smear on it from the trunk, and his cotton beach pants were stained from contact with grass, sand, and gravel. "Haven't been to my hotel since Sunday morning," he shrugged, happy-go-lucky, like a kid playing hooky from third grade.

"Sounds like you're having some kind of vacation."

"The best," he grinned, resting his hands on the Volvo's roof. He took a deep breath, forcing himself not to wince as his lungs expanded into aching ribs, then exhaled with vigor. "I always wanted to come to Martinique."

Alena laughed.

"What's so funny?"

"This is Barbados."

Eddie looked stunned. "Barbados? Oh, Jesus! How the hell did I get here?" He scratched his head, looked to be thinking hard. "You couldn't drive me to Martinque, could you?"

She reached behind her and opened the rear door. "I'll get you as far as Bridgetown. You can get a cab there."

"Why don't you fix yourself a drink?" Triacas suggested. "Relax. Alena will be back soon. With the money."

Santiago glanced at his watch. The woman had been gone about fifteen minutes. Time enough. He turned and fired three shots into the Greek's barrel-shaped chest.

The silenced blasts jerked Triacas's body, throwing his weight against the chair back. Then his lifeless form slumped forward, twitching.

Santiago went through the boat, into every closet, box, and container, dumping out their contents. He tapped walls, looking for secret compartments, finding none. In all, he came up with two gold chains to which were attached a dozen or so 18K charms, a few ladies' diamond rings of varying sizes, and a snubnose .357 Colt Python. "Garbage!" Santiago swore, but pocketed the jewelry anyway. If something happened and there wasn't any money at the shop—if Triacas had planned to dupe him—this could wind up being his entire take for a long and involved job.

He started to leave the boat, then stopped. Going to Triacas's body, he pulled the gold rings off the dead man's warm fingers.

Twenty-nine

"You drive well."

"Thank you," Alena said, "but this is as far as we go." She pulled into a parking space facing a channel of water.

Just across the azure waterway by bridge was the dark gray heart of downtown Bridgetown. Unimaginative buildings, some as high as six floors, were packed tightly together in a five-square-block concentration. The main signs advertised international banks, jewelry shops, and department stores. Vehicular traffic into the city was light by American standards, but pedestrians and bicycles took up an entire lane of the short concrete bridge, forcing cars and buses in opposite directions to battle for use of the remaining lane.

"Can I buy you breakfast?" Eddie asked.

"No. Thank you." Alena rolled up her window. "I have to go to work." She got out of the car.

"Lunch, then?"

"Would you lock the door, please?"

Eddie reopened the passenger side, pushed down the locking mechanism, then closed it again. "How about lunch?"

Alena walked away, briskly crossing two lanes of traffic, heading down a wide patio that bordered the channel. Small yachts were docked at three of the ten short piers there.

Eddie followed her, dodging a bike on which a rider on the handlebars blinded the driver's view. He jogged a few steps to catch up. "Lunch?" he asked, getting in front of Alena, walking backwards.

She smiled again, finally. "You are persistent, aren't you?"

"Does this mean yes?"

She reached into her pocketbook, bringing out a small key ring. "Unfortunately, no. Sorry." She stopped.

They were at a door in the middle of a row of small shops, yet Eddie saw no sign saying to what this particular door belonged.

Alena said, "I have to go to work." She extended her hand. "It was a pleasure to meet you. I hope you find your way back to Martinique."

Disappointed, Eddie accepted her handshake. "Thanks for the ride."

Alena turned away from him, putting the key in the glass door. "You can get a cab at the corner," she said, opening the deadbolt. But, as she entered the shop, Eddie was right behind her, pushing through the doorway.

Alena let out a startled gasp, stumbling, yet remaining on her feet.

Eddie was inside, his back to the door, keeping it closed. He pointed the .45 at her. "I'm not going to hurt you," he reassured, winded slightly from the quick burst of exertion.

"My God, you're a robber!" She was astonished, but not scared.

"No." Eddie shook his head. "But there isn't time to explain."

"Try me."

God, Eddie thought, *she's a cool one.* He looked around the shop. There was only one display case along the right-hand wall; otherwise, there didn't seem to be any merchandise whatsoever. Obviously a front for Triacas. "Jewelry store?" he asked, peering at the contents of the counter.

Alena, arms crossed, hip cocked, nodded.

"What's back there?" Eddie gestured with his head to the set of stairs that led to the doorway halfway up the center of the fifteen-foot-high wall.

"Office."

"Anyone there?"

"Not that I know of. Then, I didn't know you were going to be here, either." She looked at him more closely. "You're with Santiago, aren't you?"

"Not *with* him, *because* of him."

"What's that supposed to mean?"

"All I can tell you is that I need your help."

She considered him with doubt. "What's in it for me?"

Goddamn maniacs, Santiago swore. He stuck his head out the window. "Get over to the side or I'll run your ass down."

The man on the bicycle steered onto the rocky road edge, bouncing along there, shouting something back at Santiago as he passed by.

"Fucking bastards!" Santiago swore, then drove his right wheels off the road, throwing up stones and dust into the bike rider's face.

The Toyota's air conditioning continued its refusal to function despite repeated poundings of Santiago's fist against the dash. The heat was building already this morning, after the briefest of overnight respites; and it added to his frustration of making a wrong turn somewhere between the marina and downtown. The first three people he'd asked for directions had spoken English so poorly—and Spanish even worse or not at all—that he'd been unable to gather any help from them.

If he didn't get to the shop quickly enough, the woman would already be on her way back to the marina. She'd find Gus dead and then what would she do? Panic, more than likely. Then she'd realize she had a quarter-million dollars of a dead man's money and, if she had any brains at all—and she looked as though she did—she'd split. Damn, he hadn't considered that until now. It was happening again: all this perfect planning, and a woman threatened to screw it up.

Traffic near the harbor was clogged with tourists coming into Bridgetown to shop before midday's heat smothered the island. Parking spaces were at a premium, but Santiago didn't bother looking. He left his car with two wheels up on the curb in a tow-away zone and walked quickly down the block.

A young boy with ebony flesh made glossy from sweat came in stride with him, hawking an armful of coral necklaces.

Santiago glared. "No. Get away," he ordered sternly.

Undaunted, the boy latched onto an American couple walking the other way.

Santiago turned the corner near the channel and saw the Volvo—so it *was* Triacas's—parked there. Good, the woman was still here. He'd made it in time.

Only one of the other shops, a small café, was open along the patio. And not many people had voyaged down this little side excursion yet this morning. A lack of witnesses was always something he appreciated.

A closed sign hung down in the door to the Greek's unnamed jewelry shop, and, peering inside, Santiago didn't see anyone. He pushed on the door and it opened, but he forgot about the wind chime that dangled from the doorframe until it rang lightly, announcing his presence. He froze, slipping the MKE from his pocket, ready to fire at the rear office door if it opened.

But the woman didn't appear. Maybe she hadn't heard him.

Eddie heard the chimes. He stayed down behind the desk in Triacas's office, so close to it he could smell the rich oils of the wood. He drew back the hammer of the .45.

Santiago looked behind the display case, but saw nothing. He walked quickly, quietly, to the back of the shop, easing up the steps. On the landing, his fingers wrapped around the doorknob, turning it slightly, continuing the motion when it didn't catch, until he had turned it a full half-circle. It would be open now; all he had to do was pull.

In his mind, he reviewed the office layout quickly. Only a

desk and chair at what would be his right going in. There was another door, he remembered. A closet? No, it was a back door that led down to the alley. Other than those things, there was nothing else inside to worry about.

He closed his eyes a few seconds, wanting to better able to see in what was usually low light in there. Then he yanked open the door and went in.

He saw the woman on the floor, and the first thing he thought was that they'd been ripped off. Someone had come and robbed her—someone Triacas hadn't been careful enough not to tell about this.

The woman was on her side, knees bent, wrists and ankles tied behind her back by the strap belt from her sundress. A gag of some sort was stuffed in her mouth.

Santiago roughly pulled out her gag. "What happened? Where's the money?"

Alena coughed, gasping, drawing in a deep breath of air through her mouth. Her tongue and lips were dry.

"Goddammit! Where's the fucking money?" Santiago turned frantically, looking around the office without moving from her side.

Alena kept coughing, trying to get her breathing steady.

Santiago rushed to the back door. He pulled it open and looked down over the landing to the alley one story below: it was T-shaped, running parallel to the back of the shops with another narrow sleeve running off in a perpendicular line. Shaded from direct sunlight, dumpsters smelling ripe of rotten trash were being invaded by scrawny dogs. The only people Santiago saw were those passing by the far end of the alley as they walked along the main street.

Santiago stormed back to Alena, grabbed her thick hair. "Where's the money, goddammit? What happened to it?" He shook her head. "If this is one of Gus's tricks, I'll kill you. I'll butcher you!"

Eddie twisted around behind the desk. He couldn't tell exactly where Santiago was in relation to the woman. The sound of the Latin's footsteps and voice bounced oddly in the bare room, seeming even more disjointed from his position behind and part way under the desk. He had to make sure that when he came out he had a clean shot for Santiago.

Santiago pulled hard on her hair. "Where's the money? *Where?*"

"No!" she panted, shaking now, scared by his eyes. He looked evil, deadly. "No!"

"Where's the goddamned money?" He threw her head aside, then stood, kicking her in the back.

She cried out in pain.

"Tell me!"

Alena screamed. "Do it. Do it now!"

"What?" Santiago yelled. "Do what?" Then, somehow, he felt the movement. He didn't see it, he sensed it. She wasn't talking to him. There was someone else in the room. He spun around, aiming the MKE.

Eddie came up from behind the desk.

Santiago faced the office door, but then, quickly, spun toward him. Santiago fired. A suppressed burst of smoke and flame punched through a silencer with deceiving quiet.

Eddie dove behind the desk as the bullet ripped through the wall above him. He heard Santiago running. Then a door opened. Eddie lunged out onto the floor, landing hard on his elbows and stomach, firing at the back door.

The doorframe splintered beside Santiago's head. Eddie's second shot ripped through the door itself. Santiago kept going. He cleared the doorway and ran down what sounded like metal stairs.

Eddie scrambled to his feet, making it to the rear door in five steps. He stopped there, taking deep breaths, looking at Alena who struggled at her confines. "What's out there?"

"An alley," she said harshly, struggling, her face red from exertion.

Eddie ducked out onto the landing. A bullet ricocheted off

the concrete wall to his left. Eddie flinched, then moved right, keeping low. A second bullet followed him. Santiago fired at him from behind a dumpster, leaving Eddie without cover up on the stairs.

Another shot hit the metal landing under his feet, but there was no easy way to ground level. There was only one way, and Eddie took it. He turned his shoulder under and rolled down the stairs, feeling the hard step edges beating his ribs and legs. He hit the dirt alley sprawled outward, then quickly laid himself flat, legs pressed together, arms reaching straight forward, aiming the .45 for Santiago's hiding place. But Santiago wasn't there.

Eddie scanned the alley that ran lengthwise in front of him. The other alley that connected to this one was just ahead.

Eddie ran forward to the intersecting alley, pressing himself against the back of a stone wall. He turned part way around the corner just quick enough to glimpse the territory. Damn, no sight of Santiago. But he had to be down there. Somewhere.

Eddie ran across the mouth of the alley, taking cover behind a protruding brick wall. Immediately, there was movement along the back of buildings down to his right: feet scraped hurriedly through paper, tearing it. Eddie came out from behind the wall, down on one knee, aiming.

A scrawny dog, old newspaper tangled around his legs, limped across the alley, whimpering.

Eddie started to pull back when he heard glass shatter farther down the alley. About 100 yards away, Santiago was on the second-level fire escape of a dilapidated red-brick building, breaking a window with his gun. Eddie ran down the alley, breathing deeply, feet slapping against packed dirt.

Santiago felt panic tightening him. His hand shook as he reached inside the shattered pane of glass, feeling the window edge for the lock. Goddamn, where was it? Then, his fingers found the metal lip; it was coarse with rust, making it stick.

The man with the gun was running down the alley after

him, closing in, about 100 yards away. Santiago had only one shot remaining in the MKE, and he needed to make sure it was a good one.

His fingers slipped off the lock. It wouldn't budge. "Goddamn," Santiago urged. "Open, bitch, open!" He banged the window frame with the butt of his hand, then turned hard again on the rusted lock. Suddenly it sprang free. He raised the window then heard the shots, loud, echoing.

The bastard was going inside the building. Eddie, running hard, fired. And missed.

Santiago had one leg inside and was ducking his shoulders under the raised window.

Eddie fired again, missing. He fired a third time, and immediately blood erupted from the back of Santiago's thigh just as he was about to draw it inside.

"Fuck!" Santiago screamed, grabbing hold of the window frame, wincing. Hot pain seared through his leg as a hole burst through the front of his pants. He'd been hit.

Sweat spread immediately across his face, feeling like ice. He trembled. The pain dizzied him and was getting worse fast. He had never felt anything like it—goddammit, he'd never been shot before. Tightness gripped his chest. He couldn't move his leg. It dangled helplessly out the window.

"*Dios mio!*" Santiago cried, shaking. "*Dios mio!*" He turned sideways and tried to pull his leg in through the window. Oh, God, but he couldn't move it. It hurt so bad. And blood was everywhere, running over the windowsill, down the wall.

Sobbing, Santiago shifted his weight backward. He scraped his immobile leg over the windowsill, watching it twist sickeningly. The bullet must have shattered the bone completely.

He tried to stand on it, but couldn't. He couldn't stand at all. He braced himself against the windowsill, his hands feeling the slick warmth of his own blood.

Suddenly, the man with the gun was there, right in front of him. He had pulled himself waist-high up onto the edge of the fire escape, holding on strongly with one arm, aiming a silver-barreled pistol with his free hand. Just before the bullet splintered through his skull, Santiago had a final puzzling thought. He probably hadn't heard it right—the pain was perhaps too much for his mind to tolerate—but he was certain the man with the gun had said, "Dade-Metro police."

Thirty

Alena spun the combination a third time. The mechanism was precise, and her fingers hadn't been steady enough to hit the numbers correctly on her first two tries. She took a calming breath coming to the final digit. The lock clicked. She grabbed the handle and tugged. The heavy safe door opened.

The briefcase was inside the dark steel hole. The air in there felt cool and dry as she reached for the leather handle. She pulled the burgundy briefcase out and laid it on the floor. Her thumbs slid inside the clasps, springing them free. Lifting the top she saw the wrapped bills: used hundreds in stacks of fifty.

"How much is it?"

She jumped up, stepping back from the open case.

It was Eddie.

"How much?" he asked, standing in the doorway that led from the office down into the shop. Sweat glistened over his face and slickened the hair on his forearms against his skin. The .45 was by his side, as though his hand could barely hold onto it. "How much?"

"A quarter-million."

Eddie walked toward her. He hunched himself over as though drawn by cramps, an arm wrapped around his midsection as he knelt over the briefcase. Slowly, he lifted out a single stack of hundreds, setting it on the floor near Alena's feet. Then he put a second one on top of that, then another, and another, until there was an equal number on the floor and in the briefcase.

"What are you doing?" Alena asked when he shut the leather case.

Head hanging forward, he said, "It's your cut. Half for you. Half for me."

"What about Gus?"

"He's dead."

"How do you know?"

Eddie groaned getting to his feet. "Because I know Santiago."

Alena stared at the stacks of bills by her feet, scared of them.

Eddie said, "It's yours. Take it."

"Gus has friends."

"I told you, Gus is dead."

"You don't understand. This isn't Gus's money. He was agenting this deal for someone else. And they'll come looking for it."

Eddie loved it. Was that how they termed this now? Guys like Gus were *agenting* deals? Eddie picked up the briefcase. "Do what you want. I haven't got a lot of time to stay around here." He wiped his gun off against his shirt, then put it inside the empty safe and closed the door, spinning the tumbler.

Leaving the office, he took the steps one at a time going down into the shop, bracing his weight against the railing. His ribs hurt constantly now; each time he inhaled the pain seemed to peak, subsiding just slightly between breaths.

He was halfway to the door when Alena came running out of the office. She had the stacks of money he'd counted out for her in both hands. "In case you're right . . . about Gus. Take it back to the States for me, okay? I'd be afraid holding this around here. Gus's friends will look hard for it. Besides, I don't even know if I could get out of the country with it."

"Don't underestimate yourself," Eddie said, but allowed her to take the briefcase from his hands. He found himself staring at her thick, silky hair as she put her share inside. "How do you know I won't steal it?"

She reclasped the case shut, putting the handle back in his fingers. "You have honest eyes." She brushed a strand of hair back off his forehead. "I won't tell them what you look like— who you are." She smiled. "Look for an ad in the real-estate section of the Sunday *New York Times* about a shop for rent in Bridgetown. Reply to the box number to tell me where you've put the money. You'll be safe that way. No one will know where you are. Keep whatever part of it you need for your effort . . . expenses, too." She kissed him quickly. "You're very good."

Eddie walked outside into the hot sunlight. He expected to hear sirens in the distance, growing louder, closer, but there were none. He felt haunted by the silence.

Thirty-one

It was 2:00 A.M., a quiet Friday night, when Eddie walked into the Dade-Metro detective room. It was too dark to keep on the sunglasses that had covered his reddened eyes since yesterday, so he took them off. No one else was there. Cold cups of abandoned coffee and crushed-out cigarettes left half-smoked in tin ashtrays littered nearly every desk.

He carried a cardboard box he'd pulled out of the dumpster into Uncle Floyd's office. The window was closed, shades drawn shut, and the air conditioner hummed efficiently. One by one, Eddie took Uncle Floyd's Florida State football trophies from the shelf; he read each inscription and then set them carefully in the box. When he was finished, he found the morning newspaper and crumpled up pages to set between the trophy bases to keep them from scratching.

With the boxed memorabilia under his arm, Eddie walked to Wingate's desk and scribbled him a note: *Be safe, homme.* And he signed it: *From the wrong side of the law.*

He put his sunglasses back on once he was outside. With the trophies beside him on the passenger seat of the Chevette he'd rented at Miami International, he drove back to the airport. He took the Palmetto Expressway to 826, going out of his way so as not to have to drive past the hotel where Uncle Floyd had spent his last days.

The funeral had been Wednesday morning. Eddie hadn't been able to get back into the country until the day after.

Wendy said that the funeral was very nice. The priest hadn't known Uncle Floyd, but you couldn't tell from the warm eulogy he prepared.

There was other news from Wendy, too. Apparently things had gotten very hot around ML Engineering. The FBI had swooped in, and Anthony Marsh was being investigated for SEC violations involving securities fraud and insider trading. Marsh, however, had disappeared.

The other news involved Janice. Her requested transfer had been honored by Pan Am, and she was now flying European routes between Miami and England, Germany, and Italy.

Eddie glanced at his watch. He had four hours before his flight for London.